Delivered with Love

Delivered with Love

Sherry Kyle

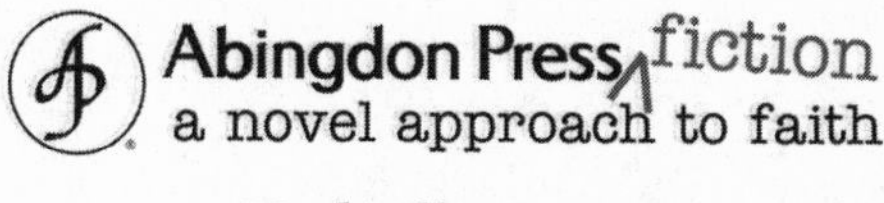

Nashville, Tennessee

Delivered with Love

ISBN-13: 978-1-4267-0866-4

Published by Abingdon Press, P.O. Box 801, Nashville, TN 37202

www.abingdonpress.com

Published in association with the Books & Such Literary Agency, Etta Wilson, 5926 Sunhawk Drive, Santa Rosa, CA 95409, www.booksandsuch.biz

Cover design by Anderson Design Group, Nashville, TN

Library of Congress Cataloging-in-Publication Data

Kyle, Sherry.
Delivered with love / Sherry Kyle.
p. cm.
ISBN 978-1-4267-0866-4 (trade pbk. : alk. paper)
1. Love-letters—Fiction. I. Title.
PS3611.Y64D45 2011
813'.6—dc22

2010045590

Printed in the United States of America

1 2 3 4 5 6 7 8 9 10 / 16 15 14 13 12 11

To Mom and Dad,
with love

Acknowledgments

With special thanks and appreciation . . .

To my wonderful Mount Hermon mentors, James Scott Bell and Brandilyn Collins, who not only helped me learn the craft of writing, but also gave me the self-confidence to finish this book.

To my CWFI critique group—Ginny, Vicki, Tracy, Amy, and Richard. Thanks for your suggestions and encouragement.

To Sarah, for her insight into the Capitola Police Department. Any errors are mine and mine alone.

To Virginia Smith, for reading every word and giving me your honest feedback. My novel is better because of you.

Thank you also to my cheerleader, critique partner, mentor, and friend, Karen O'Connor. I'm so glad God brought you into my life.

To Etta Wilson, agent extraordinaire. Thank you for believing in me.

To my wonderful editors, Barbara Scott and Ramona Richards, and the whole Abingdon team. Thank you for making my dream of a published novel come true.

And thanks to my mom, Billie Hoffman; sister, Cindy Veenstra; and sister-in-law, Karyn Hoffman, who read my manuscripts and gave me feedback.

To my four children—Carson, Brittany, Noah, and Grace. Thank you for understanding when Mommy needed to write another thousand words. What a gift from the Lord each of you is.

And to my husband, Douglas, who has been by my side supporting me every step of the way. I love you.

1

The hum of well-wishers' voices swirled around Claire James as she stood numbly in front of the brick fireplace in her mother's cramped Los Angeles apartment. Her black dress, size six and at least two years old, squeezed the oxygen out of her lungs. Claire attempted to take a deep breath and willed herself not to cry. One minute at a time. That's how she would survive.

She looked down at her feet to avoid eye contact with the so-called friends and family who came to pay their last respects. *Where were these people when Mom was sick?* Claire pushed the cynical thought to the back of her mind.

The scuffs on her black sandals were a sad reminder of her life the past few years since her mother had been diagnosed with cancer. They had spent all her college money on chemo, radiation, and natural remedies to keep her mother alive. But in the end it hadn't mattered.

She walked across the room and stood next to the small circular table in the corner that held the punch and dessert. Haley, her older sister, had insisted on a reception, saying that their mother deserved a party. Party? Yes, Mom loved parties, but today was not a day to celebrate. Claire bought the punch, while Haley baked a homemade chocolate cake with vanilla icing. The sweet smell turned her stomach. Her sister topped each of the two tiers with daisies, their mother's favorite flower. Claire picked one off the top and held it to her chest.

"I'm sorry about your loss." Geraldine, the elderly lady from down the hall, startled her back to the present. She patted Claire's hand. "She suffered a long time."

Claire nodded and blinked back tears. She hadn't seen her neighbor in quite some time.

"Well, it's probably time for me to go." Geraldine straightened the pillbox hat perched on her head. "I need to feed my cats."

Claire forced what she hoped resembled a smile. Geraldine's cats were fed better than some humans—including her. What she would do for freshly baked salmon instead of frozen dinners. The smell permeated the hallway every Thursday evening.

"Bye, Geraldine."

Claire glanced at the clock. Only half an hour more and she'd have the place to herself again.

Each minute was an exercise in patience. The condolences, hugs, and empty words wore on her. She rubbed her moist forehead and swallowed. Suddenly, the room spun and her hands trembled. She needed to get out of there.

Claire wove through the maze of people and out the back door to find privacy in her mother's old Volkswagen. The seventy-plus-degree weather hit her in the face as she slid inside the car resting by the curb. She opened the windows, leaned her head against the headrest, and sat in a crumpled heap, wishing her mother was there to remind her to sit up straight.

"Claire," Haley's saccharine voice called through the passenger side window a few minutes later. "Please come out. The Thompsons are leaving."

Mr. Thompson and his wife made a striking couple. Wealthy. Happy. Put together. A life her mom never had.

"Claire? Answer me," her older sister demanded.

"Thank them for the casserole. And tell them good-bye for me." A moan escaped her lips.

"All right, but come out soon." Haley tapped the front window with a manicured fingernail. "Mr. and Mrs. Morris and the Williamses are ready to leave too. I don't want to stand at the door by myself."

Haley never did anything by herself. The sound of Haley's stilettos clicking against the pavement grew distant. Her sister had handed over their mom's care to Claire and eloped the summer after the cancer diagnosis. It broke their mother's heart. Mark, her sister's husband, hadn't even come to the funeral.

Neither had her father. But why would she expect him to come? Dad hadn't been around since she was a baby.

Claire's throat tightened as the tears cascaded down her cheeks. She dug through the glove compartment looking for a tissue. Something white caught her eye.

Claire fingered the old envelope. Her mother's maiden name was scrawled across the front with her deceased grandparents' former address in San Diego. She ran her fingers over her mother's neatly penned name and mentally calculated how old she would have been in 1972. Seventeen. It was hard to imagine her mom as a teenager—young and vibrant—a contrast from the way she looked in her last days.

Strange. Why would her mother keep an old letter?

Claire shuddered and her eyes filled with fresh tears. *I miss you, Mom.*

She pulled the letter from the envelope. Would her mom want her to read it? Her pulse quickened as the words drew her in.

"*Dear Emily . . .*"

2

One year later

She never thought the letter would get her fired.

Claire stood in the kitchen in front of the restaurant manager with her mouth hanging open. She tucked her pen behind her ear and slipped her order pad into her apron pocket.

"It wasn't my fault Mr. Matley's pinkie finger got burned." Claire's heart sank. "He lifted his hand as I was pouring the coffee."

"Claire, the point is he *was* burned." Her boss pushed his thick black glasses higher on his nose with his right index finger. His moist forehead glistened in the fluorescent light of the restaurant. The smell of hamburgers on the grill wafted through the air.

During the months she had worked at the diner, Claire discovered food service wasn't her forte, but it paid more than the clothing shops at the mall. She averaged fifteen percent in tips, and her co-workers told her it had more to do with her looks than her ability to waitress, a fact she knew to be true. But it didn't take away the sting of their words. What else could she do?

"I need this job, Mr. Sutherland," Claire begged. "Can we give him a free lunch?"

She raised her brows and bit her lip. Today was the anniversary of her mother's death, and she was having a hard time concentrating. Her mind kept reciting the words of the letter she had discovered the day of her mother's memorial. And now she may have lost her job.

"You know as well as I do that Mr. Matley exaggerates, but he expects me to take action. He's one of my best customers." Her boss planted both hands on his hips. "Besides, you're late every day and I've had other customers complain about your service." He exhaled loudly. "You're distracted, Claire. Your mind is not on your work."

Her heart raced. Where would she find another job? "Is there anything I can do to change your mind?" She reluctantly met his gaze.

"I'm sorry." Mr. Sutherland's forehead crinkled with genuine concern. He slid his hands in the front pockets of his black slacks. "Please gather your things." He turned and walked through the door that led him out of the kitchen to the room filled with customers.

Claire followed him, untied her apron, and threw it on the counter. She reached in the left pocket and clutched the dollar bills and small change she had earned from the busy lunch hour. A familiar nausea somersaulted through her belly.

"Look on the bright side." Vivian, a middle-aged waitress, stood behind the counter cutting an apple pie into thick pieces, her upper arms jiggling with each slice of the knife. "Now may be the right time for you to pursue your dreams." She placed two pieces on separate plates. "You're college material, Claire." Vivian reached over and gave Claire's shoulder a squeeze. "Take care of yourself. I'm going to miss you."

Claire watched as Vivian's ample body lumbered through the maze of tables toward an older couple. *Pursue my dreams.*

She bent down behind the counter and grabbed her cardigan sweater and purse. Her only dream at the moment was to get out of the restaurant as fast as she could.

"Good riddance," she muttered as she pushed the door open. The sun beat down as she inhaled the smoggy air.

Her green VW bug, faded by years in the sun, sat at the far end of the parking lot. Each step toward the vehicle she inherited from her mother made the cramp in her stomach tighten. She opened the car door, threw her purse and sweater on the passenger seat, and slid inside. Her head fell forward against the steering wheel. Why couldn't she forget the contents of the letter?

Claire reached over and opened the glove compartment. The tattered white envelope wedged underneath the owner's manual mocked her. She pointed a finger at the object of her ire.

"I lost my job because of you."

She spoke to the paper as though it had a life of its own. In a way it did. The letter held clues to her mother's past. She couldn't rest or keep her mind on her work or on anything else, for that matter, until she knew who wrote it.

Now she was not only out of a job, but she had to go home and face her sister as well. Haley might be sympathetic, but her sister's lazy, no-good husband would be mad. He counted on her tip money to support his drinking habit. And today would be the last day she'd have any to give him.

The engine revved after the third try. She flicked on the radio. Kenny Chesney sang "There Goes My Life." Perfect. The sad ballad matched her mood. She backed out of the parking lot and drove the long way home.

"You're home early," Haley called from the worn chenille sofa in the small family room.

"Business was slow." Claire cringed at the lie.

Haley sat absorbed in her favorite soap opera. Her feet, covered in her fuzzy pink slippers, hung over the side of the couch. Ever since she'd been laid off from her corporate job a couple of weeks ago, her signature stilettos had gathered dust in the closet. The only difference between her and her sister, at the moment, was the severance package Haley's former boss had offered. Would her sister see it that way?

Claire needed time to plan her next move. She slipped into her bedroom and closed the door. Even though she'd lived with Haley and Mark for the past year since her mother passed away, this place was never home. She looked around her sparse room. A twin bed, a small dresser, and a desk filled the space against walls that were a dull shade of gray. She had never felt the urge to decorate. All that mattered was the framed picture of her, her mom, and her sister on the end table she'd had since childhood. She sat at her desk, turned on her refurbished computer, and scanned the job openings on the online edition of the newspaper.

She was tired of being a waitress, but was she qualified to do anything else? If she pursued her dreams as Vivian had suggested, she'd go to college and become a nurse. But what was the point of dreaming? She couldn't pay for college, and Mark and Haley would never let her live under their roof for free.

Sleep. That's what she needed at a time like this. Claire shut off her computer and slid into bed.

"You were what?" Haley stopped stirring the big pot of spaghetti. "You were fired?"

The smell of Italian spices filled Claire's nostrils. She pressed her fingers against the Formica countertop. "It wasn't my fault. Mr. Sutherland wouldn't budge."

Haley threw her an accusing look. "Your rent's due in a couple of days."

"I know. Can you talk to Mark for me?"

"Mark's going to freak out, Claire! And then you know what happens."

Guilt coiled through Claire. "Maybe he won't. Maybe not this time."

Haley snorted. "Dream on. When he drinks, he . . ." She shook her head and looked away.

He drank every night. Why did her sister put up with it? "Why don't you *do* something about it, Haley?"

"Like what? Leave?" Haley gripped the wooden spoon. "Maybe my vows mean something."

"Nobody heard you say your vows. You eloped!"

Haley shoved the spoon aside and turned on Claire. Her cheeks flushed pink. "How was I supposed to have a real wedding? Mom was too busy going to chemo appointments to even notice me."

Claire gritted her teeth. "Yeah, you're right. Why didn't Mom plan a wedding when she was fighting for her life?" Not to mention *who* drove Mom to all those appointments. Haley had no business walking away to get married.

Haley's mouth tightened. "I know what you're thinking, Claire. It's the same old same old with you. For your information, it was less of a burden for Mom to take care of one daughter than two."

"Don't give me that, Haley. You ran off for *yourself*, no one else."

"At least I did something with my life." Haley yanked open a drawer and grabbed at silverware. "You've been moping around ever since Mom died."

Claire glowered at her sister's pink slippers. "Since when is being on my feet all day in a restaurant moping around?"

Haley's hands shot up. "When's the last time you went out with friends? Or on a date?" She clattered the silverware on the table.

No. They were *not* going there. Claire threw open a cabinet and lifted out three plates. She busied herself placing them on the table just so.

"Claire." Haley's voice softened. "You've grieved long enough."

"And you didn't grieve at all." Claire whirled on her. "And now look who you're stuck with—Mark."

"Did I hear my name?" Mark staggered into the room.

"Honey, Claire has something to tell you." Haley's eyes narrowed. She ambled over to her husband and wrapped her arms around his waist.

"Yes, I do." Claire folded her arms across her chest. "I got fired today." She grinned at Haley, challenging her to deal with her husband.

Mark swore under his breath. He paced the length of the kitchen and ran a hand through his greasy brown hair. "No rent money, no room. Period." His thick drawl indicated he'd hit the bottle already.

Haley grabbed his arm and stopped him. "What does that mean?"

"It means, Haley, I want your sister gone by morning." Mark crossed the room toward the garage door and slammed it on the way out.

"I'll talk to him . . . later." Haley's eyes held an emotion Claire had seen before. Fear.

A lump clogged Claire's throat. Did she dare leave her sister alone with this man? The smell of Mark's stale breath lingered in the air. Was Haley right? Was it time to move on with her life? Mark didn't give her much choice.

"Don't bother." Claire held up her hands in defeat. "I'll go pack my bags."

3

Michael Thompson sat on the edge of the king-size bed and looked at a picture of a wedding dress from *Bride* magazine. "Sandy, just where do you think we can come up with this kind of money?"

"Michael, our only daughter is getting married." His wife of twenty-seven years stood over him. "Look at the cathedral train and the beaded lace bodice."

She was speaking another language. "It's beautiful. And Julia would look amazing in it, but the fact still remains—the price tag is outrageous." He stood and handed the magazine to his wife.

"This is only the beginning, honey. The wedding is in four months, and there is much more we need to plan and purchase." Sandy hugged the magazine to her chest.

His wife was as beautiful today as when he married her all those years ago. Her striking jet-black hair, cut just above her shoulders, and her brown eyes drew him in. "Sandy, can you keep looking? Maybe there's another dress out there that looks similar but is *reasonable*." He drew out the last word on purpose.

Her shoulders visibly drooped, and her eyebrows furrowed. "David's family will expect the best."

"Oh, so that's it." Michael strolled to their walk-in closet and opened the door. "You want Julia's fiancé to be impressed." He came out holding a navy suit, a white shirt, and a striped tie. "We're not on the same financial level as the Richards. But that doesn't mean we can't give our daughter a beautiful wedding."

"You'll sell a few houses between now and then." Sandy's silky robe clung to her waist as she tightened the belt.

He cleared his throat. "Let's hope so."

The shirt collar felt stiff, perfectly starched the way he liked. He handed his tie to his wife. The edges of the tie whipped here and there as Sandy configured the perfect knot.

Michael inspected himself in the mirror. "I'm working hard, but houses in Santa Cruz aren't moving right now." The air between them felt thick.

"I made coffee. I'll bring you a cup." Sandy avoided the conversation at hand.

"I've got a meeting. There'll be coffee there." Two could play at this game. He grabbed his briefcase.

The meeting was for new employees. Michael had been a Realtor for twenty years, but he needed an edge over the newcomers if this wedding dress was any indication of the kind of money he'd be doling out the next few months.

"But you haven't eaten breakfast." Sandy stood in the doorway. "Or read the newspaper."

Michael kissed his wife's cheek. "I've got to run. I need to put in the hours if we're going to give Julia the kind of wedding you have in mind."

"So, can we buy the dress?" Sandy quickly flipped through the magazine again, finding the page she had showed him earlier.

"Can you hold off, until we talk about it some more?" Michael walked down the hall to the kitchen and snatched his car keys off the granite countertop. "I'll see you tonight."

"What time?" Sandy followed him to the garage.

"I'll call you." Michael hopped in his BMW, started the engine, and took off.

I've got to get a new listing. And I won't come home until I do.

The sky was beginning to show daylight when Claire loaded the last of her belongings into the backseat of her car. Haley was still asleep. Claire decided to phone her later—when she had landed somewhere for the night and could think of what to say. When they were children, her mother had never liked it when her daughters fought. She would make them sit in their bedroom until they promised to get along.

"Sorry, Mom, not today." Claire took one more glance at the gloomy four-story apartment building. She wouldn't miss this place. She'd been here way too long. Maybe Haley will see Mark for who he is. Claire slipped into the driver's seat and turned the key. Her VW bug sputtered and choked, the engine refusing to turn over. Lately, she took a chance her car would start each time she got behind the wheel. Her funds didn't allow a trip to the mechanic. "Come *on*." She stepped on the gas pedal and turned the key once more. The sound of her car coming to life brought a smile to her face. Freedom. The excitement of a fresh start mixed with emotions she couldn't quite pin down made her pulse race.

She didn't want to leave L.A.—a place that reminded her of her mother. And yet, it was time to go—time for a new start. Claire drove down the street and merged onto the freeway. She'd give herself time to leave her past behind and figure out her life. And she'd drive up the coast until she wanted to stop.

Ironically, ten minutes later Claire pulled her car off the highway and into the nearest gas station. As she filled the tank, her stomach growled. She'd buy a donut or something sweet to go with a cup of coffee. Claire dumped the contents of her purse on the passenger's seat, looking for her ATM card. Receipts, lip gloss, a comb, a couple of dimes. She remembered locking her wallet in her car last night. She flipped open the glove compartment and dug her hand underneath the owner's manual. *Aha.* As she pulled out her pink wallet, an envelope fell to the floor.

The letter.

Claire tucked the envelope into her tote bag along with the contents on the seat. First, a good strong jolt of caffeine, then she'd read the letter once more before hitting the road. After walking into the gas station, she quickly purchased the tallest cup of coffee, a package of sugar donuts, and a chocolate bar for the drive. She placed her coffee on the hood of her car and fumbled for her keys.

"Claire? Is that you?"

She recognized the voice behind her. Geraldine. Claire turned around with the food in hand. "It's me." She was surprised to see her former neighbor at a gas station on this side of town. The time since her mother's funeral had not been good to Geraldine. Her white hair was thinner than before and she must have shrunk a good two inches.

"How's your sister, Holly?"

"*Haley's* fine." Claire gently corrected and gave a quick smile. Now didn't seem like an appropriate time to tell Geraldine her family troubles.

"I know your mother taught you good eating habits, my dear." Geraldine shook her head and clicked her tongue at the contents in Claire's hand.

"Oh, these?" Heat warmed Claire's cheeks.

"No need to explain. Every woman needs a little chocolate." She winked and reached into her purse. "Well, it was nice to see you." Geraldine patted Claire's hand and slipped her a twenty-dollar bill. "I should've helped you sooner when your mother was alive. Give my regards to your sister. She was always such a good girl until she met that fella."

"Thank you." Claire clutched the money to her chest. She watched as Geraldine shuffled away and climbed into a van with the help of a man she guessed to be in his mid-fifties. The side of the van read *Regis Retirement Living*. Claire hoped the adult community accepted cats. Geraldine had owned a half dozen when she lived down the hall from her mother's apartment.

Taking a deep breath, she dropped the snacks into her tote bag, grabbed the coffee, and situated herself in the seat. She reached in her purse and pulled the letter from the envelope.

Dear Emily,

Remember this . . .

Riding the roller coasters at the Boardwalk until our heads were dizzy and our stomachs felt sick.

Hanging out at the beach learning to ride the waves.

Late-night walks holding hands. Stealing kisses. Sharing dreams.

I've never met a girl who can make me smile the way you do.

Summer was fun. Meeting you was the best part.

I miss you.

I love you.

Claire stared at the letter in her hand. Someone had loved her mother. Someone who signed with only an initial. And according to the return address, someone who lived in Capitola. She folded the letter and tucked it back inside the envelope before slipping it into her purse. Claire opened the glove compartment and pulled out a map. She scanned up and down the coast until she spotted the small town of Capitola near Santa Cruz. She'd head north.

A smile tugged at her mouth. She had a plan, a destination. She would find a job and a place to live while she searched for the mysterious writer who had captured her mom's heart all those years ago.

4

With one hand on the steering wheel, Claire dug inside her bag and retrieved the candy bar she'd purchased at the gas station. She ripped open the wrapper with her teeth and bit into the rich dark chocolate. It wasn't much of a lunch. But she wanted to keep on driving. Santa Cruz was a good eight hours from L.A., and she had three more to go, maybe four if the RV ahead of her continued at a snail's pace.

The view near Big Sur mesmerized her. She snaked along the winding two-lane highway, sneaking peeks of the beautiful blue ocean lapping against the rocky shore. The San Lucia Mountains towered regally to her right.

The motor home in front of her gained speed as the road sloped downward.

Claire pressed on the gas pedal. "Finally, we're getting somewhere."

Without warning, the motor home came to an abrupt stop.

Claire slammed on her brakes, but it was too late. Metal crunched as the seat belt dug into her chest. Tears sprang to her eyes. Her car. Her inherited VW bug was damaged. And it was all her fault.

A burly man stepped out of the RV, his brows furrowed as he rushed to her door.

Claire searched his face through the windshield as she rolled down her window. Was he angry? Her hands shook and she willed herself to stay calm. She had no reason to be afraid of him.

The RV driver spat a dark orange wad on the pavement and leaned over to peer through the window. “Looks like you’ve done more harm to your little car than to my motor home.” His lower lip protruded with chewing tobacco, reminding Claire of one of her brother-in-law’s unsightly habits.

Claire opened her door and slid out to take a look, stepping over the asphalt spittoon. The front end of her car was dented and the hood buckled like an inverted V. She brushed her cheek with the back of her hand. “This is my mother’s car.”

“Does she know you’re driving it?” The man cocked his brows.

Claire stared at the damages. She tucked her hands in the front pockets of her jeans. “She died a year ago.”

The older man took off his baseball hat, revealing a bald head, and wiped his brow. “Sorry to hear that.”

Drivers honked their horns behind them. Wind stirred by the passing vehicles in the other lane. The man tapped his cap against his leg and spat a stream of tobacco juice on the pavement. “I suppose we should move ourselves off the highway.”

“But we’re not supposed to, right? Don’t we have to wait for the Highway Patrol?” Claire willed her hands to stop shaking.

“Let’s move up ahead. Then we’ll exchange insurance information.”

She didn’t have insurance. Claire watched the husky older man hitch his jeans up over his protruding belly.

“Follow me.”

She heard the RV's engine come to life.

Claire sat in her car and turned her key. She heard clicking sounds. She tried again. Nothing. She rotated her key once more. *Great! The car chooses NOW to die!* I should've had the car serviced before leaving L.A. She hit the steering wheel and covered her face with her hands.

Was someone watching her? Claire sensed a presence and turned her head toward the driver's side window. She jumped when she noticed a thin older woman. Her gray hair hung to the side and down to her waist in a long braid.

"Come child, my husband and I will haul you to the nearest campsite. It's a good thing we left our car at home this trip." She opened Claire's door and motioned Claire toward the RV she had hit.

Should she go with them? A driver honked behind them, giving Claire her answer. She grabbed her purse along with her keys and followed the woman while her husband pulled out a tow bar and hooked her car onto their trailer hitch.

The small RV had all the modern conveniences—a booth-like table with a small kitchen light, a gas stove, a TV with a DVD player, and a queen-size bed in the back bedroom with the prettiest patchwork quilt Claire had ever seen. She sat down in one of the tan leather seats.

"Welcome to our home on wheels," said the woman from the front seat. "We don't like to stay in one spot for long ever since our children flew the coop."

"I understand. I'm flying the coop myself." Claire averted her eyes, self-conscious of her admission.

The older woman grinned. "You . . . such a pretty young thing. I bet your friends and family miss you back home."

Home. Claire didn't have one. But she'd prove she could make it on her own. She didn't need anyone's help. She clutched her purse against her chest and wondered how she got into this mess. One minute she was driving north with the wind whipping through her hair and the next she was sitting in a motor home with the front end of her car in a crumpled heap and refusing to start.

"That about does it. Your car is hooked up and ready to travel." The man climbed into the driver's seat and started the engine. "I think we've stopped traffic for miles, but that's okay, people got to learn to slow down. Every one of those cars has a great view of Big Sur, if they'd take time to look."

"Now, Harry, don't start on that soapbox. This girl's been through enough." The woman patted her husband on the shoulder.

"It don't look like you'll be traveling much more today." Harry adjusted his baseball cap. "How about we camp the night at Plaskett Creek? You're welcome to join us."

Claire gulped. She'd rather not, but did she have a choice? Any accommodations for the night would be better than sleeping on the side of the road.

"We should introduce ourselves." The woman leaned over to face Claire. "My name's Pearl and this is my husband Harry. We've been married fifty-three years. Of course, we were only children when we tied the knot." She tapped her husband on the arm.

He seemed to get his wife's meaning by the smile and the wink he gave her.

"Say, how old are you, dear?"

"Twenty-three," Claire answered.

"Just a baby." Pearl turned around and looked into her eyes. "What's your name, darlin'?"

No one had ever called her darling. She stared out the window. "Claire."

"Well, Claire, we have six children, all grown and married with children of their own, except Albert. Now he's a confirmed bachelor through and through. He's the youngest of our brood and quite opinionated. He frequently marches for one cause or another." Pearl chuckled.

Claire glanced over her shoulder at her VW.

Pearl wrapped her long braid around her fingers. "Where were you headed?"

Claire shifted in her seat, tired of all the questions. "Santa Cruz."

Harry glanced at her in his rearview mirror. "Santa Cruz is a beautiful place. They have everything—mountains, ocean, redwoods, and mild weather. Have you been there before?"

"No." Claire peeled her eyes away from the mirror. "Have you?"

"A number of times." Harry swerved. Claire could see bikers on the right. "We like to camp at New Brighton Beach, a pretty spot near Capitola."

Claire's heart leaped. Capitola—the return address of the letter. "Will you be going there next?"

"We're headed to San Francisco, an hour and a half past Santa Cruz." Pearl showed Claire a family photo. "See this one, here." She pointed to a woman in her early thirties. "That's Melody, our youngest daughter, and the man standing next to her is her husband, John. She's about to have a baby any day now, and we want to be there for the arrival."

"Here we are. Plaskett Creek Campgrounds." Harry pulled the motor home into the entrance. "Let's see if our usual spot is taken."

Claire peered out the window. The main road wound in a circle, with campsites on the left and a big grassy section in the middle. She was relieved to see restrooms evenly spaced throughout the campsite. Tents and RVs filled most spaces.

"Look, Harry. Our spot." Pearl pointed to a little grassy knoll. "The Lord always provides, doesn't he?"

If the Lord provided for Claire, she'd be headed north in her VW bug without a ruined front hood.

"And land's sakes, look over there." Harry pointed. "The Andersons are here."

"We haven't seen them in what, Harry? Three, four years?" Pearl craned her neck. "What a night this is going to be." She clapped her hands together.

Are these people for real? Claire didn't know how to act around "nice" people like Pearl and Harry. How was she going to handle being around more strangers?

"Oh, you'll simply love the Andersons." Pearl leaned down, grabbed a straw hat and settled it on her head. "They're loads of fun. They have three strapping boys—why, they should almost be men by now, and one daughter, the eldest. I think she might be your age. They go camping as a family every year for a week or two. Of course, Harry and I think the world of Ed and Mary. They've raised all their children in the church, and not one of them has rebelled." Pearl cupped her hand to block her mouth from Harry's gaze and lowered her voice. "Not like our Robert. He's been around the block once or twice, if you know what I mean. But he's turned his life around."

"Now, Pearl, you don't need to share our family troubles."

Claire knew all about family troubles. She tucked a strand of hair behind her ear.

Harry pulled into the campsite. "We'll have to unhitch your car or it'll be sticking out in the middle of the road. We can ask the Anderson boys to help us move it to the grass over there."

Claire had never received so much positive attention from people she knew, let alone strangers. She thought back to her mother's friends, the ones who disappeared when they learned her mother had cancer.

"I'd say that accident of ours was a blessing in a way. If you hadn't bumped into us, we wouldn't have had the opportunity to catch up with old friends." Pearl jumped out of the RV and headed toward the Andersons' campsite the minute Harry stepped on the emergency brake.

5

Claire watched through the RV window as Pearl waved her arms and darted over to the Andersons' campsite. Three teenage boys and an older couple jumped up from their camp chairs and ran to meet her. Pearl pulled the woman into her arms, laughing. A young woman stepped out of the RV, rushed toward Pearl, and hugged her tight around the neck. They acted like relatives who hadn't seen each other in years. Claire's chest tightened. Was there a single person in the world who would be as glad to see her as these people were to see each other? She propped her chin on her hand and leaned against the window as she watched the reunion.

Pearl turned and pointed to Claire's VW bug hitched to the back of the RV. From the way she swooped her arms, Claire imagined the story she was telling. She wasn't in the mood to join such a happy crowd. She'd wrecked her most treasured possession, and yet she didn't want to be alone either.

Harry opened the side door of the RV. "Come meet our friends."

Should she? Claire let out a breath, stood, and allowed him to lead her out the door.

"Well, what do you know, it's my good friend Harry." Ed walked up and pumped his hand. "Good to see you, old-timer!"

"Speak for yourself." Harry spat a dark wad on the ground and laughed. "I don't think I've ever seen you with a beard before. You remind me of someone."

Claire quickly studied the man, trying not to make direct eye contact. Ed was tall and thin, but his beard and mustache met at the corners of his mouth, looking soft and gloriously white.

Harry rubbed his chin as if in deep thought. "Oh yeah, you remind me of a skinny Santa Claus."

Ed chuckled. "And who is this pretty girl?" He reached out his hand.

"This is Claire. We bumped into each other, so to speak, down the road."

"More like I bumped into him." Claire shook his hand.

Ed headed around the back of the RV toward the small car. Harry and Claire followed. "By the looks of your VW bug, I'd say you got the worst of it."

"We need to unhitch her car for the night and put it over there." Harry indicated a space next to the RV. "Can we get your boys to help?"

"Let's ask them." Ed smiled at Claire, looped his thumbs in his jeans pockets, and walked over to his family.

Why hadn't she seen the dent in Harry and Pearl's motor home before? Was she so concerned about *her* car that she didn't pay attention to the RV? Her stomach twisted. Claire grabbed Harry's arm, stopping him in his tracks. "I want to pay you for the damages to your motor home . . . And I *will*, I promise. As soon as I get a job. . . ."

"I'd say you have more problems with that car of yours. Why don't we take one step at a time?" Harry winked at her. "Remember, God provides."

Haley and Claire had sold most of their mother's jewelry, furniture, and dishes after Haley had been laid off, but Claire begged her sister to let her keep the VW bug. And now look at it. She'd have to find a way to get the car fixed.

Ed returned with three young men in tow. "Claire, I'd like you to meet my sons, Christopher, Andrew, and Joe."

Claire waved. "Hi, nice to meet you." She glanced at each one of Ed's teenaged sons.

The awkward moment of silence made Claire's heart race.

"Come on, boys, stop staring at the pretty lady and unhitch her car." Ed stepped forward and motioned for his sons to join him. "There'll be plenty of time to get to know her tonight."

The young woman who had hugged Pearl earlier stood a few feet from Claire with a glass in her hand. "Hi, Claire, I'm Samantha." She smiled, revealing deep dimples. Samantha looked fit in a green striped tank top and denim shorts, her brown hair pulled back in a ponytail under a visor as if she had walked off the set of a TV commercial. Fresh. Clean. Athletic.

"Would you like lemonade? I made it fresh this morning."

Claire could smell the citrus and see the fat, golden lemon slice floating in the glass. Her mouth salivated. "Thank you."

"I'm sorry about your car. I hear it was your mom's."

Claire took a long drink. "Word travels fast."

Samantha gestured toward the campfire. "We're making hot dogs and beans for dinner. You're welcome to join us. It's not gourmet or necessarily healthy, but that's camping." She shrugged.

"I'd like that." She handed Samantha the empty glass. "Thanks for the lemonade." Claire remembered last night's meal with Haley and Mark. The three of them had eaten in silence, except for the occasional slurping sound from the spaghetti.

She glanced at her crumpled car one more time before she followed Samantha to the campsite.

Michael slammed the phone down a bit too hard. His frustration level had risen with each call he'd made, and the last one had set him on edge. His highest-priced listing in the Uplands pulled out. The couple had decided they'd wait another year before selling. Michael threw a pen across his desk.

"Hey, man, what's the deal?" Eric, his good friend and colleague two decades his junior, had witnessed his tantrum.

"No deal. That's the problem." Michael leaned forward, steepled his brow, then turned toward his friend. "What is with real estate these days? I haven't seen such a slump in ten years."

"It's your attitude, man. People can tell you're tense." The top button of Eric's shirt was undone, his tie hung loose around his neck, and a glimpse of white undershirt was visible. "Professional. That's what I am." Michael straightened his tie and the papers on his desk. "Look. I know your intentions are good—"

"Of course they are." Eric slapped Michael on the back. "I'd do anything for you, you know that."

This conversation was going nowhere fast. "Say, I've got a few more calls to make." Michael picked up the phone hoping Eric would get the hint.

"Slow. Calm. Take a deep breath before you call." Eric patted him on the shoulder.

Michael let out a breath. "Thanks, Doctor. I'll take it from here."

"Can I get you a cup of coffee? A Coke?" Eric dug in his pocket and pulled out a few coins.

"I'm good. Now, get out of here." Michael turned his body away from Eric. He looked up the number for his next prospective client and punched it in.

On the third ring, a female voice answered.

"Hello?"

Michael heard children in the background. "Hello, Mrs. Johanneson. Michael Thompson here. We met at a recent open house. You'd mentioned you might be interested in selling."

"Who's this?" The voice questioned.

Michael heard a baby cry, the sound growing louder. "Michael Thompson, from Crown Real Estate."

"I'm the babysitter. I'll let Mrs. Johanneson know you called." Click.

The girl never asked for his phone number. Michael hit the "Off" button and clipped his phone onto his belt. Eric's offer of a cup of coffee sounded better as time ticked by. He stood and ambled over to his friend's cubicle.

"Five o'clock. I'll meet you there." Eric finished his phone call. He raised his index finger, indicating he needed a moment. He jotted a note on a slip of paper. "Michael, you're never going to believe this. Last Saturday, when I took your open house, I met the nicest couple. They're relocating to our area and need to buy a four-bedroom—and fast. I researched properties on Sunday and I think I found them the perfect house. We're meeting—"

"At five. I heard." Michael raked his left hand through his hair. "Are you still up for that cup of coffee?"

"I would if I could, man, but suddenly I'm swamped." Eric pointed to the stack of folders.

"Anything I can take off your hands?" Michael groveled.

"Hey, you're the best in the business. Give your clients that old Thompson charm." The phone rang on Eric's desk. "Breakfast tomorrow morning?"

Eric answered his phone before Michael could respond.

He turned and headed toward the coffeepot. The coffee didn't taste like Starbucks, but it was free. He poured himself a cup and sat down. The break room was top-notch—walnut table with chairs to match, Picasso prints on the wall—a room where a guy could feel good about working for a quality company. Michael's mind wandered to Julia's fiancé—David Richards. He was a good guy. Moral. Brilliant. Outstanding citizen. He was from a family of lawyers that represented the wealthy. *The only strike against him.* He remembered the night a couple of years ago when his daughter came home and said she had met a wonderful man at the church Christmas party. They'd been inseparable ever since.

The image of the wedding dress came to mind. His daughter would look like a princess. But it didn't take an expensive dress for her to be beautiful. She had dark hair like her mother's, and striking blue eyes like his. A good combination. Michael sighed. He loved his daughter and would do anything for her, but first he had to make Sandy understand. Julia was marrying into a wealthy family, one he and Sandy could not compete with. Michael made a decent living—but obviously, not enough. A salaried position sounded better all the time. Michael downed the last of his coffee.

He stood and stretched. He'd work a couple more hours, and then run by his rental property on the way home. If he could lease the two-bedroom ranch on Depot Hill, it would provide decent income.

On the way to his cubicle, he caught a glimpse of Eric leaving the office. "Why did I give him that open house? Just my luck." The words slipped out even though he didn't believe in luck. The fact that Eric got what should have been *his* clients rubbed him raw. Then he felt guilty for the thought. He'd been tired. Tired of sitting inside empty houses with only one or two prospective clients walking through. Eric had done him a favor, so it was his own fault he didn't get the possible sale. Michael checked his attitude.

Could people tell he was tense? He rubbed the back of his neck. Hard as a rock. The hot tub at home would relax his sore muscles. But that would have to wait.

He needed to sell another house.

6

Claire sank deeper into the camp chair as her meal of hot dogs, beans, and Mary's potato salad settled in her stomach. She nestled under a flannel blanket next to the crackling campfire and listened to Ed play the guitar while the rest of the Anderson family sang. Samantha's voice captivated her. If Claire could sing like Samantha, she'd be headed to Nashville. But not Samantha. She said she only wanted to "give God glory," whatever that meant. Claire didn't recognize most of the songs they were singing, except for *Jesus Loves Me*. Mom had whispered that song to her the night before she died as she held Claire's hand. The memory was locked into her heart.

Pearl sat across from her on a log, knitting booties for her soon-to-arrive grandchild.

Claire grinned at the blue yarn. She hoped the baby was a boy.

Harry slouched in his camp chair, his legs outstretched and his arms folded across his chest. Claire knew he was asleep by the rise and fall of his chest and the soft whoosh of air bubbling from his lips, even though she couldn't see his eyes beneath the brim of his hat.

The scene before her was picture-perfect. If her family were anything like the Andersons or Pearl and Harry, she'd still be in L.A. Life would be different. Imagine being able to relax and enjoy each other's company without fighting or quarreling.

The song ended, and Pearl tucked the knitting needles and yarn into her tapestry bag. "I'm ready for bed. And I think this big guy was ready an hour ago." Pearl nudged Harry on the shoulder.

"What's going on?" Harry sat forward, rubbed his eyes, and blinked.

"You were snoring." Pearl growled like a bear. "Just like that."

Ed tapped him on the knee, his grin gleaming in the firelight. "You were sawing logs."

Their joking manner warmed Claire as much as the fire.

"Very funny." Harry wobbled to his feet. "I only closed my eyes for a few minutes."

"It's all right, dear." Pearl kissed Harry's wrinkled cheek. "We're teasing." She picked up her bag and held Harry's hand. "Claire, I'll make up your bed. Come when you're ready."

"Thank you." Claire watched Harry and Pearl take careful steps through the darkness, their flashlight illuminating a path ahead of them.

"I think we're going to call it a night too." Ed placed his guitar in its case and snapped it shut. "Ready, honey?"

"I'm right behind you." Mary came over and squeezed Claire's shoulders. "We're headed to Santa Barbara in the morning. It was a pleasure to meet you, dear. Please give Samantha your address. I'm sure she'd like to keep in touch."

Claire had no address to give. She shivered. Would she ever get to Capitola? "Andrew, can you put another log on the fire? Our new friend is shaking." Mary stroked Claire's hair. "Unless you're ready to turn in?"

Claire's mother used to stroke her hair like that. A surge of tears threatened at the thought. She cleared her throat. "I'm going to stay up a while, thank you."

Andrew jumped up and laid a thick log on the fire. Sparks flew upward as it thudded into place. Within seconds flames engulfed the wood.

Mary patted her shoulder. "Good night, then."

"Good night." Claire watched Mary hug and kiss each one of her children and slip into the RV. Her throat constricted. It had been too long since her mother had held her in her arms.

"Now that the old folks have gone to bed, what do you say we have a good time?" Joe grabbed a flashlight. "Hey, Claire, do you want to take a night hike?" He winked at her.

All three of the brothers had been flirting with her all day, but Joe provided the comic relief. The teenagers had been treating her like a queen after they moved her Volkswagen to a grassy spot next to Pearl and Harry's RV.

"Sorry, Joe." Claire stood and sat by Samantha. "We have plans for tonight. Girls only." Claire caught Samantha in a pleading look.

"That's right." Samantha swung an arm around Claire's shoulder. "Girls only."

"You two are no fun." Joe handed the flashlight to Claire. "You don't know what you're missing."

Claire smiled. "Good night."

"Samantha, don't stay up too late." Christopher yawned. "Remember, we're leaving first thing in the morning."

"Yes, *Father*." Samantha rolled her eyes. "Brothers," she whispered. "They can be a pain."

If the years being bossed around by Mark were any indication of what a brother was like, Claire would rather not have one. "I can imagine."

"I'd say we have at least a half hour before the fire dies." Samantha poked at the log with a stick. "So, Claire, where were you headed when the accident took place?"

Samantha must have heard Pearl talk about her plans to make it on her own. Claire's hands grew moist. She rubbed them on her jeans. "Up the coast. I need to figure out a few things."

"Like what?" Samantha wrapped her sweater tighter around her shoulders.

"Like who I am. What I want to do with my life. Where I want to live. Things like that." Claire stared at the fire. Making eye contact with Samantha now would make her feel too vulnerable.

"I know what you mean. It took me a few years to pin all that down. Now I have a steady boyfriend, my own apartment, and a job I love. Four years of college paid off." Samantha leaned toward her. "Is there something else bothering you? Besides your car?"

Was Samantha a mind reader? The tenderness in her voice made Claire want to confide in her. Should she tell her about the letter? What did Claire have to lose? After tonight, she may not see Samantha again. "Wait right here. I'll be back."

Claire thought about her decision the whole way to Pearl and Harry's RV. She shone her light on the trail that led from one campsite to another. Monterey pine trees surrounded the campground. The moon was hidden from view for only a minute as she walked down the path. Then, as Claire took another step, the three-quartered-shaped crescent appeared. The moon had comforted her when her mom was sick, and now wherever she lived, no matter what town, the moon would always be there to console her.

Turning off the flashlight, Claire slipped inside the RV to find her purse. A spike of pain shot through her knee as she smacked into a bed. Her face contorted as she stifled a scream and rubbed the sore spot. Wasn't the bed a table not too long ago? Claire reached for her tote bag and pulled out the letter. Hugging it to her chest, she walked back to the campfire.

Samantha's face glowed from the firelight. "I saw a raccoon skitter across the grass. It freaked me out."

Claire laughed. She wasn't afraid of animals, big or small.

"What's that?" asked Samantha.

Claire held up the envelope. "A letter to my mother when she was seventeen." She pulled out the piece of paper.

"Who's it from?"

"Your guess is as good as mine. The person signed it with only an initial."

Samantha leaned over for a closer look. "What's it say?"

Claire read the letter out loud. When she finished, the campground was eerily quiet, except for the crackling of the small flame.

"I need to find out who wrote this." Claire slid the envelope into her pocket and edged nearer to the fire. "I wonder what it would be like to talk with him, to find out about that summer, and why they drifted apart." She watched as the fire died, the log splitting into fragments.

"I wish I could help you." Samantha's voice soothed her ears. "I'd want to know—if that was written to *my* mother. You miss her, don't you?"

"Yes. More than you know." Claire blinked back tears. "My mom and I were close. More like best friends."

"I couldn't imagine losing my mom in my twenties. You're so brave."

"Not as brave as I should be. After she died, I wanted someone to take care of me so I moved in with my sister. What a mistake that turned out to be! I ended up taking care of *her*.

But I'm on my own now." Claire rubbed her hands together and stifled a yawn.

Samantha reached into her canvas bag and produced a pen and a piece of scratch paper. "Here's my cell phone number. Call me anytime, day or night." She scribbled a note and then handed it to Claire.

"Thank you." Claire tucked the piece of paper into her pocket.

"I'm going to miss you. It was so nice to have another girl around. Too much testosterone in my family." Samantha stood and hugged her.

"You can say that again." Claire smiled, then stepped back, more at ease with space between them.

"It's late. And you look tired. I'll see you in the morning?"

Claire grabbed the flashlight. "Yeah."

Samantha waved and slipped into her parents' RV.

Claire strolled back to Pearl and Harry's campsite.

That's funny. The light was on.

Claire opened the door and stepped inside.

"There you are," said Pearl. "John called. Melody is in labor. They're on their way to the hospital! It's time to go."

7

Chicken cordon bleu. The smell of Michael's favorite dish still permeated the kitchen, but his plate sat in its place on the mahogany table, clean and empty, except for the note. Michael scanned the scrawled-on piece of paper. Sandy had gone to bed. And she didn't want him to wake her.

He wadded the piece of paper and tossed it in the garbage. He'd made a mistake. He squeezed his tight neck muscles with his right hand. He should have called at seven o'clock, when he missed dinner. Instead, he stayed at the office and followed up on a few leads, hoping to drum up business. What a waste. He opened the refrigerator door and searched the shelves, looking for the leftovers.

The blinking light on the answering machine caught his eye. He pressed the message button and heard his daughter's voice.

"Hey, Mom. Did you show Dad the picture of the wedding dress? I went to the bridal shop and tried it on again. It has my name written all over it. Oh, and I found the nicest place for the reception—Sanderlings, the restaurant at Seascape Resort. I can't believe I'll be Mrs. David Richards in only a few months. Call me. Love you. Bye."

Michael hung his head and let out a breath. He slipped off his tie and tossed it on the cream-colored leather couch, then shrugged out of his suit coat and hung it over a kitchen chair. It looked as though he'd need a higher equity line of credit. A stab of pain shot through the knotted muscles in his upper back.

He needed to relax and forget his troubles. And there was only one place that would soothe him at this time of night. Forgetting dinner, he crossed the room to the downstairs bathroom, stripped out of his clothes, and donned his trunks. He walked out to the backyard with a beach towel wrapped around his waist.

He slipped into the hot tub and hunkered low, allowing the pulsating jets to knead his sore muscles. Eric was right. He was tense, too tense for his own good. He'd have to see the doctor for blood pressure medication if he wasn't careful. Michael looked up. The moon, shining through the gazebo's glass dome, gave the water a luminescent effect.

Lord, please help me sell another house . . . or at least find renters.

Michael shifted to another seat, the jets now focusing on his lower back. Tomorrow he would run by his rental property since he had missed his chance that afternoon. The painters would be finished repainting the inside, and the carpets should be steam cleaned by now. He took a deep breath and closed his eyes.

"Honey." Sandy's voice trilled above the whir of the hot tub. "Where have you been?"

Michael bolted upright. "I thought you were sleeping."

"I was, but then I heard the garage door open and waited for you to come upstairs." Sandy wrapped the chenille blanket tighter around her shoulders. "You didn't answer my question."

Michael turned off the jets. "I was at work."

Even in the dark, he could see the look of distrust in Sandy's eyes. "You've never stayed at work this long without calling."

"I was going through files of potential clients." Michael playfully flicked water at Sandy. "Care to join me?"

"It's almost midnight." Sandy took a step back. "I'm going back to bed. Will you be long?" She flung one corner of the blanket over her shoulder to cover her exposed neck.

"A few more minutes. It's been a rough day." Michael slunk down in a corner seat.

"For me too." Sandy took another step toward the back door, her figure more of a shadow. "I'll be upstairs, waiting." She turned and went into the house.

Michael pressed the button for the jets once more. Should he stay in the hot tub long enough for Sandy to go back to sleep? He didn't feel like talking.

Didn't his wife realize he was working his tail off for her? For Julia? And for the wedding he wished he'd saved up for a long time ago? Michael laid his head back and looked at the moon. *Lord, help me relax.*

"Go? Right now?" Claire stood dumbfounded as Pearl and Harry prepared to leave the campground.

"It's a good three hours to San Francisco from here and I want to see my new grandbaby come into the world." Pearl folded the bed back into a table.

The thought of a good night's sleep vanished. "I'll let you two get ready." Claire turned to grab the door handle.

"And where do you think you're going, young lady?" Harry set his baseball cap on his head and reached out to stop Claire from leaving. "You're coming with us."

For a moment she felt as if she were being kidnapped. But the sweet look on Harry's face told her otherwise.

"That's if you don't mind hanging out with two old folks like us." Harry laughed. "Or do you have somewhere else to go?"

"No, but I can't simply leave my car . . . ?" Claire peered out the window. "I don't think we can move it ourselves to hook it onto your trailer." She thought about the letter and Capitola. Could they drop her off at the return address? Claire shook off the thought.

Harry rubbed his chin, which made a scratching noise against the stubble. "You're right about that. I'd hate to wake the Andersons."

"Why don't you two go?" Claire blurted. "Samantha's probably still awake. I'll bunk with her and then call a tow truck in the morning." Claire leaned down and snatched her purse from the tan leather seat.

"I hate to leave you." Pearl took a tissue and blew her nose. "I know God put you in our lives for a reason. And we're blessed because of you."

Claire didn't understand this couple. She had rammed into them. Their RV had a big dent because of her. Didn't they see that? "I'll be fine. You'll be hearing from me again. I'll send you a check for a new bumper when I get the money. All I need is your address."

Pearl waved her off, and then reached out with both arms to give her a hug. "Now, take care of yourself. Godspeed, my child."

Claire stiffened in Pearl's embrace. She pulled back. "You'd better hurry. That baby isn't going to wait for you."

Harry patted Claire's shoulder. "Nice to meet you, young lady."

Claire stepped out of the RV. She stood next to her car as Harry started the engine. As they drove off, Pearl's hand fluttered out the window until the RV was out of sight.

Claire turned toward the Anderson's campsite. The lights were out in their motor home. If she knew where Samantha slept, she could tap on the closest window, but she didn't feel right about waking the whole family. She scanned the darkened campground. Only one campfire glowed in the distance. Claire felt hollow and alone in the dark of the night, the sound of crickets filling the void. She needed to formulate a plan.

Claire sat in the front seat of her Volkswagen gripping the steering wheel with both hands. How she wished she could start her car and drive up the coast. She glanced in the backseat at her pillow and blankets. She could sleep in her car, but would she get an ounce of rest?

Instead, she dug through her wallet. There had to be one credit card that wasn't maxed out. Her sister had used her credit cards on occasion for her shoe fetish and had sometimes forgotten to return them. *Ah.* Her Visa. Maybe she could get to Capitola tonight after all. Claire grabbed her cell phone and punched 0 for the operator. She wrote down the number for a towing service, called the number, and huddled under her blanket to wait.

Why hadn't she thought of leaving earlier? If she had realized how easy it was to call a tow truck, she might have. Claire knew the real reason. Pearl, Harry, and the Andersons. Claire wouldn't have traded this night for anything.

A tow truck arrived within a couple of hours, and in short order the driver hooked up her car. Any other campground and she'd be stuck for the night, but Plaskett Creek didn't have a gate—cars were free to come and go when they pleased.

She glanced over at the Andersons' RV. She hated to leave without saying goodbye to Samantha, but maybe it was better this way.

"Are you ready, ma'am?" The tow truck driver called over his shoulder. His voice was low and deep, surprising for a small man.

"Yes." Claire stole one more glance, and then hopped into the truck.

The closest auto body repair shop was in Monterey, an hour north. Claire yawned and fought to stay awake as they drove the winding highway. She scooted down in the passenger's seat, and laid her head against the headrest . . .

"Ma'am?"

Claire felt a nudge on her shoulder.

"We're here."

Claire rubbed her eyes and sat up straight.

"Do you have anywhere you need to be? Mike's Auto Repair doesn't open for another six hours."

No, Claire didn't have anywhere to go at 1:30 in the morning. What was she thinking? She could've had a full night's sleep if she had stayed with Samantha. Should she call her sister? No, that would only cause more problems. If Haley knew she'd had an accident in their mother's VW, she'd call her irresponsible and tell her to come back to Los Angeles. Claire wanted to go to Capitola. And find the writer of the letter.

"Ma'am. Did you hear me?"

"No, sir, I don't have anywhere I need to be." She looked around at her surroundings. Half the lights from the repair shop sign didn't work. The place looked haunted. Few cars were on the road. And there was no one around.

A woman alone in a strange place was an invitation for trouble. Claire's heart beat wildly. Hadn't she learned anything from living in L.A.? Her throat was dry, and she tried to swallow. She was at a loss for words.

"It's the middle of the night, and you're a young lady . . ."

Claire's mind whirled. Her thoughts drifted toward the unthinkable.

"My wife and I live in the town of Capitola. We have an extra room. You can stay the night if you'd like. Then I can bring you back here in the morning."

Claire didn't realize she was holding her breath until she exhaled loudly. The driver's offer came back to her in one-word sentences. *Wife. Room. Capitola.* "Yes. Thank you. I'll get my things," she heard herself say.

Claire rummaged in the backseat of her VW for her duffel bag, pillow, and blankets. She looked over at the driver. He was talking on his cell phone. *Probably calling his wife.* A stab of panic ran through her. This might be a mistake, but what choice did she have? It would be more dangerous to hang out in her car all night in a deserted parking lot. She sized up the driver. He was about her height, and she guessed he didn't weigh much more than she did. She could take him if he turned on her.

"Ready?" He was beside her in a flash.

Claire checked his left hand. He wore a gold wedding band. "Yes."

"I'm Tom Daniels." He took her duffel bag and threw it in the truck. "My wife's name is Nancy. We should be home in forty-five minutes."

The drive to Capitola made her miss her mom all the more. She envisioned her mother as a teenager and living in the small town the summer of 1972. Had her mother driven on this highway? Claire gazed at the silhouettes of the trees as they drove past, wondering what lay ahead for her.

The pine scent from the air freshener in the tow truck filled her nostrils. Claire took a deep breath and remembered the words of the letter. *Riding roller coasters, surfing, and late-night walks.* She sighed. *Holding hands, stealing kisses, and sharing dreams.* Sounded heavenly.

"We're almost there." Tom gave Claire a warm smile, revealing a space between his front teeth. "Nancy is a nurse and works the night shift. So you don't need to tiptoe around. She's used to being up during the wee hours."

A nurse. His wife was a nurse—a career Claire dreamed about. She couldn't wait to talk with Nancy, if she existed. A nagging feeling continued to grab at her gut.

They pulled up to a small ranch-style home, the sidewalk flanked by two queen palm trees, lit by solar lights in the grass. Relief crept into her tense muscles. Surely he wouldn't bring her to a beautiful place like this if he intended to harm her. "Your home is beautiful. What I can see of it in the dark."

"Thank you. Nancy's uncle left it to us a few years ago. Wait till you see the inside. My wife's the decorator. Come on in. I'll help you with your bags." Tom reached in the backseat and grabbed her duffel bag.

Claire wrapped her arms around her pillow and blanket and followed Tom into his home.

"Nancy?" Tom dropped her duffel bag in the entryway. "I'll be right back." He left her standing inside the doorway.

Claire continued to hold tight to her bedding as she looked around the front room. A brown sofa and love seat sat against two walls. A red candle, matching the color of the pillows on the sofa, and a couple of magazines were perched on top of a black coffee table. Wrought iron lamps with gold shades stood next to the sofas. The home definitely had a woman's touch. It was warm. Inviting. Cozy.

"Claire, this is my wife, Nancy." Tom's hand rested on Nancy's shoulder.

A slender middle-aged woman with short brown hair peered through sleepy eyes, as though Tom had merely awakened her. "Nice to meet you, Claire."

"Sorry to wake you." Claire hugged her pillow and blanket a little tighter. "I appreciate this so much."

"Let me show you to your room for the night. We can get better acquainted in the morning. I bet you're exhausted."

Claire followed Nancy down the hall. A photo on the wall caught her eye. A much younger Tom smiled at her from beneath a full head of dark hair. Claire stopped and studied the picture of the bride and groom on their wedding day. Nancy, in an off-the-shoulder dress, held a beautiful bouquet of pink and yellow roses as she looked tenderly at Tom. A picture of a newborn baby hung right beside the wedding photo. Claire strolled down the hall and tried to catch up with Nancy, who'd seemed to disappear.

"Mrs. Daniels?" She passed a master bedroom and then a bathroom on the right.

Nancy poked her head out into the hallway from a room farther down on the left. Her mouth formed a straight line. "I'm sorry, I thought you were right behind me." Were those tears in Nancy's eyes?

"I was following until I got distracted by the photos." Claire hurried into the bedroom and stared. It looked like a picture straight out of a home decorator magazine. The walls were painted a shade of sage green, the same color as the quilt that lay at the edge of the queen-size bed. A picture of a meadow hung on the wall above the wrought iron headboard, and a blanket lay casually over the armrest of a chair tucked in the corner. Wispy curtains flowed from black metal rods, and floral rugs graced the hardwood floors.

Claire sighed. "This is beautiful."

"Oh, thank you." Nancy turned down the bed. "You can use the bathroom you passed on your right, and I'll come get you for breakfast in the morning. Do you need anything?" She sniffed and rubbed her nose.

Claire shook her head no. "Thank you so much."

"Well, good night, then."

"Good night."

Nancy walked out of the room and closed the door behind her.

Strange. The woman's distracted manner gave Claire the feeling she was going through a difficult time in her life. She hoped her staying the night didn't add to Nancy's burden. Claire dropped her pillow and blanket on the floor, and she sat on the bed. It had been an overwhelming day—she left L.A., saw Geraldine at the gas station, ran into Harry and Pearl, met the Andersons, and finally had to rely on a tow-truck driver and his wife. She lay back, exhausted. Could life get any crazier?

Yes, the room was beautiful, but it couldn't take away the dreadful feeling in the pit of her stomach. Her car needed repairs and she didn't have much money to fix it and she depended on strangers to take care of her basic needs of food and shelter. How was she going to make it on her own?

A knock on the door startled her. Her stomach tightened. Claire jumped up and opened the door.

"Everything all right?" Tom stood in the hall still wearing his blue pants and work shirt.

A shiver ran down her spine. *What does he want?* He seemed like a nice man, but so did her brother-in-law a long time ago.

She wouldn't let her guard down around any man, especially a complete stranger. "Yes, thank you." Claire made a move to shut the door.

Tom thrust his foot in the opening to prevent the door from closing.

8

Half of Tom's shoe protruded into the guest bedroom. What did he want? Claire sucked in a breath.

"Nancy got paged. Shortage of nurses tonight at the hospital." Tom leaned forward. "She has a twelve-hour shift."

Claire's pulse jumped. *I'm alone with Tom.* Tae Kwon Do might come in handy. She planned her defense in case he moved closer. "Thanks for letting me know." Her voice sounded shaky. She cleared her throat. What was it about this man that set her on edge?

"I'll knock at 7:30 a.m. I need to be in Monterey by nine." Tom took a step back. "Good night." He turned and walked across the hall to his room.

Claire closed the door, locked it, then leaned against the doorframe. The ticking of the small clock on the nightstand caught her attention. 2:45 a.m. Without Nancy home, every minute until the sun rose would seem like forever. Claire grabbed her pillow and blanket off the floor, flicked off the light, and lay on top of the bed. She punched her pillow a few times before settling into her usual sleep position. Would Tom come back again? The door was locked. She was safe. Wasn't she?

Her body relaxed and her eyes drifted closed.

She woke to raindrops beating against the windowpane. She looked at the clock. It read 9:56. Sucking in a breath, she bolted out of bed and ran into the hall.

"Mr. Daniels?" She passed the master bedroom. The bed was made. "Anyone here?" She approached the family room. A cat skittered past her and raced down the hall and into the couple's bedroom.

She walked into the kitchen. It was bright and cheery despite the rain outside. A red toaster and coffeemaker on the countertop made a nice contrast to the warm yellow walls. She spotted a note by the telephone.

Claire,
I couldn't wake you. Eat breakfast.
I'll check on your car and call around 10 a.m.
Tom

Just then the phone rang. Claire reached over the counter and answered it.

"Hey, you're up." Tom's voice indicated he was a morning person, something she was not.

"Sorry I slept so long." Claire held the phone between her neck and shoulder and lifted the lid to the coffeepot. There were at least two cups left. She poured the dark liquid into a mug she had pulled out of the cabinet.

"I'm down at Mike's Auto Repair on Main Street. The guys can't work on your car without your signature and form of payment." Tom sounded matter-of-fact.

Form of payment? Claire flinched. "How long will they hold my car?"

"I'll talk with Mike and let you know."

She'd have to find a job before she could afford the necessary repairs. She hung up the phone while her coffee heated in the microwave. Rummaging in the refrigerator, she found a package of cinnamon bagels. When she and Haley were kids, her mother bought bagels every Wednesday, half-price days at the bakery down the street. She missed her mom—everything about her, except when she scolded her for sleeping in late. Claire slathered a thick layer of cream cheese on her bagel, grabbed her coffee and sat down at the table. How she wished her mom was still alive. She'd be able to tell her who wrote the letter.

Claire hurried to the guestroom and pulled the envelope from her purse. She brought it to the kitchen and reread the words from her mom's admirer as she ate her breakfast. How far was Depot Hill from Tom's house? She had to find out.

Claire gulped down the last of her coffee, tidied the kitchen, showered, and straightened the guest room before setting off on foot. A bright green umbrella covered her head and rain boots kept her feet dry. She hoped Nancy wouldn't mind that she had borrowed her umbrella, but her hostess had said to make herself comfortable—and it was perched in the corner next to the door. Claire stuck the letter into her tote bag, and then hung it on her left shoulder, tucked close to her body so it wouldn't get wet.

After a fifteen-minute walk, she stopped inside Mr. Toots coffeehouse in Capitola Village. The aroma of coffee and baked goods filled the building.

A short woman, about Claire's age, stood behind the counter straightening a stack of napkins. She looked up as Claire approached. "May I help you?"

"Yes." Claire dug in her purse for the letter. "Can you tell me where I can find Saxon Avenue? On Depot Hill?"

"Sure. Are you driving or walking?" The woman grabbed a napkin and a pen.

The closed umbrella in Claire's hand dripped water on the floor. "Walking."

"No problem." The attendant drew a map on a napkin. "It's easy. And close by." She slid the paper across the counter.

Claire glanced at the napkin. Each street was clearly marked.

"Any questions?"

"Point me in the right direction?"

The woman chuckled. "Once you're out the door, head right."

"Thanks."

Claire hiked through Capitola Village before coming to Monterey Avenue. There she found the steep stairs the attendant had drawn next to the small, boarded-up theatre. She panted as she climbed the mountain of steps before reaching the top of Depot Hill, a neighborhood that overlooked Monterey Bay.

She admired the houses in the neighborhood. An eclectic mix of contemporary, old Victorians, and ranch-style homes graced the streets. She walked down Grand Avenue a couple of blocks. The view of the ocean and the coastline, even on a rainy day, was the reason she loved California. The waves crashed against the shore and the salty air penetrated her senses.

Suddenly there it was—the street she'd been looking for. Claire picked up her pace. She searched for the house among the small, older ranch-style homes. Halfway down the street, she came to an abrupt stop. Number 216. The return address of the letter. An older home with dark blue shutters stood in front of her. Claire walked up the sidewalk, her insides quivering with each step. A *For Rent* sign hung in the window. She climbed the few steps to the porch and set the umbrella down. Leaning up against the window, she peeked in. The front room was empty.

"You interested?" A male voice called from behind.

Claire spun around. A dark-haired young man wearing jeans, hiking boots, and a flannel jacket stood at the bottom of the steps. *Wow, he is good-looking.*

"Are you the owner?"

"No. I'm Blake Coombs, the neighbor." He pointed to the house directly on her left, joined her on the porch, and extended his hand.

Claire shook it. His hand felt warm, nice. "I'm Claire James." She looked up into his steel blue eyes . . . and realized she was still holding his hand. *Neighbor, huh?* Her cheeks heated. She pulled her hand free and tucked her hair behind her ear.

"Good to meet you, Claire. I told the owner I'd keep watch over the house until it was rented. Would you like to see the place?"

Would she like to see it? Definitely. Her insides danced. "Please."

He produced a key from his jeans pocket and stepped toward the front door.

She hesitated for the briefest moment. Something about the man put her at ease. Her desire to go inside the house, the place where her mother's love interest wrote the letter, jumped ahead of her common sense. "I do need to find a place." She removed her boots at the door.

"Then come on in."

Michael's wipers smeared water across his windshield, giving him a hazy view of the street. He pulled his BMW over to the curb and slid out, sidestepping a puddle. Water spattered his face as he attempted to clean the wipers. He couldn't remember when it had rained last.

He jumped back in his car and headed toward his rental property. The small sign posted in the window of the house wasn't much in the way of advertising, but it had done the trick before. The last couple had lived there for a good three years. A job transfer was the only reason for their departure.

Michael turned down Saxon Avenue. The street was only a couple hundred yards long before it reached the bluff. He had bought the house before the market spiked. Light gleamed through the front window. Either Blake had shown the place earlier and had forgotten to turn off the lights, or he was there now with a potential renter. He cut off the engine and hurried to the front door.

Wiping his feet on the mat, he saw a pair of women's rain boots leaning haphazardly against the side of the house. He turned the doorknob and walked in.

"Hey, Michael." Blake rested his arm against the fireplace mantel. "I'm showing the house to a young woman. She's in the bathroom."

"Thanks. Not working today?"

"Even police officers get a day off now and then." Blake tucked his hands into his pockets. "Lately we've been busy cracking down on graffiti. It's been a huge problem."

"I'm glad the police are involved. Do you think it's street gangs?" Michael's eyebrows furrowed. "I've seen signs and walls vandalized. It makes me think twice about showing homes for sale in certain neighborhoods."

"It doesn't appear to be gangs, but I may be wrong. The best thing to do is call 9-1-1 if you see someone destroying property. Street gangs tend to be violent and may carry weapons."

"Thanks for the tip." Michael planted his hands on his hips as he inspected the new paint job. "How's it look?"

"Armstrong Painting does good work." Blake stood next to Michael and looked at the ceiling. "The cut-in line couldn't be any straighter."

"I had the carpets cleaned in the back bedrooms as well. With Julia's wedding around the corner, I'd like to rent the place soon."

Michael heard the water running in the bathroom. He turned when the door opened. A young woman approached. She was about the same age as Julia. Blonde wavy hair spread out like a fan around her shoulders. She was petite even in a raincoat.

"Michael, this is Claire."

"Nice to meet you." Michael held out his hand.

"I've seen you somewhere before." Claire's forehead creased as she shook his hand. "Have we met?"

"I don't think so." Michael laughed. *Was this woman one of Julia's friends?* "I'm the owner. Do you have any questions so far?"

"How much is the rent?" Claire bit her lower lip.

He named a price that made the woman's eyes widen. She wrapped her arms around her midsection and had a look of discomfort on her face.

"I'll need to collect first and last month's rent as a security deposit. And run a credit check." Michael walked over to the window and looked out. "I didn't see a car out front when I came in . . ."

"I walked."

"From where?" Blake piped in.

"Not far from here."

Michael could hear a hitch in Claire's voice. That's all he needed—a homeless woman who couldn't pay rent. But she didn't look homeless by the clothes she wore. "Do you own a car?"

"Yes, a '72 VW bug." Claire's eyebrows furrowed. "But it's in the shop."

Michael's heart skipped a beat. "A '72 VW bug?" He crossed his arms over his chest and chuckled. "The last time I rode in a VW bug was well over twenty years ago."

"I was working on a VW the other day." Blake leaned against the wall. "My cousin thinks *I'm* the repair shop."

Michael made a move to the kitchen. "So, what do you think about the place?"

Claire followed along with Blake. "I'd need to find a roommate."

"It's the right size for two people. It's nine hundred square feet, two bedrooms, one bath." Michael glanced from Claire to Blake. "You'd need to pay for utilities, and I'll take care of landscaping. I've had the same gardener for years."

Claire peered out the kitchen window. "The plants are nice. Especially the daisies along the sidewalk."

"If you're interested, you'll need to fill out this application. And after I check your references, it could be yours." Michael slid the paper across the counter.

Claire picked up the application and looked it over. "When can I get back to you?"

"Here's my business card. Call me anytime." Michael glanced at his watch. "Say, Blake, can you lock up? I've got a meeting in twenty minutes."

"Sure thing." Blake walked him to the door.

Michael grinned. "She'd make a great neighbor." He kept his voice low, almost a whisper.

"You're the one she's met before." Blake raised an eyebrow.

"Nice to *meet* you, Claire." Michael gave Blake a steely look. "Hope to see you again."

Michael shut the door behind him. He hopped in his car and drove in the direction of the office. The meeting was optional, but he felt compelled to leave the rental for reasons he didn't understand. Had he met Claire before? Where? When?

9

Claire stared at the business card in her hand. *Michael Thompson.* That's why he looked familiar. He had attended her mother's funeral. His three-piece suit and beautiful wife on his arm had made him stand out. She heard the click of the door and Michael's car pulling away.

"So, that about wraps it up." Blake's voice interrupted her thoughts as he approached. "Need a ride? It's pouring."

He was nice . . . and attractive. "Sure. Thanks." Claire tucked the business card in her coat pocket, folded the rental application in half, and slid it in her purse. "Can you drop me off at the pizza place in Capitola Village? I'm hungry." She remembered the twenty dollars Geraldine gave her and the pizza parlor she passed on her way to the rental. Her cheeks warmed. Since when had she been so open in front of a guy—a stranger, no less?

Blake chuckled. "Okay. Pizza My Heart it is. I'll get my truck. Wait here." He locked the front door, jogged across the lawn, and climbed into a white Ford F-150 parked in his driveway. She slipped into her rain boots and grabbed Nancy's green umbrella as Blake pulled up to the curb.

Claire could feel his eyes on her as she descended the few stairs. She approached the truck self-conscious of every move. As she reached for the handle, the door flew open with such force that it knocked her to the ground. She found herself sprawled among the row of bushes and small plants that lined the sidewalk.

Blake jumped out of his truck and ran to her side. "Claire, are you okay?" He pulled her to her feet and tenderly picked the grass and leaves out of her hair. "I pushed the door open. So much for being a gentleman."

Claire looked down at herself. Her jeans were soaking wet, and the green umbrella was twisted and torn. At least it had broken her fall. "On second thought, drop me off at the house where I'm staying." Claire hobbled to the truck and slid into the passenger seat, her wet jeans sticking to the leather.

Blake muscled the green umbrella shut and tossed it into the bed of the truck before hopping into the driver's seat next to her. "I owe you at least a slice of pizza."

"But I'm soaked. You don't need to do that." Claire stared straight ahead. One look into his eyes and she'd change her mind for sure.

"I knocked you to the ground and ruined your umbrella. It's the least I can do." Blake turned the key and pulled away from the curb and the small rental house. "We'll get it to go."

She could think of a few things she needed—her car to be fixed, a job, and money to rent the house. Her mind turned from her selfish thoughts. She glanced at Blake as he drove. Nice profile. And his hair curled perfectly over his collar. Her stomach growled. "Okay. One slice."

"Great. I know the owner. He makes the best pizza sauce." Blake made a couple of left turns. "The lunch crowd will start coming in soon, so our timing couldn't be better."

He was wrong. Claire saw the CLOSED sign first. There were "Dangerous Surf" signs posted all along the beach. The waves crashed hard against the shore coming all the way up to the row of shops and businesses. There would be no pizza today.

"Another time." Blake merged into traffic. "Where does your friend live?"

Claire retraced her steps in her mind. What was the name of Tom and Nancy's street? Her cell phone vibrated in her pocket. Haley. Should she answer the call? Her sister must be sick with worry over her hasty departure.

"Why haven't you returned any of my calls?" Her sister's voice sounded angry, controlling, and a bit motherly. *Nothing's changed.*

"Wait a minute, Haley."

Claire motioned for Blake to take a right-hand turn, "I think it's a couple of streets down on your right." She remembered that the streets were named after jewels. She breathed a sigh of relief that the houses looked familiar. "That's it. Turn on Emerald Street."

Blake nodded.

She brought her cell phone to her ear. "Okay, I'm back."

"It's so good to hear your voice." Haley seemed to have calmed down. "I didn't think you'd leave. Where are you?"

"Capitola—a small town in Santa Cruz."

Blake turned down Emerald Street and gestured to Claire.

Claire motioned for him to keep going.

"What's in Capitola?"

Claire put up her hand for Blake to stop and pointed to Tom and Nancy's house. She maneuvered herself out of the truck. Blake joined her and grabbed the disjointed umbrella.

"Hold on, Haley." Claire held the cell phone against her chest and took the broken umbrella. "Thank you for the ride."

"No problem." Blake ran a hand through his dark hair. "It'd be nice to have you for a neighbor. Maybe we can get that pizza another time." He waved. "See you later."

Claire watched him get back in his truck and drive off. She almost forgot Haley was waiting for her. "I'll tell you what's in Capitola. Mom's old love." She stuck her hand inside her coat pocket.

The business card was gone.

10

The sound of a fire truck caught Claire's attention. She tucked her purse and the broken umbrella under her arm and walked between the palm trees toward the Daniels' front door as she finished her conversation with her sister.

"What do you mean Mom's old love?" Haley's voice dripped with sarcasm.

"It's a long story, but I'll let you know if I find him."

"So you're still stuck in the past."

Claire rolled her eyes. "Haley, I've gotta go."

"I finally get ahold of you, and you want to hang up on me?" Haley's voice rose.

"I'm starting my own life—like you said, make friends and go out on dates." Claire turned and looked down the street where Blake had driven merely moments before.

"But do you need to be so far away?" Haley sniffed and blew her nose.

Claire held the phone away from her ear. Was her sister acting overly dramatic? "Give me time. I promise, I'll let you know where I end up. Okay?"

The front door burst open. Tom stood with his hand on his hip and a scowl on his face. "There you are."

"Gotta go." Claire snapped her cell phone shut. "I'm sorry about your umbrella." She set the contraption on the porch and gave a sheepish grin. "I needed a walk. You know, to clear my head. Where's Nancy?"

"In the kitchen." Tom stepped back and allowed Claire to walk through. "We need to talk."

Claire's insides twisted. Now what? Were they ready to toss her out? She deserved nothing better. Claire laid her purse on the bench inside the door, shrugged out of her coat, and hung it on the rack. "Mind if I change first? I'm soaked."

"Nancy and I will be waiting in the kitchen."

The aroma of tomatoes, hamburger, and spices tickled her nose. Her mouth watered. She closed the bedroom door behind her, wiggled out of her wet jeans, and pulled on a pair of sweat pants.

Once in the kitchen, Nancy scooped her a big bowl of chili. "We can't talk on an empty stomach." She dished up two more servings. "I hope you like this. It's my mother's recipe."

Claire set the bowl down and took a seat. "Thank you." Tom sat to her left and Nancy to her right.

"We want the truth." Tom's deep voice startled her.

Claire dropped her spoon into the bowl in front of her. "The truth?" She gulped.

"Let the woman enjoy her food." Nancy chided. "While it's hot."

Tom glared at his bowl, dug his spoon into his chili, and shoved it in his mouth. "After we eat, then."

Claire took small spoonfuls. She wondered what had caused the interrogation. Tom's attitude toward her had changed. Nancy's eyes still held a sadness that Claire didn't understand. She picked up her glass of water. The cool liquid helped her keep her meal down, but it didn't do anything to get rid of the lump that was lodged in her throat.

Nancy stood and ladled another bowlful of chili for her husband.

Tom grunted a "thank you" and started in on his second helping.

Claire felt like running. She didn't need these people to help her. The twenty-dollar bill from Geraldine once again flashed in her mind. She could use the money to take a bus to Monterey and then figure out what to do from there. She'd deal with her car tomorrow. But the truth of her situation made her pulse race. Could she make it on her own or should she go back to L.A.? A soft moan escaped her lips. She couldn't go anywhere until her car was fixed. Claire's eyes darted from Tom to Nancy.

In a moment of panic, she jumped up from her seat and bolted down the hall to the guest room.

"Claire?" She heard Nancy's voice on the other side of the door ten minutes later. "Can I come in?"

Claire didn't feel like talking. She hugged a pillow tight to her chest.

"Claire. Everything will be all right. Please open the door."

The sweetness in Nancy's voice reminded her of her mother. Tossing the pillow aside, Claire pushed herself off the bed and made the few steps to the door. "Come in."

Nancy had a glass of milk in one hand and a small plate of chocolate chip cookies in the other. "Lunch isn't complete without dessert." She set them on the nightstand, then turned to face Claire. "I don't mean to pry, but where are you from and what are you doing here in Capitola?" Her voice was kind.

Even so Claire's palms began to sweat. "I drove up from L.A. to start a new life. Now I need a job so I can get my car fixed and rent my own place." She followed Nancy to the side of the bed. "I'm sorry. I shouldn't have come. But Tom offered, and I didn't know what to do—"

"You did the right thing. And we're happy to have you here. Oh, don't mind Tom. He's going through a rough patch lately—we both are. But we want you to know that you're welcome to stay until you find a place."

Why would these people be so friendly to her? It's as if she were a long-lost relative returning home.

Nancy sat on the edge of the bed. "The truth of the matter is Tom and I wanted to know where you went *this morning*. And when Tom looked out the window and saw you with that man, we didn't know what to think."

Claire's breath caught in her throat. "I only met him."

Nancy's brows shot up.

Suddenly Claire felt like a teenager. "No, it's coming out all wrong." She paced the room. "I went looking for a particular house this morning and found out it's for rent. By the time I wanted to come back, it was raining so hard the *neighbor* gave me a ride."

Claire could tell Nancy was deep in thought by the way she furrowed her brows and worked her lower lip. "Where is this house you're interested in?" Nancy grabbed one of the cookies and took a bite, then gestured for Claire to join her.

"Depot Hill." Claire broke a cookie in half, dipped it in milk, and popped the soggy bite into her mouth.

"Nice area. Homes for rent don't come up there very often." Nancy had a lilt to her voice. "Why don't you show me?"

Why would Nancy want to see the house on Saxon Avenue? It didn't make sense.

Fire trucks blocked Saxon Avenue. "What's going on?" Claire shifted from side to side in the passenger's seat of Nancy's Toyota Camry. "Do you want to park here and walk since it's stopped raining?"

Nancy swerved to the right and pulled next to the curb on Central Avenue. Claire hopped out of the car and fell in beside Nancy as they trekked around the corner to see the emergency.

Claire's heart pounded. If anything happened to *her* house . . . she rolled her eyes at the thought. Of course it wasn't her house yet. She'd need a miracle. But Claire didn't believe in miracles, not like her mother. "I'll get well, you'll see," her mom had said countless times, even when she was close to death. And did she? No! So much for miracles.

Claire tugged on Nancy's arm. "You're a nurse. Someone might need you."

Nancy quickened her pace. "I don't see an ambulance."

Claire spotted Blake. He was talking to a fireman. "Nancy, come on!" Claire sprinted through the puddles toward the crowd that had formed. Dark, billowing smoke dissipated as the firemen doused the right side of Blake's gray house.

"Blake!" Claire approached him with tentative steps.

He stared straight ahead. He blinked a few times and wiped his face with the cuff of his flannel shirt. Claire sidled up next to him. "What happened?" Maybe he'd rather not talk to her. After all, they barely knew each other.

"It's my fault." Blake shrugged his shoulders.

Claire touched his arm, then pulled her hand back. "What do you mean?"

"I left a dish towel too close to my gas stove while a burner was on."

"When?"

"Earlier today. I was making a pot of soup for lunch when I saw you through the window and grabbed the keys for the rental. I thought I turned it off, but apparently it was still on low."

Blake folded his arms across his chest and shook his head.

Nancy came up beside them. "I heard a fireman say you had a kitchen fire. I'm glad you weren't hurt. As a nurse I've seen far too many burn victims."

Claire's stomach churned. The fire could've been prevented if she hadn't let Blake show her the rental. Why had she bothered? She couldn't afford the house anyway. Guilt nagged at her.

"I bought the house six months ago. The kitchen is what sold me on the place." Blake sighed. "I'd better check out the damages and see if anything's salvageable." He nodded a farewell and joined the firemen standing on his front porch.

"At least the fire didn't consume the whole house." Nancy rubbed her arms. "It's chilly out here. Can we see the rental now?"

Claire pointed next door.

"*Blake's* the neighbor?"

"Can we go? I've changed my mind." Claire glanced at Blake, then walked down the sidewalk. A small white card was wedged in the bushes in front of the rental house. She leaned down and picked it up. Michael Thompson's business card. It must have fallen out of her pocket when she fell. The memory of Blake helping her up and picking the debris out of her hair brought a smile to her face. But how could she face him again?

"Claire? Wait a minute. Did I miss something?"

Claire walked down the street toward Nancy's car. "Blake does *not* want me for a neighbor."

"I didn't get that impression."

"The fire is my fault. If he hadn't shown me the place, the fire never would've started." Claire took quick steps toward Central Avenue. She glanced over her shoulder. Nancy stood with her hands on her hips in the middle of the street. Claire spun around. "What? Can we go?"

Nancy shook her head. "Not until I see the place."

"Why? I can't afford it anyway." Claire grabbed the collar of her jacket and pulled it tighter around her neck. "It's cold out here. Can we please leave?"

"Claire, I know we've only just met, but I feel God sent you to Capitola for a reason. Please, let me help you."

First Geraldine, then Pearl and Harry, and now Tom and Nancy. She'd never been helped so much in all of her life and didn't know what to make of it. Her insides shivered.

Nancy interrupted her musings. "Look, I have an idea. But before I tell you, I'll need to see the house."

11

"What's your idea?" Claire walked toward Nancy and stood in front of her.

"I'd like to see the place first." Nancy linked her arm through Claire's. "To see if it's right for my sister. We've been estranged for many years, but I've wanted her to move here and now may be the time to make things right. So, how do we get in?"

Her sister. Claire whipped out the business card from her jacket pocket and handed it to Nancy. If anything, maybe Nancy's sister will end up renting the place. "Call him."

"Michael Thompson, Realtor, huh?" Nancy pulled her cell phone out of her backpack-style purse and punched in the numbers. "How did you get his card?"

"He gave it to me."

"You've met the owner?"

"More than once." Claire thought back to her mom's funeral. Mr. Thompson had looked out of place with his fancy designer suit and tie. Claire didn't remember him being social. She had wondered why he had come.

"Hello, Mr. Thompson?" Nancy and Claire walked in the direction of the rental house as the rain came pouring down again. "My name is Nancy Daniels, and I'd like to see the inside of your rental home on Saxon Avenue . . ."

Michael couldn't believe his good fortune—two viewings of his rental property in one day. He loaded his briefcase with paperwork and swung his overcoat over his shoulders.

Eric stuffed a donut in his mouth and followed it with a swig of coffee. "Where are you headed in such a hurry?"

"Got a call on my rental." Michael pulled his car keys from his pants' pocket. "I've got to run." He waved. "I'll be back, though, so save one of those donuts for me."

"Yeah, right, Mr. Fit. When's the last time you've eaten a donut?" Eric called to Michael's back.

Michael swung around. "If I find a renter, I'll want to celebrate." He pushed the door open and slid out into the pouring rain. He covered his head with his briefcase and dashed to his car.

He saw a fire truck pass by on his left, and the neighbors milling about. He didn't see an ambulance, so decided not to be overly concerned. Two women huddled together under the eaves of his rental. Michael squinted as he studied one of the women. He'd recognize that wavy blonde hair anywhere. Claire. He turned off the engine, unclipped his seatbelt, and slid out of the car. She must really want the place. The woman beside Claire was older and looked put together, from her raincoat to her matching scarf and hat. Michael scanned the street and once again saw no car. How'd they get here?

He approached the house with his briefcase in hand.

"Mr. Thompson, I'd like you to meet Nancy Daniels." Claire blew into her hands. She appeared to be trembling.

"You must be cold out here." Michael extended his hand to Nancy. "Please, no formality. Call me Michael. Let's get you two inside." He put the key into the lock and opened the door. The smell of fresh paint wafted from the front room. "Claire, since you've been here before, why don't you show Nancy around?"

Michael kept his distance as Claire took Nancy from the living room to the kitchen. "The house has two bedrooms, one bath, and is nine hundred square feet. We'd be responsible for the utilities, and Mr. Thompson . . ." Claire glanced over her shoulder at him, "I mean Michael, will take care of landscaping."

Michael wondered if the women were browsing or serious about the place. He hoped Nancy would be the one paying the rent. Then he might not be worried about late payments. It might be good to have an older woman around to keep things in order too. No wild parties destroying his property.

"Hey, Michael? I'm sorry to barge in like this." Blake's voice interrupted Michael's thoughts. "I need to talk with you. It's urgent." He stood in the doorway with his arms tight across his chest.

Michael had never seen the man look so distraught. "Ladies, excuse me," he called over his shoulder. "I'll be back in a minute."

Michael kept in stride with Blake as they marched across the lawn. "What's up? You're making me nervous." The smell of smoke and burnt wood filled the air. They walked to the far side of the house. Michael gasped. "Blake, what happened?"

"It was an accident. I left a burner on and a dish towel caught fire." Blake opened the front door.

Michael took in the sparse setting. A black leather couch faced a simple entertainment center housing some stereo equipment. A flat screen television filled the far wall. Blake's single, all right. Reminded him of his own bachelor days.

"Thank God it was only the kitchen." Blake let out a long breath.

Michael picked up a singed potholder. "Looks like you're out of commission for a while."

"That's where you come in."

"Me?"

"Your rental house, I mean. Come, have a seat." Blake motioned him to the couch.

"I can only stay a minute, I've got possible renters." Michael gestured toward his property.

"Here's my thought." Blake sat with his elbows resting on his knees. "I'd like to use the kitchen in your rental till I can have mine repaired. I'll be glad to pay, of course."

Michael rubbed the back of his neck. "But if I have renters, how will that work?"

"Depending on who it is and what they're willing to negotiate, I'd offer to chip in on their rent for the use of the kitchen."

Michael paused.

"I've learned my lesson. You won't have to worry about *your* kitchen catching fire." Blake clasped his hands together.

"Can't see the harm in that. Sure. You'll have to work it out with the renters. Long as I get paid each month, no problem." Michael pushed himself to his feet and patted Blake on the shoulder. "You can start tonight. I'm sorry about your house."

"Thanks, man. Appreciate it."

Michael let himself out, shutting the door behind him. Poor Blake. That man loved his natural wood countertops and oak cabinets. He strolled down the sidewalk.

Michael heard Nancy's announcement the second he walked through the door.

"We'll take it."

"Great!" He joined the women in the kitchen. "I'll need the two of you to fill out the application. . . ." He fumbled through his briefcase trying to locate the paperwork. His mind drifted to his down-and-out neighbor as his eyes swept his clean, usable kitchen. How could he bring up the subject of Blake's need to use the rental kitchen?

"Michael?" It was Claire's voice this time.

He snapped back to the present. "I'm sorry. I learned that my neighbor's kitchen is totally destroyed by an accidental fire. It'll be out of commission for a couple of months, at least. He had an interesting proposition for me—and possibly for you." Michael leaned back with his hands resting against the counter. "Blake wants to use *this* kitchen while his is being rebuilt. He would pay part of the rent." Michael looked directly at Claire. "Would it be something you'd consider?"

A smile tugged at the corners of Claire's lips. "I don't see a problem, unless he cooks at weird hours."

Michael turned and caught Nancy's eye. "What do you think?"

"Well, since I'm not the one renting with Claire, I'll need to get back to you on that."

"Sure." Michael's pulse quickened. "Who *will* be renting the house with Claire?"

"Oh." Nancy chuckled. "I didn't mean to alarm you. But since I haven't spoken with my sister yet, I'd like to talk with her first. I'll most likely make the security deposit when we hand in the application, so you won't need to worry about that."

Michael liked this woman already. Any form of payment right now would be great. He wanted to make it official. Then he could relax. He'd have the money he needed to make a few payments of his own for Julia's wedding.

"Here's my card, call me when you're ready. I plan to keep showing the house until I have an application and cleared credit check on hand. I told Blake he could cook here anytime until renters move in. But after that, he'll have to work out the details."

Nancy nodded. "We understand."

Michael grabbed his briefcase. "Thanks, ladies. Unless you have any more questions, I need to head back to the office."

"Only one." Claire's voice wavered. "You were at my mom's funeral—Emily James, right?"

Michael could swear someone had socked him in the gut.

Claire folded her arms across her chest. "How *did* you know her?"

12

Claire shifted from one foot to the other as she anticipated Michael's response. Her question seemed to catch him off guard. Surprise showed in his eyes in the moment his gaze shifted away.

"Oh, Emily and I go way back. Your mom was a good woman."

A completely unsatisfying answer. Was he hiding something? Could Michael have written the letter? "How far back?"

Michael's laugh sounded forced. "A long time." Was he blushing? The lighting was dim in the house, but Claire could swear Michael looked a little warm under the collar. "We lost touch, then a mutual friend called to tell me she passed from cancer." Michael dropped his briefcase to the floor and brought his hands to his hips. "I'm sorry for your loss. How have *you* been? And from your interest in the house, you must be serious about relocating."

Smooth. He wanted to change the subject. Why? "Yeah. I've decided to give Capitola a try." She glanced at Nancy. "And with Nancy's help, it looks like I might be able to do that."

"Great. Like I said—get that application to me as soon as possible. I'll run a credit check, and then the place will be yours." Michael's shoulders visibly relaxed. He reached for the door handle. "After you, ladies."

Claire walked through the doorway. Was Michael telling her the whole truth? Whether he was or not, soon she'd be living in her own place—her first home. Of course, she'd need a roommate. And hopefully Nancy's sister would be just that person.

"Do you ladies need a lift?" Michael gestured toward his black BMW.

"Oh, no. Thank you. Nancy's car is around the corner." Claire pointed.

"We couldn't get any closer with the fire truck and people blocking the street," Nancy added.

"I see." A smile crossed Michael's lips. "I'll be waiting for your application. If you change your mind, please call." He opened his car door and slid behind the wheel.

"We'll bring it by tomorrow," Nancy called before his door shut.

Michael waved and took off down the street.

Nancy bumped Claire's shoulder playfully. "What was that all about?"

Claire frowned. "What do you mean?"

"The questions . . . and the looks." Nancy slipped the rental application in her purse as they walked down the street. "So, Michael was at your mom's funeral. Did you know all the guests but him?"

Claire had to admit there were quite a few people from her mom's past she'd never met before the memorial. The room had been packed and her mind was in a fog. Her thoughts shifted to the letter. "Before you call your sister, there's something I'd like to show you."

Nancy hugged the paper to her chest as she and Claire sat on the brown suede sofa in Nancy's family room. "I'll never forget my first love." She handed the letter to Claire. "Michael could be your mom's old boyfriend. How exciting. Are you going to show him the letter?"

"Maybe in time. He didn't seem interested in sharing any *real* details today." Claire gently folded the letter in half and slid it inside the envelope. "I wonder if the rental house has been in Michael's family for years." Claire leaned back against the couch.

"What do you mean?" asked Nancy.

Claire pointed to the left corner of the envelope. "The address of the rental house is the same one as on the envelope."

"How romantic." Nancy looked lost in her own thoughts. "And to think you're going to live in that house . . ."

"I need a roommate and a job first." Claire pulled Nancy out of her daydream as she tucked the envelope into the pocket of her jean jacket.

"Oh, yes. I need to call Vivian." Nancy sprang off the sofa.

"Vivian? I knew a Vivian down in L.A. She worked with me at a diner." Claire talked to Nancy's back as she headed toward the kitchen.

Nancy whipped around. "You know Vivian?"

Claire furrowed her brows. "You mean to tell me your sister Vivian is a waitress at a diner in L.A.?"

Nancy nodded. "She's heavyset, about this tall." Her hand came up to her chin.

Small world. Claire's jaw dropped. "I can't believe it. Vivian is your *sister*!"

Claire stood and paced the room as Nancy ran off to call her sister. How would Claire feel about renting a house with Vivian—someone twenty years older? She had seemed sweet and friendly when they worked together at the diner, but Mom once said as people age they get set in their ways. Would Vivian run the house without asking Claire her opinion? She picked up the red candle that sat on the coffee table and brought it to her nose. Closing her eyes, she inhaled the sweet apple scent. After setting the candle down, she walked to the window and ran her hand down the camel-colored drape.

Vivian might have her own ideas—on how to decorate, when to do the chores, and what to do on the weekends. Claire would have to compromise. It would be like having an older sister in the house again. She sat down on the sofa and leaned her head back.

What if Vivian still held a grudge against Nancy? Wouldn't that spill into Claire's life when she already had enough problems of her own? Maybe she didn't want Vivian for a roommate.

Claire's heart skipped a beat. She was trying to define herself as a person, become independent. She heard Nancy end her phone call.

"Vivian agreed to come for a visit! It took a while to convince her, but once she found out you were here, she agreed to come." Nancy rushed over to Claire and gave her a big hug. "Vivian said it would be nice to have a friend in Capitola—someone to run interference!" Nancy swatted the air. "That sister of mine. I'm simply glad she's coming."

"She's moving to Capitola sight unseen?" Her stomach twisted into a queasy knot.

"Well, no. I didn't have the chance to tell her about the house on Saxon Avenue."

Claire felt as if everyone else was dictating her life. She didn't like it. "So, should we show her the house first before we fill out the application?"

"No. We're going to fill out the application now and give a deposit. After all, you need a roof over your head . . . and I need my sister back. We'll take it one step at a time." Nancy squeezed Claire's hand.

Claire had a feeling at this point Nancy would do anything to make amends with her sister. Why would she put money down for someone she didn't know? Another thought wound its way through Claire's mind. Why should she question Nancy's kindness? Like the woman said, something inside her made her want to help. And at this point, who was Claire to argue?

Tom's tow truck pulled up in front of the house.

Claire joined Nancy at the window. Her Volkswagen was hitched to the back of Tom's truck. She raced through the door. Her car evoked emotions she couldn't explain. Happiness. Sadness. Joy. Fear. Without her VW, she felt lost and alone. Claire approached her car and ran her hand over the top. As pitiful as it looked, she was glad to have it back.

"I thought it'd be better to bring your car home." Tom reached down and unhitched the Volkswagen from the tow truck. "I told the guys at the shop you needed more time and that I'd bring it back down when you were ready."

"Thanks, Tom." Claire leaned against the passenger door. "I appreciate it."

"Tom, your dinner's in the microwave," Nancy called from the front door. "I've got to be at work in half an hour."

"I'll be there in a minute. You coming?"

Claire was hungry, but she didn't want to intrude on Tom and Nancy's time. "Please, go ahead. I'll be inside in a little bit."

Claire watched Tom greet Nancy with a kiss. As funny and creepy as she thought Tom was, it was nice to see his affection with his wife.

A white Ford F-150 pulled up. Blake hopped out of his truck. "Hey, Claire, how about that pizza?"

13

When she received the dinner invitation, Claire wanted to blurt out, "I'd love to," but thought better of it. Blake was one good-looking guy. But is that all he was? Someone easy on the eyes? Her mother had dated several handsome men, but when it came down to it, they bolted. "Friendship is the main ingredient for a good relationship," her mother used to say. But by the time her mother figured that out, she was diagnosed with cancer.

"Pizza sounds good, thanks," she said instead. "I'll let Tom and Nancy know." Claire sidestepped toward the house. "Be right back."

"Nancy, Tom?" Claire called as she approached the kitchen.

Tom sat at the table watching his frozen dinner spin around in the microwave. "Where's Nancy?"

"Getting ready for work. Care to join me?" Tom pushed out a chair with his foot.

"Thank you." Claire rubbed her hands together. "But Blake—you know, the guy who lives next door to the house for rent—invited me to dinner."

Nancy stepped into the kitchen wearing her nurse's uniform. "He didn't want to cook in the rental house tonight, huh?" She winked. "Have fun."

Claire ran to the bathroom to check her face in the mirror. She wasn't one for much makeup, but tonight she added a coat of mascara, a few swipes of blush, and lip gloss that held a hint of pink. Then she gently ran her fingers through the curls, attempting to tame her crazy mane. The rain had tightened her soft waves into ringlets. She raced into the bedroom and changed into her favorite T-shirt and sweater.

"Bye. I'll be back in a couple of hours," Claire called to Tom and Nancy in the kitchen, and then headed toward the front door.

"Take your time," Tom called back. "I'll leave the front door unlocked."

Claire slipped through the doorway. Nancy must have talked to Tom and softened his heart in the few minutes she dressed. Either that or maybe he had resolved whatever issue he was going through. The last time he saw her come out of Blake's truck, he glared at her. Of course, that was before he knew of her situation. Reality set in. She was *still* homeless and in need of a job—but maybe her luck would turn.

Blake inspected the dents her car had sustained in the accident. He furrowed his brow and shook his head. "I bet this was a beauty before the accident." He rubbed the top of her car with one hand. "What year did you say this was?"

"'72." Her throat closed around a lump of grief. Suddenly, she needed to get away from her mangled car.

Blake looked her way. "Shall we go?"

"I'm ready."

"I want to run something by you," Blake said the minute they pulled away from the curb in his truck. He turned left on Capitola Avenue toward Pizza My Heart. "Since my kitchen is destroyed, I was hoping you'd share yours, or the one I hope is yours in the rental." He glanced her way, then turned his eyes back on the road. "I'll do the cooking and provide the food."

Claire had never been a good cook. Macaroni and cheese was about the extent of her cooking skills, unless she counted frozen dinners or cold sandwiches.

Blake passed Mr. Toots and Pacific Coast Grille. "What time are you up in the mornings?"

"Depends if I have a reason to get up." That came out wrong. She pressed her lips together.

Blake laughed. "Believe me, my cooking will be worth getting up for. Shall we say 8:00 a.m?"

"All right. I'll do my best to look presentable."

"I bet you're cute any time of day."

"These curls? You've got to be joking." Claire tucked a stray hair behind her ear.

"And how about dinner at six?" Blake pulled into a parking spot in front of the pizza parlor and turned off the engine.

He'd be cooking for her? Outrageous. No man had ever cooked her a meal before—except a male chef in a restaurant. Her face flushed. "Every day?"

Blake held the door open. "Most days. My schedule's kind of crazy. I work ten-hour shifts four days a week."

She walked through the doorway. "What's your job?"

"I'm a police officer." He followed her inside.

"Nice." She liked a man in a uniform. A grin tugged at the corners of her mouth. "So, what did Michael say?"

"He agreed as long as the new tenant was okay with it. So what do you say?"

"Sounds good to me."

The table by the window was available. Claire sat in the chair facing the ocean while Blake ordered a medium-sized pizza—half pepperoni for him and half vegetarian for her.

Claire mulled over the plan he laid out. Good thing she was getting a roommate. Too much contact with Blake might cause her to do silly things—like fall for him. A roommate would keep her from being alone with him while his kitchen was being rebuilt.

"Here's the root beer." Blake set the pitcher and two plastic cups down on the table. "The pizza should be done soon."

Claire looked out the window. "I'm glad the storm passed. The waves are nothing like they were earlier."

"All the businesses along the beach are used to sandbagging. I'm glad Pizza My Heart reopened tonight." Blake filled both cups with soda. "There's nothing like good Italian food after a crazy day."

When their pizza came, the smell of melted cheese, pepperoni, and vegetables filled Claire's nostrils. Heavenly.

Blake held out his hand. "If you don't mind, I'd like to pray."

Claire inhaled deeply. Her mom had prayed before meals. Claire hadn't uttered one word of thanksgiving to God since he took her mom away. She put her hand in his. Blake's grip was warm, and strong. She bowed her head and listened to his words.

"Dear Heavenly Father, thank you for this food. Thank you for watching over us and protecting us. Bless our conversation. In Jesus' name, amen."

Blake gave Claire's hand a squeeze before releasing it. Surprisingly, his prayer was a comfort. She kept her eyes down as she picked up a slice and set it on her plate.

"Feel free to have pepperoni if you'd like." Blake grabbed a piece.

"Thanks. I might." Claire's eyes met his. "Can I ask you a question?"

"Sure." Blake reached for the Parmesan cheese.

"Why aren't you mad about the fire? How can you smile and make plans like nothing happened? And why aren't you angry with *me*?" Claire picked up her pizza and took a bite.

"That's three questions," Blake teased. "I'm not angry with you because it was *my* fault. I left a dishtowel too close to the flames. I'm not mad about the fire, simply disappointed in myself." He averted his eyes for the briefest moment. "But I have insurance, so I know my kitchen will be as good as new." Blake smiled and took a sip of his soda. "I'm grateful to God that my whole house didn't burn to the ground. And I'm able to use the kitchen in the rental and get to know you in the process."

Claire's cheeks heated. Was this man for real? His faith reminded her of Harry and Pearl's. "That's if I end up renting the place."

"Why wouldn't you?" Blake filled his cup from the pitcher. "Want more?"

Claire nodded. "It's only out of the goodness of Nancy's heart that I have a chance. She's going to make the security deposit with the hope her sister moves here. I need to find a job. . . ."

A man walked toward them carrying two full pitchers, one in each hand. Michael? What was he doing here? Claire stuffed pizza in her mouth, swallowed hard, and took a swig of soda.

"Blake." Michael nodded. "My wife, daughter, and her fiancé are seated at the booth in the corner. I'd like my wife to meet you. You've done so much to help me out with the house." Michael shifted. "Didn't want to cook in the rental your first night, huh?"

"I wanted to firm up plans with your new tenant." Blake gestured to Claire.

She felt invisible. Did Michael try to ignore her, or did it come naturally? Something didn't feel right. Claire stole a glance at Michael, then looked down at her purse. The letter was sandwiched between her wallet and personal items.

Michael turned to Claire. "Do you have that application for me?"

She shook her head. Michael must be desperate to rent the place. Why would she have it here at the restaurant? "Nancy's working tonight, but we hope to get it to you tomorrow."

Michael nodded, then gestured toward the corner booth. "I'm going to join my family. Stop by before you go."

Blake nodded. "My pleasure."

Michael walked toward his family and sat down. She remembered his wife from her mother's funeral. Her jet black hair matched her daughter's, although they were cut in different styles—his wife's in a bob and his daughter's past her shoulders.

"You've never met Michael's family?" Claire finished off her first slice and reached for a second.

"No, but it'll be nice to finally meet them. Now, what were you saying about a job?"

"I need one. Desperately. I can't expect Nancy to pay my rent, and there's the issue of my car—"

"I know a thing or two about restoring old Volkswagens. I occasionally work on old cars. I'd be happy to work on your VW in my spare time. It's the least I can do for barging in on your kitchen space." Blake grinned. "But you have to promise you won't tell anyone. I don't want the word to get around that I'm a mechanic."

Claire clamped her mouth shut with her thumb and index finger. "I won't tell a soul." A surge of hope welled inside of her. Maybe God did care about her . . . at least a little.

"I'll get a couple of carry-out boxes." Blake stood. "Cold pizza makes a great breakfast."

Claire agreed. She laughed as Blake headed toward the front counter. There were plenty of mornings when she and Haley had eaten cold pizza.

Blake returned and loaded the boxes with the remaining slices. "Ready to meet the Thompson family?"

"I think Michael wants you to meet his family." Claire stood and draped her sweater around her shoulders.

"Nonsense. I'm sure the whole family would like to meet their new tenant." Blake's hand touched the small of her back, propelling her forward. "Come on, Claire."

Ready or not, she was about to come face-to-face with Michael's family. Why was she nervous? She wasn't the one dodging questions. Michael had sidestepped hers. Claire moved around a few tables as she headed toward the corner booth with Blake close behind. She couldn't help but overhear Michael and his wife's conversation.

"Who's going to take care of her all day while I'm planning the wedding?" Michael's wife was asking.

"Sandy, you know Mom can't stay at Regis anymore. They'll put her in the nursing home, and that's no place for her." Michael ran a hand through his hair.

"If she keeps falling, maybe that's where she needs to be—"

"I'd rather Mom move in with us. There's no question about that." Michael leaned both arms on the table and turned to his wife. "And she also needs a caregiver while you're busy with wedding plans."

"Sorry, is this bad timing?" asked Blake.

"Hi, I'm Julia." The pretty young woman held up her hand. Then she smiled and turned to the young man next to her. "And this is my fiancé, David."

Blake shook Julia's hand first, then David's. "Nice to meet you both. I'm Blake. I live next to your parents' rental home on Depot Hill. And this is Claire." Blake nudged her forward. "She's hoping to rent the house."

Sandy's eyes lit up. "Wonderful." She linked arms with her husband. "It will be so nice to have someone living there. It is an adorable home."

"Sandy, you remember Claire, Emily James's daughter." Michael gave his wife a "just go with me" look.

"Oh, yes. How are you, dear?" Sandy's brows furrowed as she held out her hand.

Claire didn't know what to say. She reached out and shook Sandy's delicate hand, noticing the large diamond shimmering in the light. Her mom never had a ring like that. "I'm fine. Thank you."

"You don't happen to know anyone who might be able to be a caregiver for my elderly mother, do you?" Michael directed his question at Blake. "As a police officer, you must be familiar with local businesses and people around town. You've been so helpful overseeing the house . . ."

Claire's pulse quickened. Could she do it? Become a caregiver for an elderly woman? She did need a job, and the opportunity Michael presented literally felt like it was falling into her lap. Time to be bold. She cleared her throat. "I'm available."

Sandy looked at her husband.

His mouth twitched, and he tugged on his ear. "Have you ever taken care of someone before?"

Didn't he remember? "My mom, as she wasted away from cancer—"

"Of course." Sandy's eyes softened. "That must have been difficult."

Claire nodded and drew a long breath. "It was. But I learned a lot about how to take care of someone when they're sick. Not that your mother is ill." She swallowed hard. Did she just blow her chances?

"Mother's coming for a visit tomorrow. We're hoping she stays." Michael whipped out a pen from his suit coat pocket and scribbled something on a napkin. "Here's our home phone number and address. Come by tomorrow afternoon around four. We'll let the two of you meet to see if you're a good match. Fair enough?"

"You're sure, Michael?" Sandy leaned toward her husband and spoke in hushed tones. "What do you know about this woman?"

Claire took the napkin from Michael. "Fair enough."

"We'll let you get back to your meal. Nice to meet you all." Blake smiled that winning grin of his.

Claire followed Blake to his truck. He unlocked the passenger side door and opened it. "You were saying . . ."

Claire slid into the seat. "What do you mean?"

Blake leaned against the door. "You needed a job and like that, you may have one. Isn't God good?" He closed the passenger door, walked around the truck, and got inside.

"But I haven't met his mother yet." Claire raised her eyebrows. "She may be impossible to work for. Or she may not like *me*."

Blake chuckled. "So much for optimism."

Comfortable silence filled the five-minute car ride back to Nancy and Tom's house. Claire grinned. A glimmer of hope flickered inside her. Soon, she might have a roof over her head, her car repaired, and a job. Things were looking up. After waving goodbye to Blake, she walked into the house. Tom was fast asleep on the family room couch. She tiptoed down the hall to her room and saw a note attached to her door. Claire recognized Tom's handwriting.

Vivian changed her mind. She said there's too much hurt from the past. She's decided not to come.

14

Michael woke to the sound of the alarm clock. It was Saturday. Before he said a word, Sandy popped out of bed and raced to turn it off. *Bless her for trying.* He rolled over and tried to go back to sleep. Sandy, on the other hand, strolled into the bathroom to take a shower. His wife was looking forward to this day. Sandy was meeting Julia at her apartment and the two of them would go see the florist to select the wedding flowers, and then meet with the caterer to decide on the reception menu. It was a good day for mother and daughter to have fun. Sandy had impeccable taste, but she didn't always look at the price tag before making a purchase.

Michael flipped over in bed and stared at the ceiling. He wanted his daughter's marriage to last a long time—a lifetime, but did the flowers and food for the wedding need to cost more than a few months' rent on the couple's first apartment? He chided himself for the thought. Julia was his daughter—his only child. Of course, he'd give her the wedding of her dreams. He would trust his wife with the decisions—the dress, flowers, food, and whatever else they needed to pull off a wedding they'd be proud of.

Michael sat up and swung his legs over the side of the bed. He twisted left and then right to get the kinks out of his back. He was tired of worrying about money. He had other things to think about, like picking up his ornery mother at the airport and bringing her home to meet Claire, the young woman who reminded him of Emily.

Claire glanced at her watch. 3:45 p.m. Hopefully, Blake would pull up any minute. He had offered to take her to Michael's house to meet Michael's mother. *Will we like each other? Can we get along? Will they hire me?* Her stomach twisted. Claire couldn't wait to get out of the house. Nancy had been in tears all morning talking to Vivian on the phone. Apparently, whatever had happened between the two, emotions ran deep. Claire hoped they'd resolve the problem soon. She needed a roommate, but more important, she knew Nancy loved her sister and wanted her back in her life.

The slam of a car door sounded. Claire pulled back the curtain and looked out. Blake's truck was parked out front, and he was approaching the door. She grabbed her jeans jacket and purse from the couch as the doorbell rang. "It's Blake," she called.

Nancy came out of her bedroom and joined her in the front room. "Be yourself. I'm sure Michael will hire you." She pulled a tissue from her pocket and blew her nose. "When you come home, we'll talk about the rental, okay?" Her red-rimmed eyes glistened.

Claire's heart ached for Nancy. "Okay."

When Claire opened the door, Blake was standing on the front porch. "Ready?"

"Ready as I'll ever be." Claire spun around to say goodbye, but instead heard the click of the door to the master bedroom. She turned to face Blake. "Nancy's had a hard day."

"Anything any of us can help her with?"

Blake was not only handsome on the outside, but also his gentle spirit radiated from within. "No. It's something she has to work out on her own."

The air was crisp and the sun shone brightly, drying up the wet roads from the day before. Claire couldn't believe the beautiful trees—evergreens, Monterey pines, and eucalyptus flanked the highway as they headed toward Michael's home. They turned left on Freedom Boulevard, and made a few more quick turns before coming to Downing Drive. Michael and his wife lived in a beautiful neighborhood. The houses had space between them—more than Claire had ever seen. She couldn't picture Michael, a businessman, taking care of the yard. Of course, he had a gardener—someone who took care of the small yard at the rental property and probably his larger property, as well. Michael's house sat back from the road, a looming two-story structure with lots of windows.

"We're right on time." Blake's voice interrupted her thoughts as he pulled up the long driveway.

Claire took a deep breath and rubbed her hands together.

Blake cut the engine and rested a hand on her shoulder. "Lord, give Claire courage and peace. And help Michael's mother to see Claire the way I see her. In your name, amen."

Claire looked into Blake's eyes. "Is that a good thing?"

He nodded and winked. "Come on. You'll be fine."

The doorbell rang. Four o'clock on the nose. "She's prompt." Michael set the newspaper down on the coffee table. His mother sat on the corner cushion of the couch twiddling her thumbs. He strode across the room to the entry and opened the front door. "Hello, come on in." Michael lowered his voice. "My mother is in the family room. She's quite nervous."

Claire fidgeted with the hem of her jacket, looking a little nervous too.

Blake put his hand on Claire's shoulder. "We'll follow you."

"All right, this way." Michael couldn't help but notice what a striking couple Claire and Blake made. Of course, they had barely met. Blake was a good guy who enjoyed helping people, even when he was in need of help himself. And Claire. Well, he'd make sure he kept his contact with her to a minimum. No need to stir up the past. He led them into the family room. "Mother, I'd like you to meet Claire."

"Geraldine?" Claire's eyes opened wide, and her hands shot up to her mouth.

"Claire James? Is that you, dear?" She squinted and leaned forward.

"Yes." Claire raced to Michael's mother and wrapped her arms around her.

"I had forgotten you two would know each other!" Michael, his mouth open, stood next to Blake. "Remind me again how you're acquaintances."

"Michael, dear, you remember Claire's mother, Emily James." She gave a tentative smile, revealing teeth that had aged well. "Claire lived in the same apartment building as I did—the one on Gray Street—you remember."

Michael could swear Claire sat up straighter on the couch, her eyes fixed intently on him at the mention of Emily's name.

Geraldine tapped Claire's leg. "How is that beautiful sister of yours? Holly, right?"

"*Haley's* fine." Claire glanced up at Blake and smiled.

"What are you doing here in Santa Cruz?" Her brows rose.

"I moved here."

"Really? I'm moving too. My friends are passing away one by one in that retirement community. I need to hang around younger folks. Like you and your boyfriend over there." She pointed.

Claire's cheeks instantly showed pink. "Oh. Blake's not my boyfriend. He's my new neighbor . . . or at least I hope he'll be. I want to rent Michael's house on Saxon Avenue." She turned to Michael. "It looks like the woman I wanted to room with—Nancy's sister Vivian—isn't coming after all."

Michael sat down on the recliner. Emotions twisted his insides. He motioned for Blake to take a seat in the chair to his right. "What do you mean?"

"Family problems, I hear." Claire averted her eyes from him and looked down at her hands clamped tight on her lap. "I'll need to find another roommate. But I can talk to you more about that later. I'm here to see if I can help with your mother's care."

Geraldine's chest puffed out. "Oh, I can take care of myself."

"Now, Mother, you've been falling . . . and I know you need a little help with certain tasks."

"I don't want to be a bother." She touched her thinning white hair with gnarled fingers.

"You know we want you here. We wouldn't have suggested you move in with us unless we wanted you to." Michael leaned forward, resting both elbows on his knees. Did he? What would it be like to have his mother under his roof? Getting ready for the wedding would make their lives difficult enough.

"Where's Sandy? I don't see her here to welcome me." Geraldine made a sweeping gesture with her arms. "You know a two-week visit is enough for both Sandy and me. We'll fight like two cats after a while."

"Mom, you're exaggerating. You and Sandy have always gotten along—as good as a mother-in-law can with her only son's wife." He grinned, suddenly aware of the others in the room. "Let's discuss this later. . . ."

"No, dear. We'll discuss this now." She motioned for Claire to get her walker. "Help me up, Claire."

Claire did as she was asked. Michael could see Claire's caregiver instincts kicking in.

"Why couldn't I live in the rental with Claire? We'd be out of your hair so that you and Sandy could plan this wedding without worrying about me." She stood slightly stooped over, holding on to the handles of her walker. "I always loved that small house. It's the perfect size for two people. I don't think I have much more time in this world, and I would like to be close to the ocean and the salty air."

Claire's brows furrowed and she bit her lip.

"You know I have enough money to pay for the rent and for Claire too. I've been pinching my pennies, unlike most young folks today." Mother held tightly to her walker.

The truth of his mother's statement caused a lump to lodge in his throat. He wished he had saved up for his daughter's wedding years ago. "Mom, I can't expect you to pay full rent." Even though he needed her to.

"I'm not a freeloader, Son. But you may invite me over for dinner anytime you like." A smile flashed across her face.

Would Claire enjoy living with his mother? Did she like the idea? Of course, the rental was his home and he could have anyone he wanted living there. Having his mother and Claire in the house on Saxon Avenue seemed like a wild idea, but why not? It would be nice to have his mother close by, yet not living in his home. And as much as Sandy loved his mother, after a couple of weeks they would be ready to have their own space.

But then again, could his mother keep the secret? She had all these years. Would living with Claire change all that?

"Michael, dear, you look lost in your own thoughts. Do you have anything to say?" Mother scooted herself closer to him, accidentally hooking a leg of the walker on Blake's foot. She started to tumble forward when Blake caught her left arm and Claire caught her right.

Michael stood and extended his hand. "Claire, you've got the job. My mother needs a woman like you to keep an eye on her." The second the words came out of his mouth, Michael regretted them. Why had he made such a hasty decision? He hadn't even done a background check.

Geraldine harrumphed. "I'm not a child."

"No, Mother." Michael put both hands on her shoulders, leaned down, and kissed her cheek. "But you do need looking after. Let's go to the house and discuss the details."

Michael sat at the head of the table drinking a cup of decaf coffee. Sandy had prepared an amazing dinner—steak, potatoes au gratin, French-style green beans, and cherry pie with vanilla ice cream for dessert. His wife had always gone out of her way to make a good impression on his mother. He listened to his daughter describe the latest wedding plans.

"The flowers are going to be fabulous." Julia's excitement was contagious. "My bridesmaids will carry bouquets with three shades of pink roses, green hydrangea, and camellia. My bouquet will have the same flowers, but with white roses sprinkled among the pink ones."

Her grandmother took a forkful of cherry pie and put it to her mouth. "Sounds beautiful, dear."

"We also ordered my wedding dress. You remember, Dad. The one Mom showed you from the magazine." Julia tossed her jet black hair behind her shoulder. "Mom says it fits me perfectly. We even cried when I tried it on."

"Well, you looked like a princess." Sandy dabbed at the corner of her eye. "I know David will love it."

"He'd love any dress as long as you're wearing it." Michael hid a wince, remembering the cost of the gown. "But of course being your wedding day and all, I'm sure the dress you picked out is perfect."

"It is, Dad." Julia smiled. "But that's not all. We booked Seascape Resort for the reception—"

Michael choked on the last bit of coffee. *Seascape Resort.* One of the most expensive places in the area. Couldn't she have a nice, simple outdoor event? He knew an outdoor wedding would be too risky with the weather they'd been having lately. How about a church wedding with a reception in the gym? No, definitely not his daughter's style—or David's, for that matter. Why was he being such a tightwad? This was his baby. His beautiful little girl. He glanced at his wife. Should he be completely honest with Sandy about their financial situation? No. He'd always provided for his family. And he'd come up with the money now.

"Dad, are you all right?" Julia looked like a six-year-old with her doe-like eyes and fear etched across her face.

"I'm fine." Michael said between coughs. "Your wedding sounds like it will be amazing. Excuse me, I've got to go make a few phone calls." He stood and headed toward his office.

"Honey, are you sure you're okay?" Sandy asked. "Do you need a glass of water?"

"No, thank you." Michael turned and held on to the wall and coughed. "Dinner was wonderful. Now, I've got to get some work done."

Mother, still seated, stacked the dirty plates. "That son of mine always hides behind his work, doesn't he?"

Michael leaned against the doorframe. "I'm still in the room."

"I know, dear." A small smile tugged at the corners of her mouth. "Sandy, did I tell you I'm going to move into the rental with a darling young woman named Claire? Claire James. I used to live near her in L.A."

Michael shook his head. His mother had a way of changing the subject.

Sandy brought Mother her walker. "That's wonderful. I'm sure Claire will be a good helper."

She hoisted herself to standing. "Thank you, dear."

His mother swayed left, then steadied herself. It did Michael's mind good to know Claire would be taking care of her.

"Here, Grandma, let me carry those dishes for you." Julia stood, grabbed the stack of white china, and headed toward the kitchen.

"Why don't you make yourself comfortable in the family room while I clean up the kitchen?" Sandy picked up a couple of serving dishes. "Then we'll get you settled in the guest bedroom. I bought you a new comforter. It's blue, your favorite color."

"You didn't need to do that. But I appreciate it all the same."

"Feel free to take it with you to the house on Saxon Avenue. When are you moving in?" Sandy asked over her shoulder.

"Tomorrow."

Sandy's brows shot up. "So soon? We don't get to visit for at least a few days?"

"I can't wait to walk to the end of the bluff and smell that ocean air. Claire is going to meet me there in the morning.

We worked out all the arrangements." With slow and deliberate steps, his mother made it to the family room. Michael helped her sit down in the same place she had earlier that afternoon—on the corner cushion of the sofa.

He thought back to the conversation he had had with Claire while his mother looked around the rental home. They agreed she was to assist with household chores, help prepare meals, run errands, shop for groceries, do the laundry, and supervise medications. In exchange, she'd receive a small monthly paycheck from his mother plus room and board.

Mother reached over and grabbed the newspaper. She thumbed through it and found the crossword puzzle. "Got a pen on you?"

His work pen—the one with the words Crown Real Estate engraved on it—rested in his shirt pocket, where it always did. "Here you go."

"Thanks, dear. Don't you have work to do?" She smiled at him over the top of her glasses.

Michael's mind whirled as he headed to his office. So many changes. Julia was getting married, his mother would soon be living near him, and then there was Claire. A young woman who made him think of Emily and all the feelings he thought he'd stuffed deep down inside.

15

Claire lay back on her bed in Nancy's home a few hours after Blake dropped her off. He had offered to make her dinner, but Claire didn't feel up to it. She had a lot on her mind. Nancy was at work again, and Tom sat in the family room watching a football game. Cold pizza had satisfied her hunger pangs.

Grabbing her cell phone, she called her sister. Suddenly she missed Haley and everything familiar to her. So much had happened since leaving L.A.

"Hello?"

"It's me."

"Claire, it's good to hear your voice." Haley sniffed, then coughed.

"Are you sick?" Claire sat up. She fingered the edge of the quilt on the bed.

"No. Nothing like that."

Claire heard the apprehension in her sister's tone. Something wasn't right. "Are you upset? Please, Haley tell me what's wrong . . . has Mark hurt you?"

"No!" Haley yelled in Claire's ear, then softened her voice. "I'm pregnant."

A knot formed in the pit of Claire's stomach. It was bad enough that Haley had to endure living under the same roof as Mark. Now, an innocent baby would fall victim. "That's great, right?" She attempted to sound positive.

Silence filled the line. She stood and walked to the window, pushing back the curtain. Solar lights lit up the twin palm trees out front. It was a beautiful evening, but not in Haley's world. Claire felt the need to say something—anything.

"Oh, Haley, your body will get back in shape after the baby's born. Knowing you, you'll probably wear your pre-pregnancy jeans out of the hospital—with your favorite heels." Why was she ignoring the obvious? Mark was an abusive jerk.

"I'm scared." Haley's voice shook.

"Of what?" Better to let her sister voice the truth about her husband's behavior.

"I'm scared that Mark and I won't be good parents. Neither of us had good examples . . . with his parents divorcing when he was five, and Mom raising us alone—"

"Mom did the best she could . . ." From her duffel bag, Claire pulled out a framed picture of the three of them, her finger trailing lightly across her mom's smiling face.

"I know she did, but the fact is we were raised in a single-parent home. We didn't know what it was like to have both a mom and a dad who loved us. That and the fact that—"

"That what, Haley?" Claire set the picture down and sat on the edge of the bed.

"Mark is still drinking."

Claire could hear her sister crying. It pained her to know her sister was dealing with this alone. "Oh, Haley. I'm so sorry."

"It's gotten worse since you moved out." Haley hiccupped. "I don't know what to do."

"Have you talked to him about it? When he's sober . . ."

"I've tried. He says there is nothing wrong with a few beers after a hard day of work."

Claire sat down in the floral chair tucked in the corner of the room. A blanket lay folded across the armrest. She covered her bare feet. "Is he still working with his uncle?"

"Yes. Thankfully, there are construction jobs to keep him busy. At least I know Mark's insurance will cover the birth."

"Is Mark happy about the baby?" Claire couldn't picture Mark as a dad. But then again, she couldn't imagine a loving father.

"Yes. We didn't think we could have kids. So, yes, Mark's definitely happy . . ."

"Then maybe he'll quit drinking before the baby's born."

"Maybe . . ." Doubt colored her tone. "Claire, I haven't even asked you what's going on in Capitola. Have you found Mom's old love?"

"I think so, but I haven't shown him the letter yet."

"What?! Really? What are you waiting for?" Haley's voice had a sudden boost of energy.

Claire twirled her hair. "Because, like you, I'm scared."

"Scared of what? That Mom's old love still pines for her after thirty-five years? Claire, she's gone. Old memories are simply that . . . memories. It's okay to move on."

"He's my new employer. I'm scared that I'll get to know him and not like him. I'll wonder what Mom ever saw in him."

"Like I said before, it was thirty-five years ago. People change. Maybe you should forget the letter. Chances are your employer didn't even write it. Who is he, and what work are you doing for him?"

"Michael Thompson, the man wearing that fancy suit at Mom's funeral, and you'll never guess who his mother is—"

"Geraldine . . ." Haley's voice trailed off.

"Yeah, how did you know?" Claire pulled the blanket higher on her lap.

"Listen, Claire, I've got to run. Suddenly I'm feeling nauseous."

The clock displayed 1:00 a.m. Claire didn't feel the least bit sleepy. Tom had gone to bed hours ago, right after the football game ended. She slipped out of her room to wait on the family room sofa. Nancy would be home soon.

A car pulled into the driveway. After the kind of morning Nancy had had, talking with Vivian on the phone and a long shift at work, now might not be a good time to talk to her about the rental. She didn't want to break Nancy's heart further by telling her she was going to room with Geraldine, but she didn't have a choice. It was all planned out for her.

Tea. The thought popped into her mind. She had noticed Nancy drinking herbal tea this morning. Claire headed into the kitchen and opened the cabinet. She filled a cup with water and put it in the microwave to heat as her mind drifted. By the smiles Geraldine was casting Blake's way earlier today, Claire had a pretty good idea that Michael's mother enjoyed male attention and wouldn't mind him coming over to cook his meals while his kitchen was being remodeled.

"Claire, what are you doing up?" Nancy entered the kitchen through the garage door. "It's in the middle of the night. Shouldn't you be in bed?"

"I was waiting for you. Plus, I thought you might need this . . ." The microwave signaled the water was hot. Claire pulled out the cup and dropped in a tea bag. "Here you go."

"What's up?" Nancy took the cup from Claire. The skin around Nancy's eyes sagged. The woman was tired.

"Let's sit down in the family room. We'll be more comfortable in there." Claire linked arms with Nancy and led her to the sofa.

"Did Vivian leave another message?" Nancy sat down and held the cup with both hands. She brought the steaming liquid to her mouth.

"Vivian didn't call back today." Claire sat, grabbed a throw pillow and hugged it to her chest.

"You're right, I do need this." Nancy took a deep breath. "And the warm cup feels good on my hands."

"You've been so kind to me. And I wanted it to work out with Vivian. But something happened today at Michael's house."

"Did you get the job?" Nancy took another sip of her tea, then focused her eyes on Claire.

She wished she had made herself a cup. It would feel good to warm her insides. At the moment she felt cold and heartless. Nancy had been nothing but kind to her, and now Claire was going to disappoint her. "Yes, I got the job."

"That's great! When do you start?"

"Tomorrow. Geraldine wants me to help her move her things into the house." Claire clutched the pillow tighter.

"She accepted the fact she needs a caregiver? Not all seniors are that willing."

"It didn't take much convincing. Michael basically told her she needed someone to look after her. Geraldine's not stable on her feet, even though she's with it here." Claire pointed to her head. "Oh, and the best part is I know her."

"How?" Nancy sat forward.

"Geraldine was my old neighbor in L.A. We didn't talk much back then. She pretty much kept to herself."

"Interesting." Nancy put her cup down on the coffee table. "How did Geraldine seem today?"

"Like we've been friends for years." Claire slouched down on the couch. "I did see her at a gas station not too long ago—on my way up from L.A. She handed me a twenty-dollar bill. Said she should've helped me sooner."

"She sounds sweet." Nancy ran a hand through her short brown hair. "I'm glad you found a job. Things are looking up for you." She yawned. "I need to get to bed. It's been a long day—"

"Maybe I should wait until tomorrow . . ." Claire set the throw pillow neatly on the corner of the sofa and then stood.

"For what?" Nancy looked her in the eye.

"Never mind. It can wait until morning." She forced a smile.

"Claire, you might as well tell me now. I won't sleep until I know what you're talking about."

Claire picked up the empty teacup from the coffee table. "I'm going to move into the rental with Geraldine." She said it so fast she hoped Nancy heard her.

"Wait a minute." Nancy's voice caught, and she held up a hand. "Did I hear you correctly? Did you say Geraldine is going to live in the rental?"

Claire nodded. "I didn't know what to do or say. I mentioned to Michael that there were family issues going on between you and Vivian, and then all of a sudden Geraldine wants to move right in. She didn't waste a moment." Claire shifted her weight from side to side. Awful. She felt downright awful. In one respect, Geraldine provided her with both a job and a home, but on the other hand, would she have any privacy living with an old woman who needed assistance? Of course, she didn't know Vivian that well either, except for the fact that she could cut a pie in perfect triangles and serve meals at a restaurant. What a dilemma. If only she could afford to live alone.

Nancy's shoulders sagged. "I'm sure Michael was thrilled. He's found a renter—his mother no less—and a caregiver all in one. It's probably for the better. Vivian missed her chance—once again."

Claire didn't understand what Nancy meant by "once again." She wanted to ask, but thought better of it.

Nancy yawned. "I'm tired. I need to go to bed. Thanks for the tea. And congratulations. I guess I won't have to worry about the security deposit after all." She slipped down the hall and into her bedroom.

Claire stood with the empty teacup in hand. She didn't know how to feel as Nancy disappeared behind her door. But one thing was certain—she now had a roof over her head and a job in the morning. And according to Blake, she'd be driving her Volkswagen soon. She walked into the kitchen and placed the cup into the sink. Something was still gnawing at her. Was it Michael? Could be. She still didn't know if he was or even if she wanted him to be the writer of the letter. Maybe it was her sister's reaction to Geraldine. Did she know something Claire didn't? No. She shrugged off the thought. Haley's sudden nausea must be from the pregnancy. A smile tugged at the corners of her mouth. She was going to be an aunt.

A knock on the front door jarred her. Her body froze in place hoping whoever it was would go away. She heard another knock, but this time the pounding came with more force. Claire tiptoed through the kitchen into the family room. She inched the curtain back only enough for her left eye to peek through. What she saw shocked her. *Vivian.*

Could life get more complicated?

16

Claire let Vivian in, gave her a quick hug, and then knocked on Tom and Nancy's door. Tom emerged from the bedroom wearing a white T-shirt and plaid flannel pajama bottoms. Claire stood next to the brown sofa. She didn't want to pry, yet she wanted to know what would bring Vivian all this way.

"What are you doing here?" Tom paced back and forth in front of Vivian, confining her to the entryway. "Nancy's been crying all day. And now you show up to ruin what's left of the night."

"You know I don't mean any harm, Tom. I just need to talk with my sister." Vivian fidgeted with the ends of the bright pink flowered scarf around her neck. The flowers reminded Claire of the tulips she'd given her mother on a particularly hard day of chemo.

Tom ran a hand over his balding head and planted the other on his hip. "Darn you, woman. Why'd you have to come tonight? Couldn't you have worked it out over the phone?"

"Would you like tea?" Claire cut in, hoping to ease the tension. Vivian must be tired and thirsty.

"I'd love some, thank you." Vivian shifted from one foot to the other.

"Tom, can you take her coat while I heat the water?" Claire took a few tentative steps toward the kitchen. Someone had to make Vivian feel welcome.

Tom made unintelligible noises and then extended a hand.

"I don't mean to be any trouble. I've done some thinking." Vivian handed her heavy coat to Tom but kept the scarf around her neck. "I'm sorry for intruding, but I couldn't help it. I took the afternoon Greyhound bus, splurged on a taxi, and came straight here. I didn't know it would take so long."

Nancy appeared from her bedroom. Her hair was askew, and she wore her bathrobe and slippers. "Vivian?"

Vivian nodded and grinned. "Yes, it's me, Sister."

Claire slipped into the kitchen and made tea—for the second time that night. She strained to hear the conversation in the other room, but their voices were low. If Vivian had arrived the day before, maybe Claire would've roomed with her. She dunked the tea bag in the cup of boiling water. Vivian's appearance brought back memories of working in the diner. She didn't want to ever go back to that type of work. Mr. Matley and his burned finger flashed across her mind.

She grabbed a spoon from the drawer and placed it on the saucer next to the cup, then brought it out to Vivian. Their voices hushed the minute Claire walked into the room. What would cause Vivian to ride the bus through the night to see her sister? Must have been something serious the way Nancy's arms were clamped tight across her chest. Claire dipped her head. It was none of her business. She yawned and walked down the hallway to bed, leaving Tom, Nancy, and Vivian to talk in private.

Claire stuck a piece of bread in the toaster. She'd tossed and turned for the past five hours, hearing the voices drone on late into the night before she finally drifted into a fitful sleep. Tom and Nancy were early risers, and they had yet to appear from their bedroom.

"Good morning." Vivian's voice was chipper, perky even. But then again, Vivian had had a sunny disposition when she worked with her in L.A. Vivian's light blue sweat outfit clung to her full body. "Last night Tom and Nancy told me how you ended up in their home. Small world, isn't it?" She grinned.

"I know. Can you believe it?" asked Claire.

Vivian shook her head, then shrugged her shoulders. "What are you doing up so early?"

"It's my first day on the job, and I don't want to be late." Claire grabbed the toast and spread a thick layer of butter.

"Still waitressing?" Vivian pulled out a kitchen chair and sat down.

Claire scrunched up her nose. "Definitely not."

"You never did like working at the restaurant." Vivian laughed. "But you made nice tips."

Yeah. And it all went to Mark. Her mind didn't want to go down that road. "I got a job as a caregiver for an elderly woman. We're going to be living in a small house on Depot Hill." Claire took a bite of her toast.

"I've told you before, you're college material." Vivian grabbed a banana from the bowl in the middle of the table. "Maybe you could enroll in night classes." She peeled the banana and took a bite.

College. Claire thought about it from time to time, especially when she was around Vivian. She was good for the ego. "I'll think about it. But for now, I need to do a good job for Michael's mother." Claire set her toast on a plate and joined Vivian at the table. "How's everything at the diner?"

Vivian shrugged. "I quit."

"No!" Claire clapped a hand over her mouth. "The customers love you." She thought about the cute older couple who sat in Vivian's station almost every day for their slice of pie. They'd miss her.

"Mr. Sutherland took a managerial position at a big chain restaurant. It's not the same. The new manager is a drill sergeant. I thought it was a good time for me to leave too. So, here I am—in between jobs." Vivian finished off the banana and grabbed an orange.

"What are you going to do now?"

Vivian cocked her head. "I'm eager to see what plans God has for me. Too bad you're not available to room with. I'd consider living here. Nancy's been after me to move here for years."

You're a day too late. One corner of her mouth turned up in a crooked smile. "Yeah, too bad." Claire took an apple from a bowl in the center of the table and bit into the fruit. "Did you work everything out with Nancy?"

"Yeah, I hope so. The hurt's been buried deep for so many years. We probably only skimmed the surface, but I'm willing to move forward. I want a relationship with my sister." Vivian folded her arms across her large bust. "We've been fighting so long, it doesn't seem real that our relationship might be headed in the right direction."

Would she and Haley allow years to go by without reconciling? Claire pulled in a breath. "Anything I can help you with?" She placed her half-eaten apple on her plate.

"Pray."

Pray? She'd heard Blake give thanks before meals. Do people talk to God about other things too?

"I've learned to lean on the Lord. And I know Nancy does too. There's no other way this wedge between us can totally be resolved." Vivian chuckled. "Prayer and maybe Tom taking an extended vacation. That man doesn't like me much. When I hurt Nancy, I hurt him as well."

How did Vivian hurt Nancy? Claire couldn't imagine.

Vivian stood. "It was so good to see you, Claire. I hope I didn't startle you too badly last night."

"It's all right." Claire grinned. "It was good to see you, too."

Vivian lumbered into the family room. Claire placed her plate in the dishwasher and leaned against the counter. She was no closer this morning to finding out what had happened between Nancy and Vivian than she was last night. Not that it was any of her business, but she cared for both women and wanted to see each one happy.

Pray. She'd been hearing about prayer lately—Blake, then Nancy, and now Vivian. It was an interesting concept. She'd have to pay attention to how Blake talked to God. Claire smiled. Blake could teach her many things. "Look out, neighbor, here I come."

Michael parked his car in the driveway of the rental house. He opened the passenger door and helped his aging mother out of the car. He had learned once before not to pull her up, but to allow her to use her leg muscles to get to a standing position. "Here's your walker, Mom." He was missing a few hours' work—precious time to drum up business—to help his mother move into the rental.

She tilted her chin heavenward and took in a big breath. "Smell that ocean air. I'm going to like it here."

Obviously, his mother was not on his timetable. "Let's get you into the house so you can claim your room." He winked.

"Oh, you. I'm not a child, so you can quit teasing me. I'm sure either bedroom will be fine." His mother playfully swatted the air. "What time did you ask Claire to be here?"

"Ten." Michael glanced at his watch. "We're a little early." The small moving truck sat parked in front of the house. "That was nice of your friends to drive your things up for you."

"Wasn't it? They cleared my apartment at Regis Retirement Living and wanted to drive up the coast. They're going to fly back down to L.A. tomorrow." She shuffled toward the front door.

"Do you think you can manage the front steps or should I build you a ramp?" Michael surveyed the height of the steps, something he took for granted.

"I never liked the looks of a ramp. It screams 'old person lives here.' A sturdy handrail might be nice, though."

He agreed. "I'll get right on that." Or hire someone. He didn't want to fork out any more money on the house, but if it kept his mother safe, he'd do it.

Once inside, the scent of cleaner mixed with paint brought a smile to Michael's face. His mother liked things neat and tidy. The smell alone would make her feel comfortable. "I'll see if Blake's home. I should have thought about getting another man to help unload the furniture. I'll get your recliner first, so you can sit down."

"Oh, don't worry about me. My walker here has a built-in seat." She headed into the kitchen and opened the refrigerator door. "Looks like someone's been shopping."

Blake. The one detail he forgot to mention to his mother. "I took the liberty of making sure your meals were taken care of. That is, your neighbor will be coming around to cook."

"Claire doesn't know how to cook?" His mother scrunched up her nose and puckered her lips.

"Blake's kitchen caught fire the other day, and I promised he could use this kitchen until his was remodeled. Sorry I didn't run that by you sooner."

"You mean to tell me that good-looking hunk is going to be cooking in my kitchen?" His mother's eyes lit up.

Michael laughed. Mom did appreciate a handsome man when she saw one. "Until his kitchen is remodeled. And he's willing to pay part of the rent."

"Phooey on the rent, if he cooks my meals, that's good enough." She lowered a platform seat on her walker and sat.

A car pulled up in front of the house. It appeared Nancy had driven Claire. He hoped Nancy was fine with the way things had turned out. If not, he'd offer to help her find another rental for her sister. With his connections there was bound to be something else available. "Claire's here."

"Oh, good." His mother clapped her gnarled hands together. "We'll have things set up in no time. I think I would like my recliner. This seat is as hard as a rock."

"Wait. There's a tow truck out front pulling a car—" The minute he said it, Michael wished he hadn't.

"What do you mean?" Mother pushed herself to standing and turned to look out the kitchen window.

"Why that looks exactly like Emily's car—or it did before someone destroyed the hood. Emily used to drive that thing all around with you teenage boys—"

His mind raced. "Mother, please. No memories, okay." Michael walked over and stood next to her. "You promised, not a word to Claire."

"Michael, if you'd face it head-on, your heart would be so much lighter—"

"Hello, we're here," Claire called from the open doorway before she peeked inside. Her entrance saved Michael from getting into a conversation that he'd rather not have.

"Claire, great you're here." He walked over to the door. "I was going to see if Blake was home to help unload Mother's things." Michael slipped past Claire and Nancy. "I'll be right back." He sprinted out the door.

He cut through the lawn and rang Blake's doorbell. No answer. He knocked.

"Blake's not home." The tow truck driver called to him. "He told me to bring the car to the carport on the back side of the house. He'll be back later this afternoon."

So Blake's fixing that old VW. The man would do just about anything for anyone.

Walking back across the lawn, Michael had to admit he didn't want to face Nancy. How could he when he knew she had planned on having her sister live in the rental with Claire? He hadn't even looked at her as he ducked out of the rental a few moments ago. Was his mother right? Was he afraid to face conflict head-on? A memory of a past mistake jarred his thoughts. It was easier to keep it buried in the past where it belonged. Why should he stir up trouble? Michael shook it off and strolled toward his property.

"Michael, no hard feelings," said Nancy, standing outside the house. "I think it's great that your mother and Claire can live together."

"You sure you're okay—"

"I've got to run. My sister's waiting for me at home." A smile crept across Nancy's face.

That was easy. If only all uncomfortable situations ended with one person accepting things outright and getting on with life. He raised a hand and waved as Nancy drove away.

Inside, Mother and Claire were busy chatting about their favorite colors and what type of window treatments they liked.

"Blake wasn't home. Claire, you look strong enough. Ready to help move in my mother's things?" He looked down at the single duffel bag and the small pile of bedding. "Is that everything you own?"

"It's everything that's important to me, except for my car." Claire chewed her lower lip. "And this . . ." She dug into her purse and pulled out an envelope. Her eyes held a sadness, and what? Hope? "It's a letter to my mom. Do you know who wrote it?"

His mother gasped.

Heat rose in Michael's neck and cheeks. He glanced at his mother. She nodded, and her eyes pleaded for him to be brave. Michael took the envelope from Claire and pulled out the letter. He scanned it. He knew every word. His jaw muscles flexed. He shook his head. "Sorry, I can't tell you anything." He placed the letter and envelope back in her hands. He didn't have time to deal with his past. "Let's get a move on. I've got a busy day."

17

At six o'clock, Claire heard a knock on the door. Boxes littered the family room floor. The recliner sat perched next to the fireplace, and the tan chenille couch leaned against the wall adjacent to the kitchen. "I'll get it." Claire dodged cardboard boxes and opened the front door.

"In the mood for enchiladas?" Blake grinned, holding a brown bag full of groceries.

A gorgeous man and Mexican food. Who wouldn't be? "Yes. Come on in." Claire swung the door wide. "Sorry about the mess."

"Looks like you just moved in." Blake sidestepped the clutter. "Don't worry, I'll be in the kitchen."

"Need any help?" Claire sent a silent plea with her eyes. She'd much rather help Blake cook than unpack another box.

"As long as Michael's mother doesn't need you." Blake cocked his head to look down the hall. "How's it going?" he whispered.

"Geraldine's great. She's self-sufficient and only needs help standing or getting her walker. In fact, I hope I don't get bored. You should see her bedroom. You'd think she's lived here for a month the way everything is situated." Claire walked ahead of Blake to the kitchen. "So, what'd you bring?"

"The usual Mexican fare—chips, salsa, sour cream, and all the fixings for enchiladas." Blake put the bag on the counter and pulled grocery items out one by one.

"My stomach's growling already." Claire sidled up to Blake, his musky scent drawing her closer. "Mind if I open the bag of chips?"

"Be my guest. I didn't know if Geraldine would like spicy food, so I bought mild salsa."

"How sweet of you." Claire opened the bag of tortilla chips while Blake looked in the cabinet for a bowl.

"Oh, sorry. We didn't get to the kitchen yet. But I know that box is around here somewhere." Claire grabbed a chip and popped it in her mouth before she searched the family room for the plates, bowls, and silverware.

"Here it is." Blake picked up the clearly marked box and brought it to the kitchen. He opened it and pulled out the everyday dishes. "Any idea where the pots and pans are?"

"No. I'm glad Geraldine has all this stuff. I don't know what I'd do." Claire shifted boxes around. "I wonder if she had these things in storage. I didn't think a small apartment in an assisted living community would be able to hold all this."

Blake dipped a tortilla chip in the mild sauce. "Hey, come here. Tell me what you think of this salsa."

Claire came willingly. She was hungry for sure, and the sound of Blake's voice pulled her toward the kitchen. Claire allowed him to feed her the chip. As he placed it in her mouth, he held her eyes with his. A blush warmed Claire's cheeks. "Perfect. A nice blend of cilantro and tomatoes." She could get lost in those steely blue eyes.

He laughed. "You are quite the connoisseur; I can tell." His eyes drifted toward her mouth. "You have a little salsa right here." He held her chin with his index finger and gently brushed the sauce from her face with his thumb.

Her stomach fluttered.

"Well, look who's here. Claire, why didn't you tell me?" Geraldine interrupted.

Claire felt as if she'd been caught in the back seat of a car. Her cheeks heated. "Geraldine, I thought you were taking a rest."

"I'll never sleep tonight if I doze now." Geraldine ambled up to the counter. "What are going to cook tonight? Oh, looks like a Mexican meal. I love spicy food—the spicier the better."

Claire nudged Blake's arm. "Good, then I'm sure you'll love Blake's 'hot' enchiladas."

Blake winked. "You two need to get out of the kitchen so I can cook. I don't want any distractions." He placed his hands on Geraldine's shoulders and turned her around to face the family room. "Why don't you have a seat in that recliner? I'll have this ready in no time."

"If you're sure you know what you're doing." Geraldine sauntered to her chair, pushing boxes out of the way with her walker. "I don't want to hear the smoke alarm."

"I've cooked for myself for a long time. I had the best teacher in the world—my mother. And I'll make sure I turn the burners off when I'm done. The only things I need are a cutting board, knives, and pots and pans."

"Oh heavens, we should have thought about that sooner, Claire." Geraldine scooted herself around the room looking for the necessary tools for Blake.

"I think I found them." Claire motioned to a box under the oak coffee table.

"Here, I'll get that." Blake strode across the room, and picked up the box with ease. "Now I'm in business."

While Blake cooked, Claire went into her room to unpack. Nancy had let her borrow an air mattress. It would do for a while, but she hoped to purchase a queen-size bed soon. She made up her bed with her favorite sheets and comforter, then hung up her clothes. The room looked sparse. Why hadn't she brought a few things from Haley's house, such as the small nightstand and lamp? Oh, well. It wouldn't be long before she'd make money of her own and buy furniture.

The scent of Mexican food wafted through the air. A knock sounded on her door, and Blake's voice called her to dinner.

"I'll be right there." Claire pulled out the antique Victorian picture frame holding a photo of her mother, sister, and herself from her duffel bag and set it next to her bed. *So this is home.* She let her gaze circle the room. It wasn't much to look at, but it was hers. A feeling of contentment swept over her.

Geraldine was already seated at the table when Claire approached. "Are you going to make us a dinner every night?" Geraldine batted her eyelashes at Blake.

She's flirting. Claire covered a laugh with her hand. "The agreement was for Blake to use the kitchen, not make us dinner *every* night."

"It's more fun to cook for three than it is for one." Blake carried a platter of enchiladas to the table and set it down. He tossed the oven mitts on the counter and took a seat next to Claire. "If I'm not working, I'd be glad to cook."

"If you're cooking, then I'm doing the cleaning." Claire grabbed a handful of chips and put them on her plate.

"I won't argue with you on that one." Blake held out his hands. "Shall we pray?" Geraldine winked at Claire and bowed her head. Claire peeked at Blake as he prayed. Before she knew it, the prayer was over and Blake's eyes opened. He caught her staring straight at him!

"Pass the rice, dear." Geraldine's voice interrupted the awkward moment. "My, the dinner smells good."

She picked up the serving bowl and handed it to Geraldine.

The enchiladas, rice, and beans rivaled any Mexican restaurant. The smell of corn tortillas, beef, and cheese made her mouth water. Claire savored each bite as conversation flowed nicely around the table.

"I hear you're going to fix Claire's car." Geraldine took a bite of her enchilada.

"I'm going to try. I like old cars. It's a challenge to find the parts, but I'm up for it." Blake leaned back in his chair, his hands folded across his lap.

"I can't wait to drive again. It's like my left arm has been cut off." Claire stood to clear the table.

"Especially *that* old car. So many memories—"

Memories? Claire turned to Geraldine. "What memories are you talking about?"

Geraldine nudged Blake. "Hand me my walker, dear. I need to unpack my room."

Blake sat up straight. "What's your hurry?"

Geraldine looked flustered—as if she had done something wrong. "I . . . I don't know why I said that. It must be the enchiladas. You two will have to excuse me. Thank you for dinner, Blake." Geraldine stood and shuffled down the hallway.

Claire shrugged. She didn't understand what Geraldine's comment meant about her VW holding so many memories—memories for whom? Michael? His reaction to the letter had bothered her all day. It was obvious by the way his jaw muscles had flexed that he knew more than he was letting on. Claire let out the breath she was holding.

"Hey, Claire. You seem to be a million miles away." Blake stood and put the cover on the sour cream container.

All impulses told her to show Blake the letter. Claire wanted to tell him everything—about her mother's death, living with Haley, and what propelled her to move to Capitola. Instead, she stacked the dishes. "Do you want coffee?"

"I doubt that's what you were thinking." Blake chuckled. "But sure, I'd like a cup." He gathered the extra food and put it in the refrigerator.

"Should we sit outside?" Claire glanced over her shoulder and down the hall.

Blake opened the dishwasher and started loading. "How about Mr. Toots? They have the best coffee in Capitola Village."

"Oh, no, you don't. You cooked, remember? It's my job to clean." Claire grabbed him around the waist and pulled him back. The feeling of his tight abs sent a rush of adrenaline through her. *What is with me?*

Blake spun around and grinned—their faces inches apart. "If we both do the dishes, we'll be done faster." He snatched her hand and gave her the sponge. "Let's hurry. I'm ready for that cup of coffee!"

When the kitchen was clean, Claire walked down the hall and peeked her head in Geraldine's room. She was already in her pajamas and tucked in bed for the night. Claire smiled. She closed the door and turned to go into her room to grab her jacket. She opened her handbag to make sure the letter was there. She needed a good heart-to-heart talk, and Blake was the perfect person to share what was on her mind.

Perfect. Now that was one word she had never used to describe a man. She didn't know one existed. Her father had disappeared from her life, and her mother's boyfriends turned out to be flakes. Claire would need to be careful. She didn't want to give her heart away only to be crushed.

"Claire." Blake stood outside her bedroom. "I'm sorry, I've got to run." He raked a hand through his dark hair. "I'm on call tonight and just got paged."

She was sure her disappointment showed on her face. "All right. Another time." Her mind raced with all she had wanted to say to him. "See you in the morning?" Her pulse quickened when he stepped closer to her.

"Depends on the call." Blake leaned a shoulder against the doorframe. "I was looking forward to our time alone." He squeezed her hand, then slipped away. The soft click of the door echoed down the hall.

A few minutes passed before her heart rate returned to normal. She could walk to Mr. Toots to enjoy a cup of coffee by herself. Life didn't have to stand still because Blake had to go to work. Then why did she suddenly feel so lonely? Claire strolled to the family room and sat down in the recliner. She needed to talk to someone.

Samantha. She rummaged through her purse and found her camping friend's phone number. Claire grabbed her cell phone and punched in the seven digits.

"Claire?" Samantha squealed. "It's so good to hear your voice. I didn't know when I'd ever get to talk with you again. Did you find the writer of the letter?"

Claire reclined back in the chair. Boxes filled the room. "No. Maybe. I don't know. The person that I thought it was denied writing it."

"I'm sorry. Say, how did you get to Capitola? When I woke up, you were gone. My parents talked with Harry and Pearl the other night. They were so concerned for you when they heard both you and your car had vanished."

"Did Harry and Pearl's daughter have a boy or a girl?"

"A boy. They named him John Jr. But back to you . . . where'd you go?"

"I called a tow truck. It wasn't the smartest thing to do in the middle of the night, but it worked out all right. I met the nicest couple—Tom and Nancy. They gave me a roof over my head until I found a place. You won't believe where I'm living."

"I'm dying to know . . ."

"The return address of the letter."

"No!" Samantha's voice grew louder with enthusiasm. "How did that happen?"

"Once I found the place, I couldn't believe it was for rent. It's the cutest little two-bedroom house one block from the bluff overlooking Capitola Village."

"Did you find a job?" asked Samantha.

"I'm living with an elderly woman as her caregiver. She's the owner's mother."

"I'm excited for you. You're doing it, Claire. You're living on your own."

"Then why do I feel so disappointed? I thought for sure Michael Thompson wrote the letter. He was at my mother's funeral. So, when I found out he owned this house—"

"Don't give up, Claire. This means too much to you." Samantha's words were like honey to tea. Sweet. Comforting. And what Claire needed to hear.

"I have a handsome neighbor—" Claire shifted in her chair.

"Do I detect a woman in love?" Samantha teased.

"I wouldn't say love, but a strong attraction." Claire took a deep breath and closed her eyes. She could visualize Blake's handsome face and the way his eyes had penetrated her own before he left.

"Claire, my date's at the door. I've got to go . . . but thanks for calling. And please, call again."

Claire said goodbye and snapped her cell phone shut. Her muscles were sore and tired from the move. After locking the front door, she wandered down the hall to her room. That's funny. Geraldine's door was ajar. Claire thought for sure she had shut it. She tiptoed across the hall and peeked into the room. What she saw sent shivers down her spine.

18

Claire crept into Geraldine's room. The lamp on her nightstand cast an eerie glow. Geraldine was lying in bed clutching a picture frame. She looked dead—as if she were in a coffin. Slowly, Claire stepped closer until she was standing next to the elderly woman. To her relief, she saw the steady rise and fall of Geraldine's chest. She was asleep.

Claire turned to leave when she saw it—the same rare Victorian picture frame that matched the one in her room. She leaned forward to take a closer look at the photo inside. The woman, possibly Geraldine in her younger days, wore a double-breasted shirtwaist dress with a hat to match. The young boy resembled Michael with his wavy blond hair. And Claire assumed the man in the picture to be Geraldine's husband. All three were smiling.

Geraldine stirred. Claire stepped back and bumped into the nightstand, knocking over the small lamp. Grabbing the base of the lamp with one hand and the shade with the other, she set it back in place, turned off the light, and hurried out the door.

Odd. How likely was it for Geraldine to own the same style picture frame? Claire walked into her bedroom and flopped down on the air mattress. Her mother had told her that she had received the frame as a gift and that it was one of a kind. Claire fingered the ornate design on the top of the brass frame. The picture of her with her mom and sister had been taken before Claire's mother was diagnosed with cancer. All three of them looked healthy and happy, as if nothing in the world could change that. A familiar nausea somersaulted through her belly.

She turned the frame over and studied the back. Three metal wedges held the picture in place. After sliding each one to the side, she popped out the cardboard backing. What was she hoping to find? Answers to why Geraldine would own the same kind of frame? It had to be a coincidence. Claire laid the contents of the frame on her bed. She separated each layer one by one.

A picture Claire had never seen before was tucked between the more current photo and the cardboard backing. She looked closer. It was a picture of her mother leaning against her VW bug. Claire smiled. Her mom was so pretty then, with her hair feathered in a layered cut and wearing a miniskirt with a flowing top and chunky sandals. *Definitely 70s.* Claire laughed. Her mom looked so happy and carefree. Why didn't she marry her teenage love?

Claire lay back on her bed and continued to linger over the photograph. She flipped it over. *Summer 1973.* The picture was taken a year after the letter was sent. Claire turned the picture back over. Was that the corner of the rental house in the background? *Yes.* Claire bolted upright. The shutters looked familiar. Her mother had returned to this house the following year.

Claire had questions for Geraldine. And hopefully, she'd get answers . . . first thing in the morning.

Claire heard a knock on the front door. Who in the world? She turned over and reached for her watch. Eight o'clock. Blake. Time for breakfast. She smiled at the thought of seeing him again—except for the fact that she'd just rolled out of bed with morning breath. Claire dug in her purse for a breath mint. She brushed her hair, stepped into her jeans, and flung a sweatshirt over her head. She ran out barefooted into the hallway as Geraldine, who was already dressed, answered the door.

"Good morning, Blake." Geraldine welcomed him in. "What's cooking this morning?" She laughed at her own words.

"Poached eggs and pancakes." Blake walked into the house with grocery bag in hand and headed straight for the kitchen.

Claire tucked a stray hair behind her ear as she approached the kitchen counter. "I thought you might be working all night."

"One of our police officers had a flat tire. He forgot his cell phone and couldn't call in. I was only at the station for a couple of hours." Blake emptied the bag's contents on the counter. "Maybe we can have that coffee tonight?" He glanced in Claire's direction and smiled.

"Coffee, huh?" Geraldine shuffled over to them. "How come I wasn't invited?" She winked. "Why don't you two eat breakfast together? I've already had my morning tea and toast. Oh, you'll never guess where I found the toaster . . . in a box in my *bedroom*." Geraldine laughed.

Blake grabbed a pan, added a couple of inches of water, and set it on the stove to boil. "You sure you don't want Eggs Sardou?"

"I'm fine. But thanks." Geraldine waved as she headed toward her room. "Time for my crossword puzzle. You two enjoy yourselves, now."

Claire couldn't wait to tell Blake about the picture frame. For that matter, she couldn't wait to tell him everything—from her mother's funeral to what brought her to Capitola. She peeked down the hall as Geraldine closed her door.

"Do you have a griddle?" Blake stirred up the batter. "I brought blueberries to put in the pancakes."

Claire turned and looked in the family room. Only empty boxes were stacked on top of each other in the corner. Geraldine. What an amazing woman. "While I slept, Geraldine unpacked the rest of the kitchen." Claire opened the cabinets and looked for a griddle. "Here it is." The metal plate was heavy—too heavy for a frail woman in her eighties, but apparently not for Geraldine. Claire placed it on the counter. "Anything else?"

"I think I've got it under control." Blake heated the oven, whipped up creamed spinach, and prepared hollandaise sauce. He opened a can of artichoke hearts and warmed them in the oven.

Claire stood amazed as she watched a chef at work. "You know your way around a kitchen. Now I can understand how devastated you were when yours burned."

Gently, Blake cracked the eggs into the boiling water. He smiled at Claire. "Are you still interested in helping?"

"Sure. What can I do?" Claire came up beside him.

"A neck rub would be nice."

Touch him? He wants me to . . . The thought sent a rush of emotions through her. Could she help him some other way? Claire crossed her arms over her chest and playfully cocked her head. "And what does rubbing your neck have to do with breakfast?"

"A whole lot if you want to eat." His eyes pleaded with her. "I slept funny last night and I have the worst kink." He moved his head around and made a face. "It hurts like crazy right there." He pointed to a spot on the right side.

Claire moved closer. She hesitated.

He peeked over his shoulder and gave her a wry smile. "Please?"

She reached up and gently massaged his neck. He closed his eyes and let out a long breath. The feel of his skin sent tingles up her spine. She needed a distraction. Quick.

She took a whiff of the blueberry pancakes. Mmm! "Smells good." Her stomach growled. Her cheeks grew warm as she stifled a groan.

"Almost forgot about the pancakes!" Blake grabbed for the spatula and flipped them over. "Now, where were we?" He reached for her hand and brought it up to his neck.

For another minute Claire continued, moving her hands over his thick neck and pressing into his broad shoulders with strong fingers. She enjoyed the feel of him—maybe a little too much. What was happening to her? She was a different person when she was near Blake. More confident. Happy. Hopeful.

Claire whispered. "I think the pancakes are ready."

"Thanks." He took another deep breath. "That was exactly what I needed. Now let's hope the eggs turned out." Blake patted her on the shoulder.

Did he think of her as a friend, a sister—or as a woman he'd want to get to know? Claire sprinkled powdered sugar on her pancakes. She was dying to open up to Blake, but would he be interested in hearing about her life? Something about him made her want to trust. The thought scared her. Mark's image flashed across her mind. Haley had trusted him, and now she was living with an alcoholic. But . . . Claire needed a friend.

Before she took a bite, Blake held out his hand for a prayer. She was getting used to hearing him thank God for each meal. And if she was honest, she enjoyed the comfort of holding his hand.

After a few minutes of silence, she reached in her back pocket and took out the photo of her mother as a teenager. Claire scooped up her eggs with a fork and put them in her mouth.

"What do you have there?" Blake ate a bite of pancakes.

"This is my mom standing in front of this house in 1973."

"No way! Your mom's pretty." Blake picked up the photo from the table. "You look like her."

"Thanks." His compliment made her smile. "Wait right here, I'll be back." Claire slipped down the hall and into her room. Time to show him the letter. A few moments later, she handed Blake the envelope. "Go ahead, you can read it."

Blake pulled the letter out of the envelope and read silently. "Who do you think wrote this?"

"Do you want my honest opinion?" Claire propped her elbows on the table and leaned her chin on her hands.

"Yes."

"Michael Thompson."

Blake sat back in his chair. "Why do you think Michael wrote the letter?"

"He knew my mother somehow. He came to her memorial. Hold on, I have something else to show you . . ." Claire raced to her room to get the picture frame.

"Last night, when Geraldine was asleep, she was clutching an identical frame. My mother told me once that this frame is rare and that she received it as a gift. I think Michael gave it to her."

"Whoa, wait a minute here." Blake looked closely at the photograph. "You think Michael wrote the letter, took this photo, and gave your mom this picture frame?"

"Yes."

"So why not ask the man? He'd probably be happy to talk about his teenage crush. We've all had one."

"I did. Michael denied it. He looked real uncomfortable, too. What I don't get is Geraldine's reaction when I asked him . . . she gasped."

Blake shrugged. "You're kidding."

"No, I'm not. And then last night when we talked about the VW, she said it held so many memories. What was that about? She sure left for her room in a hurry."

"Where did you find the letter? Did your mom give it to you?" Blake leaned forward, obviously fascinated.

"No. I found the letter in the glove compartment of my mom's VW after she passed away. I couldn't stop thinking about it. Maybe it was the way the writer signed his name—with only an initial. Anyway, I decided to come here after my sister's husband kicked me out. I knew it was time to make it on my own. Boy, was I shocked to see this house for rent. That's when I met you."

Blake arched his brows and a smile spread across his face. "I think it was meant to be."

"What do you mean?"

"You coming here." Blake grabbed her hand. "I'd been praying for a wonderful neighbor. I think you were supposed to find that letter so that you'd come to Capitola."

"Even if I don't find out who wrote it?" Claire slipped her hand from Blake's and put it on her lap.

"Yes." Blake stood and stacked the dishes.

Claire sat there a few minutes staring at the photo. She wouldn't settle for not knowing who wrote the letter. If it wasn't Michael, then she'd keep hunting. She had to find out who had loved her mother. Claire picked up the picture and put it over her heart. *Mom, I miss you so much.*

She returned the letter, the frame, and the photo to her room, then joined Blake in the kitchen.

"You two done yet?" Geraldine's voice floated down the hall. "I feel like a walk. Who's interested?"

"If you can wait a minute while I give Claire a hand with the dishes, we'll both go with you."

"No, you two go ahead." Claire held up her hand. She wanted—no, needed—some time alone.

"You sure?" Blake came up beside Geraldine and offered her his arm.

Claire nodded. "Positive."

"I'll be the talk of Capitola." Geraldine grinned. "I can hear it now, 'Older woman catches younger man.'"

Blake laughed. "Let their tongues wag." He escorted Geraldine to the door. "You won't need that walker. Hold tight to my arm."

Geraldine winked at Claire. "Gladly."

Claire stood at the door and watched Blake and Geraldine take slow, deliberate steps down the sidewalk. When they were out of sight, she returned to the kitchen to gather the breakfast dishes and load them in the dishwasher. She scrubbed until the counters shone, and swept the floor clean. Her mind drifted to the letter and the picture frame. *I'm going to get to the bottom of this—no matter what.*

19

Claire couldn't believe she had agreed to the shopping spree with Nancy, Vivian, and Geraldine. It had been two weeks since moving into the rental. Now, sitting in the backseat of Nancy's car, she wished she hadn't decided to go. She was not a charity case.

"We'll look for a valance to match your bedding, and pictures for your walls." Nancy's eyes lit up as she glanced at Claire from her rearview mirror.

Vivian sat up front next to Nancy. "Oh, and we should stop at the paint store. A splash of color livens up any room."

"Maybe we'll find a good sale on furniture." Geraldine, her hands neatly folded across her lap, said to Claire in the backseat. "You need a bed, a nightstand, and a dresser."

Claire cringed. She appreciated all the attention from these women who had become such good friends, but she was trying to make it on her own. If they bought everything for her, it would defeat the purpose. "How about we *look* today . . . to get ideas."

"That's no fun." Nancy pulled the car into the parking lot of Capitola Mall. "Your bedding is green with a touch of yellow, right?"

Claire nodded. "Yes."

"What color do you want on the walls? And what about the valance?" asked Vivian.

Claire hadn't had the chance to think about such details. In the past, her room at Haley's apartment had been plain, with no artwork on the walls and plastic blinds to cover the windows. And now, she didn't think she'd have to face this kind of decision until she had money of her own. The silence was awkward. She needed to think of something fast.

Geraldine patted Claire's arm. "Enjoy this, dear. We want to help you."

Claire gave in. "For the walls, I'd say yellow. And the valances, white."

"I'll splurge on a can of yellow paint." Vivian craned her neck. "Did I tell you, Claire, I have an interview tomorrow with the manager of Red Apple Café?"

"Does that mean you're moving here?" She hoped for Nancy's sake it was true. Would she find out what kept these women apart for so many years?

"It sure does. I'm going to live in Nancy's guest room until I can find a place of my own."

A twinge of guilt surfaced. Vivian would have been her roommate if Geraldine hadn't stepped in to take her place. Would she have liked rooming with such a colorful woman? She smiled. It would have been interesting.

Rows of cars lined the parking lot as they drove up and down the aisles.

"There's a spot over there." Vivian gestured to an open space a short distance to the entrance of Macy's—their first stop.

"Good eye." Nancy's voice held a note of appreciation.

The sisters must have come to an understanding. Claire grinned. Sisters are meant to be close. Her mind drifted to Haley. They hadn't been close for a while. Would their relationship change now that Haley was going to have a baby? Excitement welled up inside of her. She hoped her sister was feeling well and Mark was treating her right.

Nancy parked the car. "Okay, ladies. Let's shop."

Geraldine picked up her purse. "Nancy, I'm so glad you borrowed a wheelchair from the hospital. There's no way I'd be able to keep up with the three of you." She glanced at her watch. "It's my naptime."

Nancy twisted her head to wink at Geraldine. "I was happy to do it."

Once inside the department store, Claire's stomach lurched. When her mother was ill and she was a teenager, Claire would've loved for her mother's friends to take her shopping and buy her what she needed. But now at twenty-three she felt like a failure. If only she had gone to college, she would have her degree by now and could make a decent living. She pushed Geraldine's wheelchair and watched Nancy and Vivian shop for her—feeling inadequate to manage her own affairs.

Lord, help me.

The thought, and unexpected plea for help, shocked her. Is that what it means to pray? Was Blake's spirituality rubbing off on her? She stopped abruptly, causing Geraldine to shift in her seat. Claire leaned over to check on the woman. Was that light snoring she heard? She smiled to herself. Dear Geraldine was fast asleep and they'd barely started their adventure. She set her mouth in a straight line and kept pace with Nancy and Vivian. Obviously, Vivian liked to shop. Considering how heavy she was, Claire was surprised to see her hustle through the crowd.

They rode the elevator to the second floor and made their way to the drapery department. Claire stood behind Geraldine's wheelchair, glued to the floor. What was she supposed to do? If she seemed disinterested, maybe they'd give up and go home. She pretended to yawn. Nancy and Vivian didn't notice. They were too busy digging through the mounds of packaged valances on the sale rack.

Claire didn't know one valance from another. She soon learned that valances are different lengths and made from different materials.

"How about these pretty white chiffon window treatments?" Nancy pulled them out of the package and held them up.

"And look, they're on sale!" Vivian added.

"They are beautiful." Claire touched the soft fabric. She could visualize the pretty material hanging across her window frame. "As long as I can pay you back." She remembered making the same promise to Harry and Pearl about their bumper, one that she hadn't yet been able to keep. Her enthusiasm for the new valance dwindled.

Nancy patted Claire's shoulder. "Please don't worry about that." She folded the valance, placed it inside the package, and tucked it under her arm. "I don't have any children of my own, and shopping for you is a real pleasure." She sniffed and rubbed her nose.

"On to pictures now." Vivian's voice was curt. She led the way, pumping her arms as she walked.

Was Vivian mad? Claire pushed Geraldine's wheelchair as both she and Nancy attempted to keep up with Vivian. She glanced Nancy's way. Nancy mumbled to herself and wiped away a stray tear. Claire was curious to know what had happened between the sisters. Would they ever tell her? She took a deep breath. She didn't have the energy to deal with Vivian and Nancy when she was confused about her own current emotions.

Picking out a valance was easy compared to finding a picture for her walls. The difference in everyone's taste was overwhelming.

Vivian held up a bold piece of contemporary artwork. "Claire, isn't this painting amazing?"

It reminded Claire of a picture she made in the first grade. A stroke here, another colorful stroke there until there was no white showing on the canvas.

"I'm thinking more subtle hues might be better." Claire shrugged a shoulder and continued flipping through the overlapping pictures on the display shelves. The last thing she wanted to do was hurt Vivian's feelings. This shopping trip was more difficult than she could have imagined.

She envisioned shopping with Blake, holding hands as they discussed their likes and dislikes. With money in her purse, she could buy whatever she wanted—without that gnawing feeling that she needed to pay someone back.

"Did you see these black wall cubbies?" Nancy pointed to a boxed set of three, pulling Claire out of her daydream. "Decorators say to put a touch of black in every room. Plus, you can put books in one, a potted plant in another . . ."

Claire studied the box. She liked the idea. "Let's get them." It was easier simply to go along with these women. She could always return items if things got out of hand. A black easel floor mirror caught her attention. She looked at the price tag. Seventy dollars. She mentally calculated the hours it would take to earn that amount of money.

Nancy ran her hand over the wood. "Oh, you have to have this. It would look so cute in the corner of your room. When you have a hot date you can make sure you're looking your best. Not that you need any help in that department." She rolled her eyes. "I'd do anything to be in my early twenties again."

Vivian scowled. "You have nothing to fret about. You are quite petite, my dear sister, and you have a man who loves you. What more do you want?"

"Claire, look at this." Geraldine's voice surprised Claire.

"I thought you were still asleep." Claire placed a hand on Geraldine's shoulder. "What did you find?"

The floral tapestry—a collection of vases filled with colorful wildflowers and pink tulips with a scenic countryside in the background, drew her in. "Geraldine, this is beautiful."

"Well, then, it must go in your room."

The matter appeared to be settled as far as Geraldine was concerned.

"What about a lamp?" Vivian grabbed the handles of Geraldine's wheelchair and turned down the next aisle. "I think they're this way."

Geraldine held the wall tapestry on her lap, Nancy carried the box of wall cubbies, and Claire grabbed the mirror. Claire never had such nice things. With these added decorations, her room would be a place to relax and enjoy. The women stopped at the checkout counter.

"Would you mind holding these for us?" Nancy handed her box to the clerk, gathered the remaining items, and piled them on the counter. "We're not quite finished."

The young woman nodded and then answered the ringing telephone.

"Come on, ladies, follow us." Vivian lumbered toward the lighting department as she steered Geraldine's chair in the right direction.

There were so many lamps to choose from, it made Claire's head spin. But after twenty minutes, she settled on a white glossy milk-glass lamp, topped with a natural colored drum shade.

Nancy nudged Claire's elbow. "I think you picked the right one. This is fun, isn't it?"

Claire smiled. "I didn't think so at first, but I'm getting used to it—as long as you know that I'm going to pay you back for every purchase."

"Okay, Claire, I won't fight you on this. I respect your decision." Nancy wrapped an arm around Claire's shoulder. "My chance at motherhood was snatched away from me—I would have loved the chance to spoil my little girl."

Claire's mind whirled at Nancy's statement as they headed toward the furniture department. What did she mean? The photo of the baby in Nancy's hallway crossed her mind. Her throat constricted. Nancy may have lost a daughter. She had lost a mother. Claire blinked back tears as they walked toward the bedroom furniture. She spotted a darling twin bed set with a matching dresser—just right for a little girl. Claire eyed Nancy as they walked past. She would have wanted only the best for her daughter.

After much discussion, Geraldine ordered a mahogany bedside table and dresser, along with a Victorian metal headboard to be shipped and ready for pick-up in a couple of weeks. The furniture was beautiful and exactly what Claire would have chosen.

"On to the paint store!" Vivian rubbed her hands together. "I'll even come over and help you paint."

Claire searched Geraldine's eyes. "Will Michael mind?" She didn't want to do anything to risk the new relationship she had with her landlord.

"Oh, phooey." Geraldine swatted the air with her hand. "When will Michael ever see your room? I know he recently had the whole house painted, but it's ours to do with as we wish now. In fact, I was thinking my room would look nice in blue."

Claire laughed out loud. Geraldine was a kick. She wished they had gotten better acquainted when they both lived in L.A.

The hard days when her mother was ill could have been a little brighter with Geraldine's sense of humor.

Geraldine fanned her face as they left Macy's and headed to Nancy's car with purchases in hand. "I'm exhausted. I think I'll stay in the car while you shop at King's Paint. I don't drive so you don't have to worry about my highjacking your car, Nancy." She chuckled. "Claire, you know the color of my comforter. Can you help Vivian pick out a nice blue for my room?"

Geraldine trusts me to make a decision. "I'd love to." A sense of pride welled up inside her. She opened the door and helped the elderly woman get in the car.

The minute the women walked into the paint store, Claire could see Vivian's excitement. She continued to rub her hands together, as if she couldn't wait to get hold of a paintbrush. Vivian walked directly to the color strips, pulled out several samples of yellow and blue, and flipped through them, discarding those she didn't like.

Claire walked over to the historical display swatches. She liked the warm, subtle hues. The colors reminded her of peace and harmony. She fingered several swatches and finally decided on Hawthorne Yellow for her room and Jamestown Blue for Geraldine's.

Nancy stood next to Claire. "You've got great taste. The inside of my house is painted with historical colors, too."

Vivian positioned her arms across her ample bosom. "Are you sure you don't like these?"

Claire burst out laughing. She wouldn't be able to sleep with the bright yellow Vivian chose. And Geraldine would faint if she saw the blue that Vivian picked—bright turquoise. "Sorry, Vivian. But Hawthorne Yellow and Jamestown Blue it is."

"Okay, then." Vivian snatched the swatches out of Claire's hand and brought them to the counter for the paint to be mixed and purchased.

Claire carried both cans of paint as they exited the paint store.

"Do you have time for coffee?" Vivian asked as they reached the car.

"I've got to be at work soon." Nancy glanced at her watch. "It's close to six o'clock."

"Vivian, do you want to come over for dinner? Blake cooks enough for ten people." The minute the words were out of her mouth, Claire cringed. She hoped Vivian didn't take offense.

"I've heard about your handsome neighbor." She flexed her eyebrows. "Do you think he could drive me back to Nancy's afterward?"

Claire loaded the paint next to the wheelchair in the trunk. "I'm sure he wouldn't mind."

Nancy unlocked the doors. As the women climbed in, Claire's pulse pounded. Something was drastically wrong. "Where's Geraldine?" She seemed to have disappeared into thin air.

20

The phone call set him on edge. "What do you mean my mother isn't with you?" Michael's jaw flexed.

"Has she been known to take off by herself?" Claire's voice was shaky, obviously upset.

"On occasion," Michael said flatly. "She doesn't go far." He paced the family room. "Where are you?"

"King's Paint."

"I had the house painted. Why are you there?" Michael's voice was louder than he planned. "Never mind, I'm on my way—"

"Mr. Thompson, I mean, Michael, wait a minute . . ."

He heard women's voices in the background. Then, his mother came on the line.

"Michael, dear, I'm fine. I stepped out of the car for fresh air, then I spotted a furniture store. I'd like a new chair in my bedroom."

His mother sounded chipper, like her usual self.

"You went by yourself?" Michael couldn't hold back his agitation.

"I had my cane with me. I can't lose *all* my independence. Claire didn't see me is all. Go back to what you were doing."

"Mother?" Michael knew his tone was reprimanding. "What are you and Claire doing at King's Paint?"

"We have a little project going, so mind your own business." Her voice held a teasing tone.

"Okay, I get the point." Michael sat down on the couch. "How's it going with Claire? Are you two getting along?"

"Splendidly. Now I need to go. Blake will be showing up at the house any minute to make dinner. My, that man can cook. Nice-looking, too."

"I think he's more Claire's age, Mom." Michael laughed into the phone, the conversation shifting to lighter things.

"You're right. There are sparks there. I'll weave my magic like I did on you."

"That's right, you're the one who introduced me to Sandy." Michael remembered the day he met his wife. He was graduating from UCSC in a week, and his mother thought he needed to give a tour of the campus to her friend's niece. Sandy would be a junior at UCSC when she transferred from a school back east.

His mother whispered into the phone. "I was thinking more along the lines of the summer after you graduated from high school."

"I've got to run. Tell Claire I'm glad you're all right. I'll check in with you later in the week. Love you, Mom." Michael hung up the phone before his mother had another chance to remind him of his past mistakes—especially in front of Claire. He tossed the phone on the couch. Why couldn't his mother leave him alone? It was bad enough that the letter had resurfaced after all these years. He didn't want to be reminded of that time in his life. And he certainly didn't want to admit he knew exactly who wrote that letter.

Michael stomped up the stairs to his bedroom. He opened his closet and saw the box of memorabilia. Was it time to face things head-on? He pulled the box from the shelf and placed it on his bed. With sweaty hands, he slipped off the lid. A musty aroma hit his nostrils. He hadn't opened the box in a long time. A scrapbook of his high school years greeted him. His mother had spent countless hours cutting and pasting newspaper clippings, photos, and souvenirs to create the book. He ran his hand over the cover. *1968-1972*. So long ago.

Michael turned the scrapbook over and opened it from the back. A picture of his friends, the *Rat Pack*, like the popular entertainers of the 50s, brought a smile to his face. He chuckled at his bell-bottom pants and disco shirt. Martin, Willie, and Glen all wore the same style. They were quite the foursome. They hung out together, worked on cars, and chased girls. Michael touched the photo, running his index finger over Martin's face.

"Honey, I'm home," Sandy called, her voice interrupting his recollections from the past.

Michael shut the scrapbook, placed it in the box, and shoved the memories back in the closet.

He walked down the stairs and into the kitchen. "How's my wife?" Michael greeted her from behind, grabbed her around the waist, and pulled her toward him. He nuzzled and kissed her neck.

"What's gotten into you?" Sandy reached into a grocery bag and pulled out lettuce, carrots, and tomatoes.

"What do you mean?" Michael turned her around and cupped her face with gentle hands. "You, my dear, are the most beautiful woman on the planet." He lowered his face to hers and gave her a tender kiss, then wrapped his arms around her. "I haven't been the best husband lately, and I want to change all that."

"Oh, yeah." Sandy glanced up at him with a smile. "And how are you going to do that?"

"First of all, I'm going to show you how much I love you." Michael leaned down for another kiss. "And then, I'm taking you out on the town. Anywhere you want to go."

"What *has* gotten into you?" Sandy squinted her eyes. "Do you have bad news to tell me and you're buttering me up?"

He pushed the guilt away. "Now, why would you say that? I'm trying to be a better husband to you." He ran his hands down her arms, and hugged her close.

Sandy looked deep into Michael's eyes. "What are you afraid of, Michael?"

"What are talking about?" He took a step back, the intimate moment gone. She had no idea of his long list of fears—one of them buried in his closet.

"Is it because your baby girl is getting married?" Sandy closed the gap between them and brought her arms up, clasping her hands behind his neck. "You've been on edge. It's natural to feel sad and old. Remember the movie *Father of the Bride?*"

He let out an exasperated sigh, his shoulders sagging.

Sandy's face softened. She stood on her toes and kissed his chin. "I'm sorry. Forget I said anything. Now where were we?"

Michael put his hands in his pockets. "Forget it. Another time. Think I'll go shoot hoops with Eric. He's been wanting to get in shape."

Sandy let go of his neck, clearly wounded. She turned away from him and continued to unload the groceries. "You'd rather spend time with your coworker?" She grabbed the milk and put it in the refrigerator, slamming the door shut.

He felt his guard slip a notch. Why was he making such a big deal of the letter? The answer was clear—he couldn't risk Sandy knowing the truth before Julia's wedding.

"Go ahead. If that's what you want." Sandy turned away from him and placed the dried fruit and canned tuna fish in the pantry.

No, that's not what he wanted. He wanted to make love to his wife. Why couldn't he say so and fix what was wrong between them? *Pride.* It had gotten him into more messes than he could count. He inhaled deeply and let out his breath. "I'll be back in an hour."

Michael threw the basketball to Eric. "Okay, man, show me what you got." Michael didn't want to poke fun of a man attempting to get back in shape, but the sight of Eric had doubled him over with laughter. Long white athletic socks came up to his knees, his knit shorts clung to his body, and his T-shirt was a few sizes too big.

Eric bounced the ball. "Before you called, Jennifer had asked me to get the kids ready for bed. But when she found out you wanted to work out, she shooed me out the door." He threw the ball, missing the hoop by a good two feet. "Wow, I'm rusty."

Michael jogged over to the ball and picked it up. He dribbled as he ran toward the hoop, stopping abruptly to take a shot. It bounced off the backboard and swished through the net. "Do you want to run around the gym a few times to loosen up?"

"Anything to get my body moving." Eric stretched from side to side.

"Great. Let's go." Michael allowed Eric to set the pace.

"So, what's been going on with you?" Eric's breath came out in short, quick bursts. "You've been reclusive lately."

"What do you mean?"

"We're friends, right?"

"Yeah. Of course we're friends."

"Then answer this. Where've you been hiding out?"

The slow run hurt Michael's knees. "Work. Home. Setting my mother up in the rental. Planning a wedding. Life's been busy."

"Hey, everyone's busy. That's not what I mean." They rounded a corner of the gym and kept running. "You seem to be deep in thought all the time."

Leave it to Eric to drill him. He was a good man, husband, and father who seemed to take things in stride. Michael liked that about him. Eric would say it was his faith that kept him going and gave him peace. Did that mean he didn't have enough?

"Do you have any regrets?" Michael voiced the question that filled his mind. Did he just dig himself a hole?

Eric laughed. "Are you serious? Of course, we all have."

They completed a lap. "Do you want to keep running?"

"Oh, yeah!" Eric waved them on. "I need to show my wife a sweat-soaked shirt when I get home." He flexed his biceps.

Michael laughed. "Okay, your call." He hoped Eric had forgotten his question. No such luck.

"So, what do you regret?" Eric pumped his arms and legs.

"I wrote a letter." The words slipped out before Michael could stop them.

"Who'd you write to?"

"A young woman I had a crush on a long time ago."

"Whoa. When did you do that?" Eric's forehead creased.

"1972."

Eric stopped abruptly. "That's over thirty years ago." He laughed. "Let it go."

Michael grabbed the basketball and ran to the free-throw line. "I wish I could." He cradled the ball, bounced it a few times, and then took the shot. The basketball hit the rim and dropped through the hoop.

"What do you mean?" Eric ran to get the ball. He dribbled it down the court, turned suddenly, and took a jump shot. Once again he missed. Eric shrugged his shoulders and retrieved the ball. He tossed it to Michael.

"I thought the letter was long gone, and then it showed up. I denied writing it or knowing anything about it." Michael took off running and made a layup. He picked up the basketball and passed it to Eric. "I'm surprised this ol' body can still make that shot."

"Back to this letter . . . If you signed it, why would you deny writing it?" Eric held on to the basketball and motioned for them to sit down on the bleachers.

"I didn't sign it. I wrote my first initial. But that's the least of my problems. I have other skeletons in my closet."

21

Claire dug her toes into the soft sand. Seagulls squawked overhead as the waves crashed on the shore. Geraldine had given her the afternoon off. She told her that she didn't expect Claire to be at her side twenty-four hours a day and insisted she take time for herself.

The afternoon turned out to be sunny and warm, a perfect day to walk along the beach. With her sunhat on her head and her tote bag over her shoulder, Claire had walked through Capitola Village and down to the shore. She kicked off her flip-flops and tucked them in her bag, then wandered up the beach close to the water's edge, feeling the cold water swirl around her feet. Two joggers ran past. A woman with a golden retriever walked in the opposite direction. Claire breathed in the salty air. Time alone felt good.

She didn't have a plan for how far she'd walk, but she'd keep going until she'd collected enough shells or was too tired to go any farther. As she rounded the cove, she spotted an elderly couple sitting on beach chairs. The man was reading a magazine while the woman knitted. They looked strangely familiar. Claire picked up her pace. "It couldn't be." *Harry and Pearl?* She darted up the beach.

"I thought it was you." Claire stood in front of them, blocking the sun's rays.

Pearl looked up. "Land's sakes, Harry, it's our friend Claire." She scrambled out of her beach chair, dropped her knitting needles, and hugged Claire so tight she could barely breathe. "How've you been, darlin'?" Pearl finally let her go.

A couple of months ago, Pearl's use of the word *darling* had made her uneasy, but today it felt comfortable. In fact, she would have been disappointed if Pearl didn't call her by that name. "It's so good to see you two." Claire tucked her hands in the pockets of her shorts. "I'm renting a house on Depot Hill."

Harry sat forward. "And how's that car of yours?"

"Almost fixed. Blake, my neighbor, is working on it."

"Blake, huh? You sure he knows what he's doing?" Harry crossed his thick arms over his chest. "That car of yours is a classic. You wouldn't want just anyone tinkering with it."

"Oh, Harry, for goodness' sake. Leave Claire alone." Pearl tugged on the bill of his baseball cap. "I'm sure this Blake knows what he's doing."

"Congratulations on your new grandson." Claire grinned. "Samantha told me." She reached into her bag, grabbed her flip-flops, and slipped them on.

"We're coming from San Francisco. We helped John and Melody with our new grandbaby. But it was time to go. You know that old saying, 'When the fish start smelling, it's time to leave.'"

Claire laughed. Pearl was a woman of wisdom. "I'm surprised to see you here."

"New Brighton Beach has always been one of our favorite spots. We've already been here a week. Our RV is right up there on the bluff." Harry pointed behind him.

"About your RV . . . I still need to pay you for the repairs."

"Oh, honey, we're not going to get a new bumper for a little scratch." Pearl twirled her long braid between her fingers. "You keep your money and put it toward something you've been saving up for."

Savings? It would be a while before she could save for anything. With all the new stuff for her bedroom, she'd be paying her friends for a long time.

Claire took off her sunhat and wiped her forehead. "How long are you going to be at New Brighton?"

Harry finally stood. "We leave first thing in the morning." He tugged on the waistline of his jeans. "We're heading south to L.A. Our son Albert wants us to pay him a visit."

"Who knows what cause he's marching for now." Pearl shrugged her shoulders. "I can't keep up. Say, have you ever been to L.A.? Albert's about your age and if I do say so myself, quite good-looking."

"There you go, woman." Harry grabbed his baseball hat and slapped it against his thigh. "Albert will find himself his own bride. Stop matchmaking. Although, Claire would be a nice catch." He grinned.

"Yes. I've been to L.A." She wrinkled her nose. "And I'm not going back there anytime soon if I can help it." *Unless I can't make it on my own.* The thought unnerved her.

"I know I've said this to you before, Claire, but I firmly believe it. Remember, the Lord provides." Pearl winked and patted Claire's arm. "Ready to go, Harry. I'm done baking in the sun." She reached over, folded her beach chair, and picked up her knitting supplies. "Claire, can you come up for dinner? We have plenty."

"Thank you, but I—" Claire pointed down the beach.

"We understand." Harry folded his beach chair. "You need to check on Blake and that car of yours." He gave her shoulder a grandfatherly pat.

Claire momentarily toyed with the idea of following Harry and Pearl to their campsite. It would be so nice to be in their company for a while longer. But Harry was right. She needed to check on her car.

"Nice to see you, Claire. Keep in touch." Pearl smiled.

Claire watched as the couple ambled up the beach toward the path that led to the campground.

The Lord provides. Pearl had said this to her before. At that time, Claire didn't have a job or a place to live. Did she believe it now? Maybe. But did God really care about her? She still had unanswered questions, such as who wrote the letter to her mother? Why was her picture frame the same as Geraldine's? And why did her heart skip a beat whenever Blake was near? Claire's breath caught in her throat. Where did that come from?

She walked home so deep in thought she nearly ran into her favorite neighbor on the sidewalk in front of her house.

"There you are." Blake fit the image of a mechanic. He wore blue pants and a button-down shirt with a few tools sticking out of his shirt pocket. "Can you come over and take a look at your car?"

There was a magnetic pull between the two of them that she couldn't describe. At that moment she'd follow Blake almost anywhere.

"Claire, what's wrong? You have a silly look on your face." Blake walked closer, grabbed her hand, and pulled her toward his carport.

"Oh, it's nothing." The last thing she wanted to do was ruin any chance she had with this man. Not that she thought she had a chance with him. If chemistry had anything to do with two people getting together, then they were the perfect match, but she knew there was more to love than physical attraction. Her thoughts drifted to Haley and Mark. They married before they knew each other. Mark's addiction to alcohol has been an ongoing problem since their first year of marriage. No amount of flirting on Blake's part would force her into an irrational decision.

"Take a look at the bumper and hood I found at Gino's Auto Recycling."

Claire picked up speed. She couldn't wait to sit behind the wheel of her car and drive again.

"Now, I haven't been able to work on your engine yet." Blake led her to the carport. "But your car will look better once I get the new bumper and hood in place."

Claire gasped when she saw her dismantled car. In a way, it was a relief—she didn't have to look at the evidence of her neglect. She ran her hand over the side of her VW.

"Here they are." Blake pointed. "The color of the hood doesn't match your car, but it fits perfectly." He picked up the hood and laid it on top. "And this silver chrome bumper was an amazing find."

Claire bit her lower lip, then smiled. "Blake, it's going to look perfect." She touched the new hood. "I can see you know what you're doing." Harry's words echoed in the back of her mind.

"It's a hobby, but I've been at it for years." Blake grabbed a rag from his back pocket and wiped a dirt spot off the front window. "The engine's what may cause me trouble . . . oh, and I found replacement headlights. I noticed yours were cracked."

"Thank you, Blake." Her eyes filled unexpectedly, and she turned her back. Blake was so considerate. She didn't want to take advantage of his kindness. "I'll have to figure out how to pay you for all this."

"Let's figure that out when I'm done." Blake walked over to Claire and nudged her arm. "In the meantime, you can cook *me* dinner. After tonight, I'm working the next four days."

"I better get going, then." Claire bumped his arm back, and a smile tugged at her mouth. "I'll check the fridge for leftovers." She tossed her hair over her shoulder and walked away.

"Hey, I like my steak medium rare." Blake called to her retreating back. "I'll be by at 6:30."

She walked up the sidewalk hoping Blake was watching her. As she reached the sidewalk, she took a quick glance over her shoulder. No! He was working on her car instead.

Claire cut through Blake's front yard to her own. The UPS truck was stopped in front of her house. A postal worker hopped out with a wrapped brown box in his hand.

"Your package, Miss." The man had a friendly smile that reached his eyes.

Claire took the parcel from him, signed her name on the tracking device, and looked at the return address. *Haley.* She ran to the front door and burst through.

Michael and Sandy Thompson were sitting in the family room talking with Geraldine. All three craned their necks at her noisy entrance.

"I'm sorry." Claire retrieved a pair of scissors from the kitchen drawer and scooted past them to her room. She sat down on her bed and quickly tore open the package.

She found a note on top from her sister.

> Claire,
> I know these were your favorite stilettos, so I'm giving them to you.
> I thought you'd like to see this journal. Hopefully it will answer the questions you have about Mom.
> And here is a small portion of what was yours in the first place . . .
> I miss you.
> Haley

Claire peered inside the box and found the bright red stilettos. She pulled them out and slid them on her feet. She stood up and wobbled across her room, positioning herself in front of her full-length mirror. There was something about a pair of high heels that made a woman feel glamorous. She posed in different positions, admiring the look.

Claire walked back to see what else was in the box. An envelope sat wedged against the side. When she grabbed it, a handful of twenty-dollar bills tumbled out. Claire stifled a scream as she counted the money . . . two hundred dollars! Why was her sister sending her cash? Money she knew Haley couldn't part with right now with a baby on the way. *The Lord provides.* Claire smiled, remembering Pearl's words. She'd give each person she owed—Harry and Pearl, Geraldine, Nancy, Vivian and Blake—forty dollars. It was a start. She tucked the money inside her wallet.

At the bottom of the box was a journal in her mom's own handwriting dated from September 1972 until May 1973. She flipped through the pages, then turned to the first entry.

> I'm in love with Martin DeWitt. We had a fun summer together, and today I received a letter. He signed it with his first initial. Isn't he cute? He's trying to keep his identity a secret, but I know it's him.

Claire tossed the journal across her bed. *Martin DeWitt?* Who in the world was this man and how did he know her mother? What about Michael? She thought he had written the letter. Claire kicked off her heels and paced the room. She could come right out and ask Michael again, but with Sandy sitting next to him it might be awkward. If she waited until Michael, and Sandy left, she could show Geraldine the journal and ask her. Claire opened her door a crack and peeked out.

Geraldine, Michael, and Sandy appeared to be in the middle of a deep discussion.

Claire leaned back against her door. Were the answers right in front of her in the journal? She dove back on her bed, grabbed the journal, and turned to the first entry. Claire shifted against the pillows and reread the opening line again.

I'm in love with Martin DeWitt.

22

Claire heard Geraldine's voice on the other side of her bedroom door. "Claire, dear, may I come in?"

She set the journal down on her nightstand, crossed the room, and opened the door.

"Michael and Sandy invited me out to dinner and to spend the night." Geraldine leaned on her walker and grinned. "It's so nice to be wanted. So, you have the evening to yourself."

She hoped her company wanted her too. "Thanks. Blake should be coming over soon. I'm making him dinner."

"I have candles in the top right-hand drawer in the kitchen. You're welcome to use them." Geraldine winked. "Can you help me get my bag packed, dear?"

"Yes, but first I have something for you." Claire opened her purse and took out her wallet. "Haley sent me money. Here's my first payment for the furniture." She handed Geraldine forty dollars.

"Are you sure you can part with it?" Geraldine tucked the money into the neckline of her dress.

Claire nodded. "Come on. I'll follow you. Let's get you packed."

She glanced at Michael and Sandy sitting comfortably in the family room. Her eyes met Michael's, and she quickly turned away. Why couldn't she look at the man without feeling vulnerable? She wondered what kind of relationship he shared with his daughter. A shiver ran through her. She couldn't imagine having him for a father. But then again, how would she know? Her father left before she could remember him.

Once Geraldine's bags were packed, Michael, Sandy and Geraldine took off. For the first time, Claire had the house to herself. She dimmed the lights and turned the radio to her favorite country station. She swayed to the music as she moved to the kitchen. The candles were right where Geraldine said they would be. She pulled out two red ones and set them in candleholders on the table. She opened the refrigerator and looked at the contents inside. She didn't want to admit to Blake she wasn't a good cook, especially after all the wonderful meals he'd been making, but she could barely boil water. When her mom was ill, she'd call for take-out and have dinner delivered to their door.

She *could* make a delicious sandwich. She pulled out the roast beef, provolone cheese, lettuce, tomatoes, wheat bread, and condiments. What would Blake think? Cold sandwiches by candlelight. That was an interesting combination. She whipped up the light supper, adding potato chips and carrots to each plate. As she poured the soft drinks, the doorbell rang.

The musky scent of Blake's cologne hit her before he walked into the house. Did he have to smell so good? With his damp hair combed back and his face clean-shaven, he had a way of making her knees grow weak. "Come in. It's you and me tonight." Her voice sounded eager.

Blake entered the house and looked around. "Where's your cute roommate?"

"I'm glad Geraldine is in her eighties, or I'd be jealous." Claire bit her lip. What was it about this man that made her speak her mind?

"Jealous, huh?" Blake teased.

Claire smiled and motioned to him to join her at the table. "It's not steak . . ."

Blake followed her. "I'd enjoy eating cold cereal alone with you." Once they were seated, he held out his hand and bowed his head. The words of Blake's prayer soothed her spirit.

"There is something you should know about me . . . I can't cook."

Blake chuckled. "Geraldine warned me earlier."

"But I can make my first payment." Claire pulled out two twenty-dollar bills and laid them on the table. "I received a package from Haley today. She sent me money." She plucked a baby carrot off her plate and popped it into her mouth.

"Don't you need this money for living expenses?"

"I like to pay my debts. I'm sure it will take me a while to cover all that I owe you."

"The dinner is your first payment."

"It's nothing like what you fix."

"You can pay me another way. How about another neck massage?"

Claire's pulse quickened. She remembered the feel of Blake's skin against hers. She'd have to be careful. The last thing she needed was to complicate her life with a man who was too good for her. The women in her family didn't go for guys like him. Blake was confident, secure, and close to God—three things she was not. No, men who left their families or were alcoholics were what she was used to. At least, that's what happened to her mother and sister.

She needed to change the subject fast. "Haley sent a couple other things too." She swallowed a swig of her soda.

"Like what?" Blake appeared to be enjoying his sandwich—either that or he was starving after working on her car all day.

"A pair of red stilettos—"

"Hmmm. I'd like to see you in those!"

"Really?" Claire laughed.

"Why not?" Blake smiled.

"Now?"

"Sounds good to me."

Heart racing, Claire pushed her chair away from the table and went to her room. She took the heels out of the box and placed them on her feet. Now, if she could walk without falling on her face. With tentative steps, she rejoined Blake in the dining room.

He leaned forward and flashed her a smile. "Wow. Nice. How about I take you to dinner in those." The look in Blake's eyes sent chills down her spine. "Bella Roma after my four-day shift."

"Bella Roma?" Claire's eyes widened. She joined him back at the table.

"It's a quaint little Italian restaurant here in Capitola." He placed his hand on top of hers and brushed his thumb across her fingers.

The momentary excitement disappeared when she thought of her responsibility to Geraldine. Claire wrinkled her brow. "I don't feel comfortable leaving Geraldine alone."

"I think she'd be fine for an hour or two. I won't keep you out all night." He grinned and sat up straight. "How about we ask Nancy or Vivian to stay with her?"

Claire's heart fluttered. One thing she knew about Blake—he was persistent. He seemed to have everything figured out. "Bella Roma sounds wonderful." She was giving in and enjoying it. Claire glanced at her own half-eaten sandwich. She had lost her appetite. This man was making a path to her heart. It was exciting and disturbing.

"Did your sister send you anything else?" Blake took the last bite of his sandwich.

Claire wiped her hands with a napkin. "A journal."

"Sounds intriguing. Who from?"

"It's my mother's journal from 1972, after she received the letter." Claire kicked off her heels and retrieved the book from her bedroom.

She motioned Blake to join her on the couch. "Come, and I'll show you."

Blake sat down, resting his arm behind her.

Claire scooted closer to him. His nearness made her wish she had remembered to dab her neck with perfume. She opened the book and read. "I'm in love with Martin DeWitt—"

"Didn't you tell me you thought Michael Thompson wrote the letter?"

Claire closed the book and set it next to her on the couch. "I thought he did. It all made sense until this journal showed up. And now I don't know what to think. Why does Michael look as if he's hiding something? The way he dodged my question about the letter still makes me uncomfortable. And then, there's the picture frame. How come Geraldine has the same one?" She stood and paced the floor.

Blake rose from the couch. "Are you sure you're not making too much of all this?"

Claire's hands flew to her hips. "What do you mean?"

"Claire, you have your answer. Martin's name starts with the letter *M* and your mom says she was in love with him. It's time to move on with your life." Blake led her back to the couch. "She won't be forgotten."

"Don't you see, I can't quit. I need to understand this part of my mom's life." She swallowed the lump that formed in her throat. "There is something more to this letter. I can feel it."

Blake pulled her close, tucking her head securely against his chest. "I know you miss your mom, but missing her is one thing, being obsessed with this letter is another." He let out a frustrated sigh.

His words stung. He didn't mean it—he couldn't. How could such a caring man be so unkind? Claire bolted upright. "You don't understand me at all." She stood, marched to the dining room table and blew out the candles. "You sound like Haley. 'Move on. Make friends. Go out on dates. Stop being stuck in the past.' Until you're in my shoes, don't judge me."

"Claire, I didn't mean to hurt you. I think Haley is right. It's time to move on." Blake came up beside her, placed both hands on her arms. "And I want to help you." He leaned in for a kiss.

Instinctively, Claire's hands shot up to his chest and pushed him away. A memory of her mother and one of her deadbeat boyfriends popped into her head. Claire dropped down on a dining room chair, unable to look Blake in the eye. He was not like those men Mom used to date. When Claire had turned sixteen, her mother swore off men altogether. "Friendship," she had said, "was the only way to go." Heat crept up Claire's neck to her cheeks. "Please leave."

"Come on, Claire . . ." He laid a hand on her shoulder.

"I said go!" A knot started in her throat and burned its way to her heart.

Blake walked to the door and turned the handle. "I'll make a reservation at Bella Roma for six o'clock on Saturday." He walked out to the landing and half-closed the door, then stuck his head back in. "Oh, and wear those red stilettos!" He smiled, then closed the door.

Persistent. Claire exhaled. The man sure was persistent.

Claire lay in her bed with the comforter drawn up to her chin. The sun's rays shone through the window. She had tossed and turned most of the night, replaying the attempted kiss and the subsequent shove. How humiliating. She covered her eyes with a hand, forcing her thoughts to less embarrassing things.

Geraldine had called last night to tell her that she and Sandy would pick her up at eleven so she could help them find a "grandmother of the bride" dress for the wedding. Claire looked forward to spending time with Geraldine and Sandy. Michael's wife seemed like a nice woman, someone she'd want to get to know.

When was the last time she wore a dress? She couldn't remember. Wouldn't Blake be surprised to see her in a dress that matched her heels? That's if she decided to go on their date. Maybe Nancy had one she could borrow; they were about the same size.

The clock displayed ten o'clock. Way past time to get up. Pushing the blankets aside, Claire stretched, then stood and walked to the mirror. Her long wavy hair was askew, and her nose was pink from the previous day's walk on the beach. She rubbed the sleep from her eyes, pulled her hair back in a ponytail, and dug in her closet for something to wear. She settled on her ivory pants and light blue sweater.

Once in the kitchen, she put a slice of four-grain bread in the toaster and pulled the honey from the cabinet. After she heated water in a mug, she dropped in a tea bag and brought her small breakfast to the table.

She ate in a trance without tasting her food. Her evening with Blake had been a disaster—from the meager dinner of cold sandwiches, arguing over the letter, to pushing him away when he tried to kiss her. Claire would be surprised if he showed up to take her to Bella Roma. Did she want him to? Even after the way he dismissed her interest in finding the writer of the letter? He'd been downright rude implying she was obsessed. Was she? She discarded the thought. The smell of her lemon tea brought her comfort as she drew the cup to her lips.

There was nothing wrong with wanting to meet someone from her mother's past. There had to be one man her mom dated who was decent. How else was she going to believe in love? Or keep the memories of her mother alive? As it was, she could barely remember the sound of her mother's voice. Martin DeWitt, huh? She grabbed the phone book from the cabinet above the table and was thumbing through it when a car horn startled her.

Sandy. Grabbing her purse, she stuck a piece of gum in her mouth and locked the door behind her.

"Claire, hi. Come on in." Sandy called from the driver's side window of her Lexus. "I would've come to the door, but we're running late. Julia is waiting for us at the bridal shop."

Claire opened the door and stepped inside. The tan leather seats smelled new. "I like your car."

"Thank you. Michael got a great deal from a friend of his." Sandy pulled out of the driveway and drove down the street. "The car's a few years old, but the previous owner took good care of it."

"How was your evening, Geraldine?" Claire reached forward and touched her shoulder.

"Fine. Just fine. I should ask the same of you, my dear. How's that handsome man of yours?"

"Blake is not my man." Claire squirmed in her seat. "But the candles were a nice touch. Thanks for warning him about my cooking."

"When Blake's kitchen is put back together, I'll teach you a thing or two. A man likes a woman who can cook." Geraldine held up a gnarled finger.

Fifteen minutes later they arrived at Bridal Veil Fashions. After walking to the back of the store, Claire helped Geraldine sit in a chair as Julia entered the room in her wedding gown. She was stunning. The exquisite beaded bodice hugged her slender figure, and the cathedral train trailed elegantly behind. Claire hoped *she'd* have the chance someday to have a real wedding, not a rushed ceremony as her sister had had. Claire pushed her envious thoughts away. How could she be jealous of someone she barely knew?

"Julia, you look beautiful. I don't think you'll need much in the way of alterations." Sandy wiped tears from her cheeks.

"Mom, don't start crying." Julia fanned her face with a hand. "If you start crying again, I know I will too." Her eyes softened. "You think I look beautiful?"

"You're gorgeous, honey." Sandy reached into her purse, pulled out a tissue, and dabbed at her eyes. "Don't you think so, Mom?"

Geraldine had the cutest grin on her face. "You make a beautiful bride, Julia."

"Grandma, we need to find you a dress." Julia made quarter turns to accommodate the seamstress.

"My friend here will help me." Geraldine patted Claire's hand. "Won't you, dear?"

Claire nodded. "I'd love to."

"I'm sorry, Claire. You remember my daughter, Julia." Sandy blew her nose. "I don't know why I'm falling apart . . ."

"Nice to see you again." Claire lifted a hand.

"Thanks so much for caring for my grandmother. She speaks highly of you."

Claire's face warmed at the compliment.

Julia turned for the seamstress once again. “Feel free to find a dress, Grandma. And remember, the bridesmaids are wearing pink.”

Geraldine grabbed both handles of her walker and slowly hoisted herself to standing. “Okay, Claire. Help me find a knockout dress.”

Claire giggled and followed Geraldine to the front of the store. Rows of gowns filled the small room.

“What size do you wear?” She guessed Geraldine to be less than five feet tall, and not much more than one hundred pounds.

“Good question. I think I’ll have to try them on.” Geraldine stopped abruptly and pulled on the skirt of a pale pink dress. “I like this one. Look, it has a lace jacket to match. Help me try this one on, dear. If it’s too big, I’ll have the seamstress take it in.”

Claire liked Geraldine’s no-nonsense approach. She carried the dress and helped Geraldine to the fitting room.

After disrobing, Geraldine sat down on the seat and stepped into the pink gown. She stood, and Claire zipped the back of the dress. “This one was made for me. Hand me the jacket, dear.”

Claire held up the lace fabric while the elderly woman placed her arms inside the sleeves. “You look beautiful.”

“Aren’t you sweet.” Geraldine slowly twirled around, then opened the door. “Let’s see what Sandy and Julia think.”

Remembering the photo from Geraldine’s antique picture frame, Claire could picture Geraldine getting dressed up for a man. She was quite the romantic at heart.

“Claire, dear?” She interrupted Claire’s thoughts. “How’s it going with Blake?” The elderly woman scooted toward her. A smile was plastered across her face.

"He's taking me out to dinner on Saturday . . . if Nancy or Vivian can stay with you." Her feelings about Blake were a jumbled mess. Did she want the sisters to be available? Her heart skipped a beat.

"Don't you worry. Perch me in front of a good movie and I won't budge." She motioned to Sandy.

"Mom, that dress looks nice on you." Sandy eyed her from all directions. "A few alterations are needed, but otherwise it's perfect."

Geraldine grinned.

"Mom, remember I'm meeting my friend for lunch. We should get going soon."

"Oh, that's right. Claire, please help me get changed." Geraldine shuffled back into the fitting room. "We wouldn't want Sandy to be late. Her friend Debbie DeWitt is always on time."

Claire was close behind. Her mind raced. "Did you say DeWitt?" her palms were suddenly moist. "Any relation to Martin DeWitt?"

23

Michael drove his BMW into the parking lot in front of Pacific Coast Manor. He hadn't seen his friend Martin in three years. He pushed his guilt to the back of his mind as he slid out of the seat and locked the door.

He hoped Martin's brain stem injury didn't keep him from remembering the good times. Knots formed in his stomach as he approached the double doors. He wiped his sweaty palms on his slacks and hesitated before going in. Before he could change his mind, he stepped through the doorway.

"Can you tell me the number for Martin DeWitt's room?" He leaned his arm on the front counter.

The young secretary looked him over. "I can ring his room to see if he's up to visitors." She fiddled with her shirt collar. "Your name?"

"Michael Thompson," he answered. "A friend from high school."

The woman nodded and punched in a series of numbers on the telephone.

Michael looked around the room. A couple of chairs flanked a potted ficus tree. A coffee table perched in front of the chairs held various magazines. The place seemed neat and clean.

"He'll see you now. Room 131." The secretary gave a curt smile. "To your left, and down the hall. You can't miss it." Her fingers flew over the keyboard sounding like raindrops on a windowpane.

"Thank you."

The antiseptic smell filled his nostrils the moment he stepped into the hallway. An elderly woman pushed a walker as a nurse stayed close to her side. The place was quiet, except for the squeak of a lunch cart. He continued down the hall.

Michael froze the minute he located Room 131. Was this a mistake? Why'd he come? It was Sandy's idea. She had suggested he visit his high school friend today while she went out to lunch with Debbie. He had a feeling Sandy wanted his relationship with God to get back on track. Martin's faith never wavered.

He peeked inside the doorway. A curtain draped the opening so he couldn't see inside. The last thing he wanted to do was startle his old friend. He'd have to make his presence known. "Here goes," he muttered under his breath.

"Martin?" Michael pulled the curtain back a few inches. "Are you there, Buddy?" The endearing name slipped off his tongue. The sight of Martin in a wheelchair made him cringe. Even now years after the car accident, the thought of a man in his fifties wasting away caused him heartache. He had to give Debbie credit for sticking by a man who could never walk again, much less anything else.

He approached with cautious steps. Would Martin be worse? By the blank look on his face, Michael wondered if he remembered him.

"What are you doing here?" Martin's words slurred together like a man who's had too much to drink. "Your wife make you come?" He blinked as if in slow motion.

Got me there. "I wanted to see you." Michael pulled up a chair and sat mere inches from his high school chum. "I know it's been a while." He might as well acknowledge the obvious.

"I've been here." Martin's brows furrowed.

"Our wives are having lunch today." Michael attempted to avoid the jab.

"I know. They have lunch *every* Thursday." Sweat trickled down Martin's forehead; the exertion from a simple conversation was apparently too much for a man in his situation.

Michael jumped up from his seat, walked to the window, and slid it open. "Our wives have become close friends." Debbie had approached Sandy twenty-five years ago when Michael and Sandy were having marriage problems. Sandy had been amazed at the timing of their friendship. Michael knew better. "Look, Martin, we've got to get past this wedge that's grown between us. It's gone on too long."

Martin looked past him toward the open window. The wind pushed the vertical blinds back and forth, casting shadows on the wall and floor. He seemed to be fascinated with the movement. "It's up to you." The words burst from his lips.

"Yes. It's my fault." Michael sat back down in the chair, rested his elbows on his knees, and clasped his hands together, causing his knuckles to turn white. "How can I make it up to you?" He glanced down at the floor.

"Not me. Sandy."

A nurse walked in. "Time for physical therapy."

A sense of relief washed over Martin's face. Michael sensed his friend was eager to get away from him. The thought soured Michael's stomach. If he'd come to visit him more often, Martin would believe he cared for him. The thought jarred Michael. Of course, that's it.

He glanced at his watch and noted the time. Martin had physical therapy at 12:30. Next time he'd come a little earlier.

Michael stood and placed a hand on Martin's shoulder. "I'll come again next Thursday, I promise."

Martin turned away. "No promises."

"I will, you'll see."

The nurse unlocked the brakes, grabbed the handles of the wheelchair, and pushed him out of the room.

Michael pinched the bridge of his nose with his thumb and index finger. A headache was forming. He'd tried to prepare himself for such a meeting, but the reality was like a knife to his heart. If only he could reverse time. He'd change so much about the past—and maybe a little about the present too.

Geraldine's stunned expression told Claire all she needed to know. Debbie DeWitt was related to Martin. She had to find out how. "Is Debbie Martin's wife?" Claire slipped the lace jacket off Geraldine's shoulders.

"Why, yes. How did you know?" Geraldine pointed to the back of her dress. The zipper was well hidden.

"Haley sent me Mom's journal. She mentioned Martin's name. So, when you said Sandy was meeting Debbie DeWitt, I guessed."

"I can change the rest by myself, dear." Geraldine pushed Claire out the door and locked the dressing room behind her.

Interesting. She had a feeling the older woman knew more than she was letting on. She had avoided the conversation on more than one occasion. And they all pertained to her mother.

"Julia left to go back to work. You ladies ready?" Sandy approached.

"Almost, dear," Geraldine's voice piped in.

"I'll drop you both off at home before I meet Debbie for lunch. We're going to Gayle's Bakery and Rosticceria." Her voice oozed with enthusiasm. "Say, why don't I call Debbie and tell her you and Claire will be joining us? I know you'd love this place, Mom—"

"That's sweet of you, dear, but I'd like to go home. I need a nap." Claire heard Geraldine shuffling around in the fitting room. "I hope you don't mind me saying so, but the bed in your guest room is a little lumpy."

Claire stifled a laugh.

Geraldine stepped out.

"Well, then, why don't you take a nap . . ." Sandy tapped her chin with a manicured fingernail. "And Claire can join Debbie and me."

What would it be like to meet Martin's wife? Claire smiled. But one look into Geraldine's eyes told her she'd better return home. She didn't want to upset her employer. "Maybe another time. I'd like to get Geraldine settled. I have plenty of food in the refrigerator. Blake keeps us well stocked." Her stomach fluttered at the mention of Blake's name. "Can we have a rain check?"

"Most certainly. I meet Debbie for lunch every Thursday, so we can plan it another time." Sandy held her hand out to carry Geraldine's gown to the cash register.

Once home, Claire helped Geraldine settle into bed for a nap. Then she reached for her mother's journal and situated herself in the recliner in the family room.

Since that first mention of Martin DeWitt, her mother wrote about teenage life as a senior at San Diego High. But mostly she wrote about boys—those who were cute and athletic, the ones she liked, and the one who took her to the prom. Michael's name wasn't mentioned once. In fact, Martin was referred to only a handful of times. Carrying on a long-distance romance would have been difficult for a teenager.

Her thoughts turned toward the letter. Claire couldn't identify her feelings. Was she disappointed? Relieved? Maybe Blake was right and she was obsessed with it. The caring look in Blake's eyes last night made her shudder. She couldn't believe she had pushed him away. Claire set the journal on the coffee table, stood and paced the floor. Was it time to let go of the past? She fingered one of the red candles left on the dining room table. Why had Blake tried to kiss her? To help her move on with her life?

Claire inhaled, then let out an exaggerated sigh. She didn't have much practice with men. In fact, she couldn't remember the last time a man had kissed her.

She heard footsteps on the front porch. Then, as quickly as they came, they disappeared. Claire rushed to the kitchen window and looked out. Her heart skipped a beat at the sight of Blake walking toward his house in his police uniform. She continued watching him. He slid inside his white truck and drove down the street. Why did he come to her door? Claire raced to the door and opened it. A long-stemmed red rose stood in a tall, thin vase. Claire reached for the vase and brought it inside before reading the note that was attached.

> To the Lady in Red,
> Until Saturday night.
> Yours, Blake

Goosebumps ran up and down her arms. Right there and then, she decided she'd go to Bella Roma.

And forget about the letter. At least for now.

24

Michael tried to concentrate on his wife's words. He dug his hands in the soapy water as she rambled on about her lunch date with Debbie. He rinsed the pan and handed it to Sandy.

" . . . and you should see Debbie's new van. It has all kinds of features for the handicapped. She plans on picking up Martin tomorrow and taking him for a drive." Sandy wiped the pan dry with the towel and set it on the counter.

The uncomfortable visit with Martin replayed in his head. Martin's distrust of him had been palpable. He didn't believe for one minute Michael would return. That didn't say much for how he treated people. He'd prove Martin wrong. But paralyzed or not, Martin had been his best friend for thirty-five years. And Michael planned on visiting him again next week.

"Honey, did you hear me?" Sandy took a step toward him, a frown creasing her forehead.

Michael pulled the plug from the sink and watched the dirty dishwater disappear. "Did you say something?"

"I told Debbie it will be like old times." Sandy turned and stacked the pots on the counter. "We could make a picnic lunch, meet them at New Brighton Beach, and hang out for a while. The weather's supposed to be gorgeous on Sunday."

"Sandy, I told you my meeting with him didn't go well. He doesn't want to see me again." Michael threw his hands up in the air, water spraying the already dried pans.

"Did he tell you that?"

"No. He turned away from me when I told him I'd visit him again."

"It'd been three years."

Ouch. Michael wiped his hands on a towel. His wife was right.

"You can't expect Martin to be like he was before. He's a different man." Sandy leaned against the granite counter, her arms folded across her chest. "Goodness knows Debbie's had to make adjustments." She approached Michael and rested her hands on his shoulders. "The more time you spend with Martin, the more comfortable you'll be. Please?"

Michael didn't think it was possible. The secret Martin had been hanging on to would hopefully go to his grave. Debbie had been sworn to secrecy too. Martin had told Michael for years to come clean and ask his wife for forgiveness, but he didn't want to risk it. Not now with Julia's wedding around the corner—maybe not ever.

Michael looked down at Sandy's chocolate-colored eyes. She was beautiful—inside and out. He didn't want her to suspect anything. He'd have to concede.

"Okay, honey. Sunday. We'll have a picnic with the DeWitts."

Sandy reached up and pecked him on the cheek. "Let's invite your mother and Claire too."

"My mother? Really? Wait a minute. You didn't say anything about making this a family affair—"

"I thought having them at the picnic would be a nice buffer, you know, in case there's a moment of awkward silence. Your mom usually keeps the conversation going."

Thoughts of the past month swirled in his mind. He liked having his mother around. She was fun, caring, and always ready to share a good laugh. But there was the serious side of her too. She was stubborn, proud, and took the high road with relationships. She wanted Michael to take care of his past and was here to make sure he did.

Michael clenched his fist, then slid it into his pocket. Did he want his mother involved? She might say something she would later regret. And Claire. Why should she have to know his mistakes from the past?

"Honey? What do you say?" Sandy's brown eyes pleaded. A clear indication that she wanted his answer to be "yes."

"Why not?" He said it more like a question than a definitive answer. As long as his wife was happy and unsuspecting. Michael would need to bend over backward to keep his mother busy. And Claire. Hopefully, she'd forgotten about the letter. Michael's stomach tightened into a hard knot. He was not only going to face his past head-on, but bring his mother and caregiver to watch his life unfold.

"I told Debbie I'd go to church with her in the morning. She doesn't want to be alone her first time back." Sandy's face softened. "Thought you'd understand. Honey, the accident shook *both* yours and Debbie's faiths."

The accident wasn't the only thing that had shaken his faith. Michael's insides twisted. The news he had shared with Martin before the accident had triggered his downward spiral away from God. Sure, he shot arrow prayers every now and then, but that was the extent of his relationship with the Almighty.

Michael flopped down on the couch and grabbed the remote. "I'm not ready." He flipped channels until he found a college football game. He didn't care who was playing.

Sandy came up behind him. "Think about it." She massaged his shoulders and neck. "We'll take one week at a time. Okay?"

Making an appearance at church was as intimidating as looking Debbie in the eye. He felt as though everyone would see straight to his soul. And they wouldn't like what they saw. Darkness. A hole. A spot that he knew only God could fill.

And yet, he couldn't go there. It had been years. He didn't feel worthy.

But he couldn't make excuses any longer. He was tired. Tired of the mess he'd made.

"Maybe next Sunday." He stared at the television as the football passed the goal line for a touchdown.

Sandy swung around the couch and sidled up to him.

Michael knew he had scored a few points himself.

Claire hadn't thought about the letter in a couple of days. She had wedged it between the pages of her mom's journal and tucked the book in her dresser drawer. It had been nice to concentrate on her own life—taking care of Geraldine, and dreaming about her upcoming date with Blake. Life had taken on a nice rhythm.

As she doled out the pills into the seven sections of Geraldine's pillbox, her cell phone jingled in her back jeans pocket. She quickly completed the row before she reached for the phone and answered it. "Hello?"

"Claire, it's me, Samantha."

"Samantha, it's so good to hear your voice! What's been happening with the most put-together woman I know?" She envied Samantha's life—her family, her college degree, and her ability to make it on her own. And she had a boyfriend to boot. Some women had all the luck. Claire needed someone in her life to inspire her to keep going. And Samantha was that person.

"Oh, not so put together. The opposite, in fact." Samantha let out a breath. "Would you believe me if I told you my landlord is selling my house, I've been laid off from my job, and my boyfriend told me he's in love with someone else?"

"NO!" Claire's voice lowered. "You can't be serious." She twisted the lid back on the medicine bottle.

"Yes, it's true."

Claire stared at the row of pill bottles. She would hold off finishing her task until her phone call ended. She didn't want to mess up when Geraldine was counting on her to keep track of her medications. "Don't keep me in suspense." She heard shuffling noises in the background.

"My landlord put up a for sale sign yesterday. I discovered it when I came home after being laid off."

"So, what are you going to do?"

"Move. I'm packing right now. Mom and Dad want to help me out until I land another job and find a new place. Nice of them, huh?"

"Speaking from experience, don't stay too long." One year with Haley was more than enough.

"Oh, no. It's definitely only temporary."

"Capitola is a beautiful place. You should move here." The idea popped out. "We'd have so much fun!"

"Thanks, but I don't know if I'm ready for a drastic change. I want to stay here in case Jason changes his mind." Samantha's voice sounded desperate.

"Jason, as in the guy who thinks he's in love with someone else?" Claire placed a hand on her hip. "Any man who dumps *you* for another woman is crazy. He's not worth the effort." She swatted the air as if she were shooing away a fly. "Forget about him and come to Capitola."

"Two years of dating down the tubes. A promising career cut short. Life is the pits."

"Samantha, you sound like Eeyore." Claire slouched down in her chair.

"I guess I do seem pretty miserable . . . but I am."

Claire would be miserable too if she dated Blake for two years and then he dumped her. She panicked. Should she cancel their date tonight before their relationship progressed any further? No. She couldn't do it. Geraldine was looking forward to a visit from Nancy and Vivian. And if she was honest with herself, she was looking forward to spending time with Blake.

"Hello?"

She realized Samantha was waiting. "Hey, look on the bright side."

"And what could that be?"

"Things could be worse." *Your mom is still living.*

"How's it going for *you* in the love department? Any chance encounters with the handsome neighbor?" Samantha teased.

"Since you mentioned it, yes." Claire took hold of the rose from the vase sitting in the middle of the table, brought the lovely flower close to her face, and inhaled the sweet fragrance. "We're going out tonight."

Samantha's tone lifted. "What if he tries to kiss you?"

"I don't want to think about kissing—yet."

"Wise woman."

Butterflies danced in Claire's stomach. She hoped they'd fly away by six o'clock. "I'm not ready for anything—you know—serious."

Claire could hear the sincerity in Samantha's voice. "I can't wait to hear all about it. Have a good time, friend."

"Thanks. You hang in there. And think about Capitola, okay?"

"Will do."

Claire clicked her phone shut, set it on the table, and continued counting Geraldine's pills. Samantha's words played over in her mind. "What if he tries to kiss you?" The thought sent a shiver down her spine and a smile to her lips. Would she let him this time?

At 5:00 p.m., Nancy and Vivian appeared at the door with a red dress, a stack of DVDs, and a large pepperoni pizza.

"Here you go." Nancy handed her the dress. "It's an Ann Taylor. Simple, yet elegant."

"Thank you. I knew you were the right person to call." Claire held the dress under her chin. "How do you think it'll look?"

"Beautiful."

Claire grinned. "Thanks again. I'll go hang it in my closet."

After she hung up the dress, she remembered the two hundred dollars she received from Haley. Now was a good time to make her first payment to the two sisters. As she entered the kitchen, the smell of cheesy pizza wafted through the air. Her stomach growled. All of a sudden a relaxed girls' night in sounded more fun than a fancy night out.

"Movie night with Geraldine." Nancy laid the Meg Ryan flicks on the coffee table. "Too bad you can't join us." She winked at Claire.

"Of course, she'll be in the presence of a handsome man." Vivian pulled out paper plates and plastic forks. "I'd rather be in her shoes."

Shoes that were too high and uncomfortable? Claire walked over to the pizza and took a whiff. "Do you have to torture me? This smells good." She handed Vivian two twenty-dollar bills. "For the paint," she whispered.

Vivian tucked the money in her pocket.

"Help yourself to a slice. But I wouldn't if I were you. Bella Roma has the best Italian food in town." Nancy looked around. "Where's Geraldine?"

"In her room. She's folding laundry. I told her I'd do it, but she insisted on doing it herself." Claire shrugged.

Nancy approached the kitchen and grabbed plates from the cabinet. "That's how she stays young—by keeping active."

Claire slipped forty dollars into Nancy's hand. "For the valances," she spoke in a hushed tone.

"Claire." Nancy's eyebrows were arched, her voice soft. "We can work this out later."

The ends of Claire's lips turned up in a mischievous smile.

"I'd let Nancy fold my clothes anytime." Vivian let out an unladylike snort. "I'm willing to fold Nancy's laundry, even Tom's boxers, so I figure we're even."

Nancy placed both her hands on the back of Claire's shoulders and pushed her to the bathroom. "Take a bubble bath, pamper yourself. Don't worry. I'll check on Geraldine right now."

A night off sounded better with each passing minute. "Thank you for coming. And for letting me borrow the dress." Claire tucked a strand of hair behind her ear. "I think I'll take that bubble bath now."

"Oh, that reminds me. I brought you something." Nancy reached into her purse and pulled out two small bottles of bath oils. "One is rose and the other lavender. I couldn't decide which one you'd like better, so I brought both."

"Nancy, you didn't have to do that." Claire glanced down at the expensive-looking bottles. "But thank you. I think rose is the right scent for tonight." She glanced at the single flower on the dining room table, gave Nancy a quick hug, then went into the bathroom and closed the door.

Twenty minutes later, Claire wore her cozy blue bathrobe with a towel draped around her head. She felt like a new woman. Clean. Fresh. And ready to dress up.

Nancy, Vivian, and Geraldine sat close together on the couch drinking soda, eating pizza, and watching Tom Hanks and Meg Ryan in *You've Got Mail*.

"I love that movie." Claire clutched the top of her robe. "Are you sure you want me to leave, Geraldine?"

"If you want, I'll go out with Blake." Geraldine smirked. "But I don't think *I* am what he's got in mind. I wouldn't look right in that adorable red dress, and those red heels would kill my feet."

Geraldine was something else. She envied a woman who could act young even in her eighties. Claire laughed as she took the towel off her head. Her wet hair hung down in a tangled mess. "You three look quite comfortable sitting there."

"I want to see how the dress fits." Nancy took a bite of pizza.

"Shhhhh," Vivian scolded. "This is a good part."

"I'll be out as fast as I can." Claire slipped into her bedroom. She blew her hair dry in sections, straightening each piece. Would Blake like the new look? He had only seen her hair wavy. She applied a thin layer of foundation, a few strokes of blush, a coat of mascara, and a few swipes of lip gloss, then slipped the dress on over her head and stepped into her red high heels. The only thing she needed was a jacket. She thumbed through the few choices in her closet. A black cardigan wouldn't do the borrowed dress justice, but she grabbed it from the hanger and put it on.

The doorbell rang. Her stomach lurched. Blake was right on time. As usual.

25

Blake, come on in." Vivian grabbed him by the arm and pulled him into the house. "Don't you look handsome . . . and that cologne—" She leaned in, a smile tugging on her lips.

"Vivian," Nancy called from the couch. "Leave the man alone. You're embarrassing him."

Claire giggled from her bedroom doorway. Blake did look handsome in his polo shirt, pants, and sport coat. She could see him scan the room. He turned his head in her direction and caught her eye.

It was time she made her entrance. She glided into the room in her red high heels.

"Claire, don't you look like a princess." Geraldine fumbled with the remote and paused the movie as Tom Hanks and Meg Ryan moved in for the kiss. Was that planned?

"Your hair is beautiful. And the dress fits you like a glove." Nancy walked over to her and gently laid a hand on her shoulder. "Don't worry about a thing. Geraldine will be well looked after," she whispered.

A tingle rushed down her spine when she saw the grin on Blake's face as he watched her come toward him. Her mouth felt like a desert on a hot day. She attempted to swallow, but instead she croaked, "Blake, you're right on time."

"I wouldn't be late for this night." Blake lifted his elbow and flashed her a smile. "Ready to go?"

Ready? That was a loaded question. Ready to get out of the house from all the staring eyes? Yes. Ready to be alone with one of the most handsome men she had ever seen? Debatable. She didn't trust herself after their last encounter together.

"Claire?" The look on Blake's face shifted to concern.

Claire shook the bad feelings away and slipped her hand in the crook of his arm. "Ready."

"You have your key?" Geraldine motioned.

"Oh, Geraldine. Claire won't be late. She's going out to dinner." Nancy winked at Claire. "Besides, we'll wait for her to return before heading home."

"For goodness' sake, they're not children." Vivian reached behind Claire and Blake and guided them through the doorway. "Have a great time, you two. See you later." She shut the door behind them.

"Well, that was awkward." Claire stepped carefully down the front steps holding tight to Blake's arm. "Sorry about that."

"Nothing to worry about. Those women care about you." Blake placed his hand on top of hers.

"I'd say the same for you." Claire chuckled. "Did you see the way Vivian ogled?"

"I think it's time Vivian had her own date."

"Got anyone in mind?"

"No." Blake shook his head. "It would take a strong man to handle that woman. You look beautiful, by the way." Blake's steely blue eyes shone with admiration as he opened the passenger door to his truck.

"Thank you. You're not so bad yourself." Claire sat down, then swung her legs inside. Blake shut her door, dashed around the truck, and hopped in the other side.

"Oh no. My purse!" Claire blurted the minute Blake inserted the key into the ignition. "I'll be right back." She kicked off her heels, opened the car door, and ran back into the house barefoot.

"Back so soon?" Vivian stood in the kitchen dishing up three hefty bowls of ice cream.

"Remember, I don't want much," Geraldine called over her shoulder. "Claire, what are you doing? And where are your shoes?"

"In Blake's truck." She took off toward her room. "I forgot my purse."

"Don't leave that man for long," Vivian called from the kitchen. "The way he looks tonight, another woman may appear out of nowhere and join him . . . like me, for example."

Claire snatched her purse from her bed and headed toward the front door. She caught Vivian licking the ice cream spoon as she peered out the window. "Thanks for the tip. See you later."

She skipped down the steps and rejoined Blake in the truck. "A woman can't go anywhere without her purse."

"I don't get it." The truck's engine roared to life. "What do you carry in there that's so important?" Blake chuckled.

"Oh, I don't know." Claire clutched her purse to her chest. "Personal things like lipstick, a hairbrush, a wallet—"

"That's one thing you won't need tonight." Blake grinned at her with warm eyes. "I'm old-fashioned. When I take a woman out to dinner, I pay."

Claire could feel the heat rise in her cheeks. "I wasn't sure." She looked straight ahead through the window. "These days couples our age expect to go 'dutch.'" Did she call them a couple? She hoped Blake didn't notice.

"Couple, huh?" He turned left onto Monterey Avenue. "I like the sound of that."

He had noticed. Claire slipped her bare feet into her heels and kept her eyes away from him. "What I mean is—"

"No need to explain." Blake turned right on Capitola Avenue. "I hope you're hungry. Bella Roma has won awards for its cuisine."

Her stomach growled—loudly. Claire sunk deep in her seat. "I'd say I was hungry."

"Good." Blake pulled against the curb in front of the restaurant. "Wait right there. I'd like to open your door."

Claire's heart thumped in her chest. *Is this the kind of date you had in mind, Haley?* She doubted Mark ever opened Haley's door or treated her sister to a fancy dinner. The thought brought a mixture of satisfaction and sadness. She quickly composed herself.

Blake opened the door and held out his hand. "Watch the curb—"

Claire swung both legs out of the car, grabbed onto Blake's warm hand, and hoisted herself to standing. Stepping forward, she caught her heel on the edge of the curb . . . and fell into Blake's arms. "Sorry. I'm such a klutz."

"No need to apologize." Blake's eyebrow arched. "I kind of liked it."

Claire quickly righted herself and ran a hand down the skirt of her dress. She could hear her mother now, "*Chin up, back straight.*" She clutched her purse with one hand and stood erect.

Blake closed the truck's door and held tight to her arm. "You're cute when you're nervous."

"Who's nervous?" She giggled.

Blake led Claire up the steps and through the doorway.

She looked around the room. Italian paintings graced the peach faux-finished walls. Columns separated the dining room tables, each set with white tablecloths, cloth napkins, and goblets rimmed with gold.

"Welcome to Bella Roma. Do you have a reservation?" The host, wearing a white chef's smock with blousy sleeves, looked up from behind the reservation desk.

"Yes," Blake answered. "For 6:15. Blake Coombs."

"Ah, yes." The man ran a finger down the list of names. "There you are. Please follow me." The host led them to a table in the corner by the window. After Claire and Blake were seated, he handed them each a menu. "Your waiter will be by to take your order." He smiled, then walked away.

Claire was overwhelmed. She didn't know what to order. "What do you recommend?"

"You can't go wrong here." Blake studied the menu. "The lobster ravioli is amazing."

Claire fidgeted with the hem of the tablecloth away from Blake's view. She loved Italian food. The spaghetti joint down in Los Angeles was her favorite—a long shot from the classy atmosphere of Bella Roma. "Sounds good to me."

She'd have to come up with more stimulating conversation. A nagging feeling pulled at her middle. What kind of women did Blake usually go out with? She imagined the model type—thin, beautiful, someone with manicured nails and well traveled. Claire was far from that. Capitola was the only place she'd been outside of L.A.

"Blake, tell me about your family," Claire opened the conversation after the waiter took their order.

"My parents own a coffee shop in Boulder, Colorado—where I grew up. And my sister Candy is married with twin boys."

"Does she live in Colorado?"

"Yes. She wanted to stay close to my parents." Blake dug into his suit coat pocket, pulled out his wallet, and revealed a picture of two little boys with dark brown hair and blue eyes, like their uncle.

"They're adorable. Don't you miss them?" Claire took a closer look at the picture and then handed Blake his wallet.

"I do. But I see them every year at Christmas, sometimes more often when I get the urge to drive out there."

"What brought you to California?" Claire liked the way the conversation was going—easy, light, and comfortable.

Blake shifted in his seat. "My fiancé."

Claire's eyes widened. She felt as if she'd been socked in the gut. *Fiancé?* She didn't have a right to be so jealous. Blake wasn't her boyfriend. And yet . . .

The waiter appeared with two large plates of ravioli. "Enjoy. I'll be by to check on you shortly."

Claire stared at her plate. Each ravioli square was perfectly striped and covered with a white cream sauce. She picked up her fork and sliced one in half.

Blake reached for Claire's hand. "Shall we pray?"

Claire winced. Another reminder that they weren't meant for each other. Blake's relationship with God was so much closer than hers would ever be. She couldn't remember to thank Him for a meal—even a fancy one from a beautiful restaurant.

"Heavenly Father, thank you for this food. Thank you for Claire's company. Guide our conversation and help it to be glorifying to you. In your name, Amen."

Instead of a gentle squeeze, he held on.

"Claire. I wanted to explain—"

She pulled her hand free. "We should eat. Our food will get cold." She wasn't ready to hear about the other woman in his life. One that she was sure was better suited to him than she.

Picking up her fork, she stabbed a ravioli and shoved it in her mouth.

Blake leaned forward in his chair. "She broke it off three years ago. I haven't seen her since. I stayed in California because of my job . . . and the nice weather. Of course, I enjoy the beach, too." He fumbled over his words.

There was more to the story, Claire was sure of it. Did Blake's ex-fiancé know something about him she didn't? Her mother was blind to men, and so was Haley. Would she be that way too? They ate most of their meal in silence.

Claire decided to keep the conversation light—and safe, avoiding what was on her mind. "I've lived in California all my life. Colorado sounds adventurous with the mountains and all."

"It's a beautiful place." Blake nodded between bites. "Housing is less expensive, too."

"Then, why not move back?" *And save me from falling for you.*

"Because, I have a house and a great job." He shrugged his shoulders. "That reminds me, I need a woman's opinion. Can you help me pick out new cabinets and hardware?"

Claire's cheeks flushed. He was asking her opinion—as if they were an item . . . dating . . . or married. A feeling of panic engulfed her—like the other day with the attempted kiss. She took a forkful of ravioli—to distract herself from the rising fear—then nearly choked trying to swallow it. She reached for her glass and took a long sip, then looked directly into Blake's eyes. She had to know.

"Why did your fiancé break off your wedding?"

26

The question hung in the air like a lead-weighted balloon.

"How long did you date your fiancé before you proposed?" Claire blurted out. "And did you ask her to help you pick out furniture?" She straightened her spoon next to her plate, her voice escalating. "And why did you move to California? Doesn't the woman usually follow the man?"

Blake stared at her with his mouth hanging open. "Claire . . . Claire, slow down." He reached out his hand to touch hers.

She slithered hers back and dropped it into her lap. "Oh, no you don't. You're not going to charm me with your good looks and gentle touches. I don't want any part of dating someone who acts like he cares about me without getting to know the real me."

"What are you talking about?" Blake leaned back in his chair.

"You're right when you said I was nervous. I've never been to a restaurant like this, and probably never will again." She swiped at her mouth with her napkin. "I'm more of a pizza and burger type girl. I hardly wear makeup, and I've only straightened my hair once before—at my mother's funeral so no one would recognize me. I can count on one hand how many times I've been on a date in the last five years and you're the only one who's attempted to kiss me. Speaking of kisses . . . I don't take them lightly, so if you were planning on trying it again tonight, you might as well forget it unless you want—"

"Another shove?"

"I was going to say . . . oh, it doesn't matter. Blake, I'm not ready. I'm not ready to date, to kiss, or to pick out kitchen cabinets."

"Okay, Claire. You've made your point." He lifted his hand to get the waiter's attention. "I'm not asking you to marry me, only to help me pick out a cabinet or two. And the kiss—well, I'm not going to apologize for that."

Claire's hand shot up to her mouth.

"And to answer your question." Blake covered his plate with his napkin. "My fiancé left me for another man. Her childhood sweetheart."

Claire's heart twisted. *Oh.*

"I'm over it, but it took a long time."

Claire laid her hand on the table. She reached over and touched Blake's fingertips. He didn't budge. "I'm sorry. That must have hurt you deeply."

Their waiter returned with the bill and placed it on the table. "Whenever you're ready."

Blake reached into his suit coat pocket, pulled out his wallet, and produced a credit card. "We're ready now."

A lump formed in Claire's throat. She had misjudged him. He wasn't like her father. Or Mark. And now she had probably ruined her chances with him.

"I'll take you home." Blake stood after the transaction was complete, came to her side of the table, and helped her up.

"If you don't mind, I'd like to visit the ladies' room."

"I'll be right here." Blake touched her elbow, then recoiled.

With unsteady feet, she walked to the back of the restaurant. *This is not going well.*

Claire entered the ladies' room, locked the door behind her, and stared at herself in the mirror. How would she face Blake after going off like that? He was obviously taken aback and couldn't wait to drive her home. Was it better this way? She washed her hands, dabbed a paper towel into cold water, then patted the back of her neck. She couldn't go home yet. Nancy, Vivian, and Geraldine would ask questions. Better stall for time. She reached into her purse and applied a fresh coat of lipstick and popped a mint in her mouth.

She left the ladies' room holding her head high as she joined Blake. *Does he have to take my breath away?* A sigh escaped her lips.

They walked out into the cool night air, with stars above and the smell of the ocean coming at them full force. It was romantic, the perfect evening for—

"How about a walk?" Claire filled her musings with a question.

Blake glanced down at her feet. "Are you sure? In those heels?" He led her to his truck.

"We can park around the corner at the beach. I can walk barefoot." Claire's eyes pleaded. "It's too early to go home. Nancy rented three Meg Ryan movies."

Blake opened her door. "Okay, as long as we've got one thing straight."

Hope swelled within her. "What's that?" Claire situated herself in the seat.

"I'm going to treat you like a lady, no matter what." Blake leaned down. "And I won't kiss you again until you say so." He shut her door and walked around the back of the truck.

She wanted to kiss him—now. Claire's palms grew moist. Why were her emotions all over the place? Friendship. Isn't that what her mother recommended?

"The beach it is. I have a blanket in the back in case your legs get cold." He turned the truck around. "We don't have to walk if we find a good spot to park. The view is beautiful on a clear night."

Blake pulled into a parking space overlooking Capitola Beach. He was right. The view was breathtaking. The moon cast a romantic glow on the ocean, the waves lapping on the shore. Claire could see the lights from Santa Cruz on her right and the smoke stacks of Moss Landing on her left. She must be crazy. How could she think of bolting when she not only had one of the kindest and most patient men sitting next to her, but also gorgeous views on both sides? But she did think about bolting—because she was afraid.

She crossed her arms over her chest and shivered. All the men in her life had treated her mother or sister with disrespect, and her experience was limited, to say the least. Her mom's boyfriends had never hurt her physically, but once they realized she and her sister were part of the package, they'd take off. Then there was Mark. He milked her out of her tip money and made sure she knew he was doing her a favor by letting her live with him and Haley.

Blake cracked the window open. A slight breeze wafted through. Claire remained perfectly still and quiet, for fear of ruining the moment. He reached over and grabbed the blanket from the backseat. "You look cold." He gently laid it across her lap. "I don't know what you've been through. I hope someday you'll tell me. But for now, you can lean on my shoulder and listen to the waves."

A comfortable silence filled the truck. What was he—a mind reader? How did he know her thoughts had drifted to the past? As she scooted over and rested her head on his shoulder, a knock startled her.

"Blake, is that you?" Two brunettes stood on the other side of the door. "Where've you been? We haven't seen much of you lately."

Blake glanced at Claire and shrugged. Was that irritation in his eyes? He lowered his window. "Claire, this is Amber and Kristy. Amber is a police officer in my division, and Kristy is her friend." His voice definitely held a hint of frustration.

Claire felt like melting into the seat. Was this her competition? She forced a smile. "Hello."

Kristy pouted. "What do you mean I'm Amber's friend? *We* used to be friends, remember?"

"Ladies, I'd like you to meet Claire James." Blake grabbed her hand and held it possessively against his chest.

"Say, why don't you two join us?" Amber leaned against the truck and winked. "We're meeting several off-duty officers at Mr. Toots. We'd have a great time."

Claire nudged Blake's shoulder. "I'm not feeling so well. Why don't you bring me home and then join your friends?"

"That's an excellent idea." Kristy rested her arms on the window frame. "We can hang out another time, Connie." Her earrings dangled near her shoulders.

"Claire. Her name is Claire," Blake shot back. "Ladies, tonight's not a good one." He started the engine. "See you at work, Amber."

"I'm looking forward to it." Amber smiled, revealing straight white teeth.

Blake shifted the truck in reverse and backed out. He rolled up his window and took off down the street and out of sight of the two voluptuous women.

Perfect. They were perfect for him with their manicured nails and dyed hair. Claire tucked her hands under the blanket. "Amber seems nice—"

"I don't mix business with pleasure," Blake cut in. "Plus, she's not my type." He glanced in Claire's direction. "I'm sorry you're not well. I was looking forward to our walk." He pulled up to her house. All the lights were on. She didn't feel like talking with anyone—especially the three women inside. They'd want to hear every detail of her date.

"Mind if we hang out a while at your place?" The moment the question slipped off her tongue she wanted to take it back. "No, what I mean—"

"Yes, I mind." He answered a little too quickly.

Her cheeks heated. What must Blake think of her?

He placed his arm across the back of the seat. "Honestly, I don't think we should be alone." Blake's eyes lowered to her mouth. "I might do something I'll regret. We better say good night."

27

Sunday afternoon Michael sat on a rock, allowing the sun to warm his body. He had to admit New Brighton State Park's setting was tranquil with its beautiful Monterey cypress, oak, eucalyptus trees, and wild berry vines. People came from all over the world to visit the ninety-three-acre park and take in the spectacular view of the Monterey Bay. But Michael was anything but peaceful. He didn't want to be there waiting for Martin and Debbie to show up. He'd rather be on his couch watching football.

Michael glanced at his mother and Claire, who stood near the fence overlooking the towering bluffs high above the Pacific Ocean. Sandy was busy setting the picnic table. She hummed as she worked, probably enjoying the thought of getting old friends together.

The crunch of tires caught his attention. A blue Toyota Sienna pulled up next to his BMW. Debbie was behind the wheel while Martin sat next to her in the passenger's seat. The time had come. Michael cracked his knuckles and pushed himself to standing.

"They're here." Sandy dropped silverware on the table and rushed to the van.

Debbie stepped out and greeted Sandy with a hug.

"You made it. What can I help you with?" Sandy's voice sounded eager.

"Can you grab the food from the back while I get Martin settled?"

"Sure."

Michael walked up to the front of the van. "Anything I can do?" He forced a smile.

Debbie walked around and pressed a remote. The sliding door opened and a ramp appeared. "I can get Martin out if you'd like to help Sandy with the food."

"Hey, Martin." Michael nodded. He didn't want to make the situation any more awkward than it was.

Martin passed him a look. Michael remembered that look from when they were teenagers. Martin had used it to challenge him in a game of basketball, dare him to ask out a girl, or as he did today—make him face his mistakes. With one glance, Martin said all he needed to say.

The look reminded Michael of the message Martin left on his cell phone earlier that morning. "Today's the day to make things right—that's if you have the courage." Martin's slow speech came through loud and clear.

It's complicated. Didn't his high school friend understand that?

Michael stared at the floorboard where Martin's wheelchair was held in place. "When did you buy the van?"

"Just last week. It's going to make a world of difference. I'll be able to take Martin out more. Won't I, honey?" She rubbed his arm.

Michael respected Debbie. She was a bright spot in Martin's otherwise seemingly dark world.

Sandy approached, carrying an aluminum-foiled covered bowl and a plastic-wrapped plate of fruit. "Michael, can you grab the cooler?"

"Certainly." He walked to the back of the van and drew in a deep breath. Every time he saw Martin in that wheelchair, he felt sad and helpless. Why did God allow this to happen? He wiped his brow and watched as Debbie maneuvered the wheelchair. God had a plan and was in control, right? His shoulders sagged. People make their own choices. And the drunk who hit Martin's car had a choice whether or not to get behind the wheel. Martin was in the wrong place at the wrong time. Michael's stomach churned. If he hadn't asked Martin to meet him that night, his friend wouldn't be in a wheelchair today. Michael hoisted the cooler out of the back of the van and slammed the rear hatch.

Claire and his mother helped Sandy arrange the food. Mounds of fried chicken sat heaped on a plate. Sandy placed a vegetable tray in the middle of the table next to the potato salad and fruit. Michael set the cooler off to the side and opened the lid to find cans of soda and bottled water mixed in with the ice. "Who wants one?" he offered.

Claire's hand shot up. "Is there diet?"

Michael pulled out a Diet Coke.

"You young things worry too much about your weight." His mother leaned over to take a peek. "Diet soda has just as much sugar. Give me a dew, son."

"Mountain Dew?" Michael chuckled, then handed his mother the soda.

Sandy placed the napkins on the table. "Bottled water, please."

"Me too." Debbie chimed in.

Michael pulled out two water bottles. "Martin?"

Martin was situated at the head of the table. "You don't remember?" he asked with slurred speech.

Had it been so long since they've shared a meal that Michael couldn't remember what they used to drink? He dug his hand in the cooler and pulled out a Dr Pepper. "How about one of these?"

Martin nodded.

Michael passed the soda to Debbie and grabbed a Dr Pepper for himself. It was a lucky guess. He couldn't recall the last time he had had the soft drink. Then, like a punch in the gut, he remembered. It was that night. The night Martin's car got hit after Michael spilled out his past. He dropped the lid shut and took a deep breath to steady himself. He would make it through lunch—and keep his emotions in check. Michael sat down next to his wife at the picnic table, reached over, and grabbed a drumstick.

Claire couldn't believe her good fortune when Nancy had called and invited her and Geraldine for a picnic lunch. She never imagined she'd meet Martin DeWitt—the man from her mother's journal. And the letter.

Since Debbie and Martin arrived, Claire couldn't stop staring in Martin's direction as he sat in his wheelchair by the picnic table. Probably he had been a good-looking man when he was in his early twenties. He had a nice head of dark brown hair, and mysterious hazel eyes. She tried to picture her mother falling for him when they were young. What did the letter say? They rode the roller coasters at the Boardwalk, hung out at the beach, and held hands as they strolled under the stars. Claire tried to imagine Martin as a romantic all those years ago.

Claire mulled over the conversation she'd had with Geraldine as they took in the view a short time ago.

"A drunk driver plowed into Martin's car." Geraldine's voice shook. "Left him paralyzed from the waist down and slow from the brain injury."

Claire's eyes misted.

"Debbie and Sandy have been best friends ever since. They're kindred spirits."

They had appeared that way when Sandy introduced her to Debbie when the couple first arrived. "Claire, I'd like you to meet Debbie DeWitt." Sandy had gestured to the woman standing next to her.

So, this was Martin's wife. "Hi, nice to meet you." Claire shook Debbie's hand.

"Nice to meet you too." Debbie smiled and placed an arm around Geraldine's shoulder. "And it's good to see you too, Geraldine."

"The good Lord has yet to call me to my heavenly home." Geraldine grinned.

Claire had studied Debbie as the women chatted. She was a beautiful woman—with her straight teeth, blonde hair, and a dainty nose. She must be approaching fifty, but Claire didn't think she looked a day over thirty-five. Debbie was one of those women who aged gracefully and naturally.

At this point, Claire was more interested to get to know Martin and whether he was the writer of the letter. Now with lunch finished, Claire had to find a way to talk with him alone. She tossed the paper plates in the trashcan. How could she orchestrate a few minutes of his time? It didn't look like it was going to happen. She glanced at Sandy and Debbie chatting and laughing together as they folded the tablecloth. And Geraldine, bless her heart, had closed her eyes as she sat on the rock enjoying the sunshine. Michael was packing the picnic basket in his BMW.

"Photo time!" Sandy cheered. She grabbed her digital camera from the car. "Debbie, stand close to Martin so I can get a picture of you two first."

Michael moaned. "You have boxes of pictures to put into albums as it is, plus the ones in our computer."

"Come on, it'll be fun." She snapped a photo of the DeWitts.

"Okay, let's get it over with." Michael placed a hand on Martin's shoulder. "Cheese."

Claire's mind whirled. Michael was obviously ready to leave. How could she stall? An idea hit her. "There's a perfect place for a picture down the trail."

Sandy smiled. "The one down to the beach?"

"Martin and my mother can't go down there." Michael shook his head.

Claire saw her chance. "I'll stay here with them. Go on ahead."

Michael's brows furrowed.

"Thanks, Claire. That's sweet of you." Debbie placed her hand on the back of her husband's neck. "Okay, Martin? We'll only be a minute."

Sandy grinned at Michael. "And when we get back, Claire or Debbie can take a picture of you and me with your mom." She hooked her small camera around her wrist.

Claire hoped it'd be more than a minute. She wanted to find out all she could about her mother and Martin's relationship. She sat down at the picnic table and watched Debbie, Sandy, and Michael disappear down the trail.

"Martin, do you remember my mother, Emily James?" The question popped out like a kernel of corn in a popcorn machine the minute the three were out of view.

Martin's eyebrows shot up. "Emily was your mother? Yes, I couldn't forget her. She was my teenage crush." His halting speech was painful to listen to. Claire's heart went out to him.

Now she was getting somewhere. She moved closer and focused on Martin's caring eyes.

Martin continued. "We spent time together one summer." A grin tugged at his mouth. "She came to visit from . . ."

"San Diego." Claire finished his sentence. She didn't want to be rude, but she didn't have much time. "Martin, do you remember writing my mother a letter?" Claire leaned forward, her elbows resting on the table.

"A letter?" Martin's eyebrows furrowed. "No, I don't."

Claire reached into her jacket pocket and pulled out the tattered envelope. "This one. Someone with the initial 'M' wrote this to Mom back in 1972." She handed the letter to Martin.

Her heart pounded as she waited. She glanced over her shoulder. Geraldine stood and headed in their direction. *Hurry, Martin.* What did she see in his eyes? Confusion? Embarrassment? Guilt? He flipped the envelope over.

"July 1972." He shook his head.

"Claire, dear, is there any fruit left?" Geraldine called as she ambled toward the table. "It keeps me regular."

"In the cooler." Claire pointed. Her voice held a hint of annoyance. She shouldn't treat Geraldine that way, but at the moment she needed to find out all she could from Martin.

"I didn't write this." Martin's eyes reached hers.

His words registered in her brain. "If you didn't, then who?"

"Claire, can you help me, dear?" Geraldine held on to her walker with one hand as she reached down with the other. "I can't seem to grab the grapes."

Debbie, Sandy, and Michael approached. Claire closed her eyes and exhaled. She felt the heat rise in her cheeks. *Lord, help me.* She jumped up from the picnic table, leaned down, and picked a bunch of grapes for Geraldine.

"What do you have there, honey?" Debbie came up beside her husband. "May I?"

Martin gave Debbie the letter. She read it aloud.

"That is so romantic." Sandy's hand touched the side of her face. "And sweet."

"I agree. But—" Debbie bit her lip.

"I didn't write it." Martin glared at Michael. "But I can guess who did."

Michael shook his head.

Sandy looked from Michael to Martin and back again. "Can I see the letter?"

Debbie handed the piece of paper to Sandy. "Michael. This is *your* handwriting."

The weight of the truth pushed on Claire's shoulders. She was right. Michael had been hiding something all along. It was time he faced the truth.

Michael looked over his wife's shoulder. His laugh sounded forced. "Martin and I hung out with Emily one summer. You know, teenagers. I probably got those sappy words out of a book. I didn't mean anything by it."

Sandy handed the letter back to Claire. "I received quite a few love letters myself when I was a teenager. Of course, I didn't keep them." She snuggled into Michael's side. "They didn't mean anything to me once I met the love of my life."

"I thought it was from Martin." Claire tucked the letter back in her purse. "My mother wrote about him in her journal."

Sandy turned to Michael. "Michael, I thought we went to Emily's funeral because we were down south visiting your mother." Sandy folded her arms across her chest. "How come you never told me you knew her when you were a teenager?"

"Look, baby, I didn't think it was important." Michael wrapped his arm around his wife. "Can we talk about this later?" He gave her a peck on the cheek.

The air felt thick.

Claire saw Debbie touch Martin's hand and pass him a tender look.

Sandy turned toward Geraldine. "Mom, did you know Michael and Emily had a relationship?" She frowned.

"Vaguely." Geraldine picked a purple grape and popped it into her mouth.

Claire could see the hurt in Sandy's eyes. She never intended for Sandy to see the letter, let alone upset her. Claire felt like crawling down the nearest gopher hole.

Twenty minutes later, after saying good-bye to the DeWitts, Claire sat in the backseat of Michael's car next to Geraldine. The silence in the front seat was unnerving. Michael gripped the steering wheel with white knuckles, while Sandy leaned against the passenger-side door. Neither of them said a word. Geraldine, on the other hand, talked nonstop.

"Your fried chicken was amazing, Sandy. You'll have to share your recipe with Blake." Her hands flew here and there like a chicken trying to escape beheading. "And those snickerdoodles . . . my, my, my, were they delicious."

Claire looked out the window as Geraldine rambled on. The older woman knew a thing or two about Michael and her mother's relationship, she was sure of that. What was her part in all of this? Claire folded her arms tight across her chest. If she hadn't shown Martin the letter, Sandy and Michael might be talking and laughing about how Michael ate *four* drumsticks or how Sandy forgot the salt and pepper. Instead, they were at odds with each other.

Suddenly Claire had the urge to call Blake. He had become such a confidant the past month. He would know what to make of the situation. Either that, or he'd tell her to move on with her life. But she couldn't do that now. She would get to the bottom of this even if it caused Sandy or Geraldine discomfort. Tonight she'd talk to Geraldine about the letter, and then she'd show her the picture frame—the one that looked strangely similar to the one Geraldine had in her own bedroom. Maybe it wasn't so strange after all.

28

Claire paced the floor in the family room while Geraldine napped. Once they had arrived home, the older woman had gone straight to her room complaining of heaviness in her chest. Claire wondered if it had anything to do with the letter and her part in keeping it a secret.

Claire plopped down on the couch and flipped through Geraldine's *Senior Living* magazine. How long would Geraldine sleep? She scanned an article on the importance of exercise as people age, then tossed the magazine on the coffee table.

Outside, a car door slammed. She stood, walked to the kitchen, and looked out the window. Who was that? It couldn't be! "Haley?"

Her sister's beat-up Chevy hugged the curb.

Claire raced through the doorway and down the sidewalk. "Haley." She squeezed her sister tight the second she stepped out of the car. "What are you doing here?"

"It's good to see you too." Haley teased. "I thought I'd check on you. You know, make sure you had a roof over your head and food in your belly."

"Don't I look like it?" Claire twirled around. "Hey, wait a minute." She stepped closer. "It's Mark, isn't it?" She looked into her sister's eyes.

"We're fine." Haley brushed her blonde hair back. "I needed a break, is all."

"A break from what?" Claire pulled the heavy suitcase out of the trunk. "From Mark's drinking?"

"He was doing so well." Haley swiped the stray tears from her cheek, opened the passenger door, and grabbed her pillow, a blanket, and her purse. "But last night he relapsed. A high school buddy came into town—Brett Wilder."

"Wilder?" Claire's mouth dropped. She remembered Brett from high school. He had been known as a partier. She rolled her eyes. "You let Mark go out with Wild Man Wilder?"

"Mark is a grown man, Claire. I'm not his mother. He can make his own decisions."

Claire set the suitcase down. "So, why are you here?"

"They went to a bar." Haley's mouth formed a straight line. "He broke his promise."

Claire touched Haley's shoulder. "That low-down, horrible—"

"Wait a minute." Haley held up her hand. "He's still my husband."

Claire took a deep breath, shut her eyes, and counted to three. "Okay, I'll keep my opinions to myself . . . for now." She picked up the suitcase. "I'm glad you came."

"I'm also here to make sure you're moving on with your life. No more talk of mystery letters, journals, or Mom's past. Plus, I want to see this hunky neighbor of yours."

Haley's timing couldn't have been worse. Just when she was getting to the bottom of her mom's relationship with Michael, her sister showed up. "Blake's at work. He's a police officer. You'll have to wait till tomorrow." Claire shrugged. "Oh, and

Geraldine is asleep, so we'll need to be quiet." She pushed the door open with her foot. "You'll be sharing my room, okay? The house is small."

Haley nodded. "Small and adorable." She looked around. "Where did you get all this nice furniture?" She ran a hand over the back of the Victorian-style couch.

"It's Geraldine's. I'm fortunate she furnished the place." Claire set the suitcase down against the family room wall. "My room's the first door on the right." She walked toward the kitchen. "Anything to drink? Coffee? Soda? Water?" She opened the refrigerator.

"Water's fine. I've cut back on caffeine." Haley patted her belly.

"The baby, of course." Claire pulled out two water bottles. She joined Haley in the family room. "How are you feeling?"

"Nauseated most of the time, but I always carry crackers with me." She unzipped her purse and took out a small plastic bag filled with Saltines.

"Claire, you have company." Geraldine appeared, pushing her walker, her hair slightly askew. "Is that Holly?"

"Haley." The sisters spoke at once, then laughed.

"Haley, of course." Geraldine's cheeks flushed pink. "How are you, dear? I didn't know you were coming for a visit."

"Claire didn't know. I surprised her." Haley sat down. She crossed her long legs, a pair of black stilettos peeking from below her designer jeans.

"You didn't have to dress up for me." Claire pointed to Haley's shoes. "How did you drive in those? I can barely walk in the red ones you sent."

"Practice." Haley's mouth twisted into a teasing smile.

"You should have seen Claire the other night, she was breathtaking." Geraldine sat down in the recliner chair next to the fireplace. "I offered to go out with Blake—he's quite smitten with me, you know, but I wanted to give Claire a chance." Geraldine tossed a small blanket over her feet. "Claire, mind getting me water? In a glass, with ice, dear. All those plastic bottles will end up in a landfill." She leaned in Haley's direction. "I like to be environmentally friendly."

Claire walked back to the kitchen. The sight of Geraldine made her heart race. She was a sweet woman, funny even, but her part in keeping the truth from Claire stung. Why would Geraldine hide something as important to her as Michael's relationship with her mother? She exhaled and grabbed a glass from the cabinet. They had been close—like grandmother and granddaughter—and now this rift between them. Claire pressed the button on the freezer door and a few cubes of ice dropped into the glass.

She paused. So, Geraldine left out a few details. Did that make her an ogre? Claire picked up the water pitcher and filled the glass. No. Not an ogre, but definitely a mother covering up for her son. Claire tossed a look over her shoulder.

"Claire, dear. My mouth is parched." Geraldine clicked her tongue.

"Here you go." Claire hurried to the family room, handed her the glass, and sat down on the sofa.

"Oh, thank you, dear." Geraldine took a sip of water.

"Where's Haley?"

"She needed to use the bathroom." Geraldine cupped her hand over her mouth, "She's in the family way."

Claire leaned back against the couch. "And I'm going to be an aunt." What was taking Haley so long? Maybe now was her chance. "Geraldine, can we please talk about Michael and my mother—"

"What's there to talk about, dear? They knew each other when they were teenagers, went out a few times, and wrote letters." Geraldine's hand trembled. She set the glass on the end table.

"But there has to be more . . ."

Claire could hear the water running in the bathroom. Haley would return any second. She glanced down the hall, then back at Geraldine.

"You never forget your first love." Geraldine's voice was low. She kicked the blanket off her feet. "Is it hot in here? I'm sweating."

"You have the cutest bathroom." Haley came toward them, walking like a model. "Seashells and starfish, how adorable." She glanced at Claire, then Geraldine. "Did I miss something? You two look like you've seen a ghost."

Claire popped up off the couch. "Why don't we get you settled?" She linked arms with her sister. "I bet you're exhausted from your drive." She pulled Haley toward her bedroom. Claire wanted to tuck her sister in her room and get back to her conversation with Geraldine.

"I *could* kick my heels off and rest a while." Haley pointed. "I left my suitcase in the other room."

"Don't you worry about a thing," Claire smiled. "I'll take care of it." She guided Haley to her bedroom.

"Wow, Claire. Where'd you get the furniture?" Haley sprawled across her bed. "Comfortable too."

"Long story." Claire walked backward toward the door. "After you rest a while, I'll tell you all about it."

"You're right." Haley yawned. "Maybe I do need to rest."

"Take as long as you need." Claire blew a kiss and closed the door. She turned and walked back into the family room. Geraldine looked pale, her eyes were closed, and her lips were a light shade of purple. "Geraldine?" Claire ran to her side. She touched the woman's arm.

No response.

"Haley, come quick! Something's happened to Geraldine." Claire checked her neck for a pulse. It was faint, but it was there. Thank God she was still alive.

"What's the matter?" Haley came running.

"Call 9-1-1. I think Geraldine has had a heart attack."

Michael plopped down on the couch and grabbed the remote. He had missed most of the football game because of the picnic. The scoreboard read ten minutes to go. Enough time to catch the last quarter.

Sandy walked into the family room wearing her exercise clothes, her iPod nano clipped to her red form-fitting top. She placed the earpieces in her ears. "I'm going for a run." Her tone was chilly. Michael nodded without saying a word.

Now with the game over, he flipped through the channels. His mind raced to the past. So he wrote Emily a few letters. So what? He was a kid at the time. Michael ran a hand through his wavy hair. He knew that was the least of his worries. His thoughts drifted back to that day so long ago.

"Michael? Is that you?" Emily's sweet voice had risen an octave, and a smile spread across her face.

Michael glanced over his shoulder down the hall at his mother's apartment, then back at Emily. "Mind if I come in?" He heard a toddler in the background.

"Sure, of course. Give me a minute, okay?" Emily shut the door.

Five minutes later, she welcomed him in. She had let her hair down, and her lips were colored a lovely shade of pink.

"Who is this?" Michael leaned down and ruffled the little girl's hair.

"Haley. She's almost two."

"And your husband?" Michael stood close enough to Emily to take in her perfume.

"Separated." Emily leaned down and picked Haley up.

"Want to go out for dinner?" Michael smiled. "Like old times. I'm sure my mother would be more than happy to watch your little girl."

Michael shook off the memory. How could he look his wife in the eye and tell her that his relationship with Emily had gone beyond his teenage years. A knot formed in the pit of his stomach.

He turned the television off and threw the remote across the room. *Lord, how will she ever forgive me?* He paced the floor. He had to get out of there before Sandy came home. Where would he go? He eyed his car keys sitting on the kitchen counter. Crossing the room in a few steps, he reached for them as the front door opened.

Sandy's breath came fast and hard. Her hands cradled her hips. "A good hard run was what I needed." She walked into the kitchen, grabbed a glass from the cabinet, and filled it with filtered water. "I thought about the letter while on my run."

"Oh, yeah—" Michael slipped his keys in his pocket.

"I'm sorry I overreacted." She took several big gulps of water. "We all have people from our past. Right?" She raised her eyes.

Michael nodded. "So, you're not mad?"

She cocked her head and pursed her lips together. "Mad, no. A little jealous, definitely."

Michael came up beside her and eyed her up and down. "I like the way you look in those tights." He touched her thigh, then walked his fingers up her arm.

She responded to his touch with a grin. "You, my dear, are quite the charmer."

A feeling of dread wormed its way into his heart. Is that what happened between him and Emily? Did he charm his way into her arms? Michael coughed. He brought his hand to his mouth. "Emily, you are quite charming yourself." He leaned against the counter.

"Emily?" Sandy glared at him. She tossed the remaining water at his chest and set the glass on the counter.

"Sandy . . . Sandy." *How could I—?* Michael grabbed both of her shoulders. "You know I didn't mean it. Of course, I meant to say your name."

"Well, you better get it straight. We have a daughter getting married soon, and—"

"Everything's fine and it's going to stay fine, I promise."

"No." Sandy took a step back. "It's not. It hasn't been for a long time—especially the last six weeks. I don't know what's gotten into you, but I have a feeling it has something to do with Emily."

"What do you mean?" Michael gripped the edge of the counter.

"Ever since Claire and your mother came into town, you haven't been yourself."

"That's ridiculous." Michael raised his voice. "You're imagining things." He turned and looked at the floor. "I'm stressed about work."

"No, Michael. You can't use work as an excuse. I'm right and you know it."

"Sandy, come on." He couldn't look her in the eye. She'd see right through him.

"So, what went on between you and Emily? Huh, Michael?" She folded her arms across her chest.

"Emily is gone." Michael slammed his fist on the counter.

Sandy let out a long breath, then walked away and stomped up the stairs.

Michael took off his soaked shirt, grabbed a clean one from the laundry room, and put it on. How could he have called his wife of twenty-seven years the name of an old girlfriend? He massaged his temples. Should he come right out and tell Sandy everything? No. He'd wait until after Julia's wedding. He pulled his keys from his pocket and headed out the front door.

The fresh air filled his lungs. He exhaled slowly and slid into his car. He started the engine, glanced over his shoulder before backing out, then slammed on his brakes. Sandy rushed toward him wrapped in a towel with streaks of mascara running down her face.

"Michael, STOP!" She whipped around to the driver's side door. "It's your mother. She's in the hospital."

29

Claire sat in a hard-backed chair leaning her head against the wall in the waiting room of Dominican Hospital.

"Coffee?" Haley grabbed her purse and stood. "The doctor told us it could take a couple of hours."

"A mocha, please." Claire reached for her purse. She needed coffee *and* chocolate at a time like this.

"My treat." Haley winked, then turned and walked down the corridor.

Claire glanced at Michael and Sandy sitting across from her. Michael leaned forward with his head resting in his hands. Was he praying? Now would be a good time. Claire had talked to God on and off since she found Geraldine slumped over in her recliner. Sandy sat pin-straight, her hair pushed back behind her ears, and her face void of makeup. Her eyes held a faraway look.

The last hour had been crazy. Claire was relieved Michael had been there to sign consent forms and give his mother's medical history.

"Claire." Nancy came toward her in her nurse's uniform and sat down in the empty seat beside her. "I just heard."

"I was so scared." Claire laid her head on Nancy's shoulder. "Geraldine was so pale. And her lips were blue."

"You did the right thing." Nancy stroked Claire's hair. "An angioplasty can only be done within the first 90 minutes after a heart attack—you saved her life."

Claire sat up straight. "If she dies . . ."

"Now, now." Nancy wrapped her arms around Claire. "We're not going to go there. God knows the number of our days. You can rest in Him."

Claire rubbed her nose and leaned back. "I hope Geraldine has many more days ahead. I love her so much."

"I know you do. She's like a grandmother the way she dotes and talks about you. The other night," Nancy chuckled, "when you were on your date with Blake, she talked about how much you remind her of Michael—the way you tug at your ear when you're nervous, or the determined look in your eye when you want something bad enough. She's impressed with you."

Like Michael? The thought sent a ripple of fear through her. "I'm afraid I put stress on her today." Claire's eyebrows furrowed.

"How so?"

"I pushed her about the letter." Claire opened her purse. "Remember this?" She pulled out the envelope only enough for Nancy to see.

"Yes. The letter to your mother." Nancy nodded, then shook her head. "I don't get it. Why would Geraldine know anything about it?"

Claire leaned in and whispered in Nancy's ear. "Because Michael wrote it."

Nancy's eyes widened. She glanced at Michael, then back at Claire. "When did you find that out?"

"Just today." Claire tucked the letter inside and zipped her purse. "And I pressured Geraldine to tell me about their relationship this afternoon, right before her heart attack."

"Oh, sweetie." Nancy hugged her. "Geraldine is on heart medication. She's had a heart condition for a while. It could've happened anytime."

Haley approached. "Your mocha, sis."

"Thank you."

Nancy grinned. "Is this—"

"My sister Haley." Claire took the steaming drink. "Haley, I'd like you to meet Nancy. You remember the story of my first night in Capitola. Nancy is the tow-truck driver's wife."

Acknowledgment flashed across Haley's face. "That's amazing how you took my sister into your home."

"Well, to tell you the truth, Tom has never invited someone to come home before, so it startled me. I didn't know what to think. But then I saw the scared look in Claire's eyes and knew she wasn't a serial killer." Nancy smiled.

"I had no other options at that point." Claire took a sip of her mocha.

"You could have called *me*!" Haley held up a hand.

The thought turned her stomach. "No way. I don't ever want to live under the same roof as *you-know-who*."

"You told me you wouldn't talk about Mark that way." Haley glared at Claire. She crossed one leg over the other and bobbed her foot up and down.

"Don't get me started, Haley." Claire accidentally tipped her cup and spilled a few drops of coffee on her jeans.

Haley handed her a napkin. "I'm carrying Mark's child. Nothing will change that."

The truth consumed Claire like a tidal wave. It didn't matter if Haley was able to get away from her husband. The baby had Mark's blood flowing through his or her veins.

Claire's eyes softened. "Truce." She held up two fingers, making a peace sign.

"You two need a walk?" Nancy stood and pulled both women up by the hand.

Michael looked over.

"We'll be back in a little while," Claire offered.

"Come with me to the nursery." Nancy linked arms with both women. "I want to tell you about my relationship with *my* sister—"

"Nancy's sister Vivian worked with me at the diner in L.A.," Claire interjected.

"We didn't speak to each other for years—too many years—years that were wasted on anger and bitterness." Nancy led them down the hall.

"What happened?" Haley's heels clicked on the linoleum floor.

"I had a little girl," Nancy choked out. "Her name was Erica." The three now stood in front of the nursery window. Two baby boys wrapped in blue blankets and three baby girls in pink filled the room.

"Had?" Claire blinked back the tears that threatened to spill down her cheeks.

"Yes." Nancy gripped the window ledge. "She was two years old when the Lord called her home."

Claire's heart sank. Nancy would've made a wonderful mother. "I'm so sorry." Claire placed her hand on her friend's arm.

"Thank you." Nancy dabbed at the corners of her eyes. "For a long time I blamed Vivian. She was babysitting Erica while I was at work. Vivian fed her grapes, and Erica choked. By the time the ambulance arrived, it was too late."

"That's horrible." Haley's eyes narrowed. "How could Vivian do such a thing?"

"For a long time, I thought the same thing. I blamed Vivian for Erica's death and I also blamed God. Vivian and I didn't speak to each other for many years. I realized that *I* was Erica's mother and ultimately responsible. I should have told Vivian to cut up the grapes." Nancy sighed. "I was at work when it happened. What kind of mother was I?"

"I'm sure an amazing one." Claire pulled Nancy close. "Like a mother I'd like to have."

"The day you arrived was Erica's birthday." Nancy looked deep into Claire's eyes. "I was sad, grieving over what could have been. Then, you showed up. A woman close to my daughter's age in need of care."

The Lord provides. Pearl's words filled Claire's mind. "I'm so grateful you took me in. Who knows where I'd be—"

"Maybe back home in L.A." Haley tapped her manicured nails against the wall.

Didn't Haley understand how much God was doing in her life here in Capitola? No, probably not. Claire herself didn't realize it until this moment. How could her sister understand? She had wasted the past seven years with an alcoholic husband who didn't have the decency to quit drinking when he had a baby on the way. *What kind of father is that?* The thought tightened Claire's gut. How did *she* know what a good father was like? She hadn't had a father figure in her life since she was a baby—and according to her mother, he'd only come around when he needed money or a place to sleep for a few nights. But she could try to imagine a loving Heavenly Father—the one from the verse Geraldine showed her the other day. 1 John 3:1. "How great is the love the Father has lavished on us, that we should be called children of God."

Haley stepped closer. "I'm sorry for your loss, Nancy."

Nancy peeked into the nursery once more. "Vivian and I—well, we made up a short while ago. It took all these years for us to see the importance of forgiveness. We are going to be sisters for the rest of our lives. Nothing is going to change that. And the wall that separated us would only have gone higher unless *we* took it down."

Claire felt a rush of emotions spiral through her body like a tornado. Would it take years to make things right with Haley if they allowed their differences to come between them? Claire bit her lip and kicked the toe of her shoe on the linoleum floor. It was something to think about. "Thanks for sharing your story, Nancy."

"Oh, look at the time," Nancy glanced at her watch. "I better get back to work." She hugged Claire tight, then extended her hand to Haley. "I hope you can stay a while. I'd like to get to know you."

"We'd better get back." Claire tugged on Haley's arm. "Geraldine may be out of surgery."

"Only two at a time, please," the nurse from the cardiac ward instructed.

Michael took his wife's hand and headed toward the door, leaving Claire and Haley in the hallway. With tentative steps, Michael approached the side of the bed. His mother looked old and frail. Her eyes were closed, and her short white hair fanned away from her face. He squeezed Sandy's hand before letting go.

"Mom?" Michael leaned in and gently kissed her cheek.

Her eyes fluttered open.

"Hi, Mom. You gave us quite a scare." A lump formed in Michael's throat. "How do you feel?"

"Like I awoke from the dead." His mother's voice sounded raspy.

Michael pulled up a chair and sat down. "Well, I'm glad you're all right."

"I thought I was going to see your father. I've been waiting to see him for over twenty-four years." She turned her head and looked directly at Michael. "I almost made it to heaven."

"We're not ready to let you go just yet." Sandy picked up his mother's hand.

Michael cocked his head to look at his mom square in the face. "Dad's going to have to wait a while longer."

"You look so much like your father." His mother's eyes misted. "Your wavy blond hair and strong jaw remind me so much of him."

Michael relaxed his shoulders as he listened to the steady beat of the heart monitor. His mother was going to be okay—for now. "The doctor said they placed a stent in your heart to keep the artery open." He smoothed her hair. "You're going to be in the hospital a while—at least a week."

"Julia and David will be here soon." Sandy stroked his mother's wrinkled hand. "The wedding wouldn't be the same without you, Mom. I'm so glad you pulled through."

Her eyes drifted closed. She had fallen back to sleep.

30

Claire rolled over and hit the hardwood floor with a thud. The couch wasn't a good substitute for her queen-sized bed. She had insisted Haley sleep in her room. A pain shot through Claire's right shoulder blade—the side she slept on all night. She sat up and arched her back. Why hadn't she thought to sleep in Geraldine's room?

Geraldine. Claire glanced over at the recliner, remembering the events from the day before. *Thank you, Lord, that she's okay.* The simple prayer slipped off her tongue. She didn't know what she'd do without Geraldine in her life. The older woman had wormed her way into Claire's heart. If anything happened to her, Claire's life would change. She'd have to look for a new job. Would Michael rent the house to her anymore?

A knock on the door brought her to her feet. Eight o'clock. Must be Blake.

Claire grabbed the blanket from the couch and wrapped it around her shoulders, hiding her rumpled clothes from the day before. She swung around the couch and opened the door.

Blake leaned one hand against the doorframe, the other in his pocket. Would she ever get used to the sight of him? "I get the feeling I woke you." He smiled.

There was so much to tell him. Where should she begin? There was church, the picnic, the letter, her sister, and Geraldine's heart attack. Thoughts swirled in her head.

"Where's Geraldine? Still asleep?" Blake inched closer to the doorway and tried to see past her into the family room.

"I'm sorry. Come in." Claire stepped aside. "Geraldine isn't here."

"What?" Blake walked through the doorway. "Did she spend the night at Michael and Sandy's?"

"No." Claire led him to the couch. She spotted Geraldine's water glass sitting on the end table. "Geraldine's in the hospital. She had a heart attack." Hearing her own words sent chills down her spine.

"Is she all right?" Blake scooted closer. He laid his hand on her shoulder and gently squeezed.

Tears formed in Claire's eyes. "Geraldine had an emergency angioplasty yesterday."

"Oh, no." Blake's brows furrowed over his steely blue eyes.

She licked her dry lips. "She made it through surgery."

"Thank the Lord," Blake raised his hand heavenward. "Were you here by yourself when it happened?"

Haley sauntered into the room—her arms outstretched wearing her baby doll pajamas and her fluffy pink slippers. "Claire, what's for breakfast?"

Classic. Leave it to her sister to make a grand entrance. Claire jumped up and wrapped the blanket around Haley's shoulders. She looked at Blake, then back at her sister.

The minute Haley saw Blake sitting on the couch, she turned and ran back into Claire's bedroom, the blanket flying behind her like a cape. She slammed the door.

"Who's that?" Blake laughed. "Why didn't you tell me you had a visitor?"

Claire sat back down and grinned. "I didn't get around to it yet. That's my *married* sister, Haley."

Blake placed his arm on the back of the couch and twirled a strand of Claire's hair. "I only have eyes for one woman." He tapped her chin. "Someone who's definitely not married."

Me? The thought excited and unnerved Claire.

"So, what *is* for breakfast?" She stood and glanced down at her wrinkled clothes. Her blouse looked as though she'd been wearing it for days, and the coffee stain on the right leg of her jeans seemed to have grown overnight.

Blake stood. "That's what I was going to talk to you about. Workers are coming any minute to install my new kitchen cabinets. Do you think you'll be okay on your own?"

"Yeah, sure. Cold cereal works." *No, Blake, please stay.* "Will I see you later?"

Blake flashed her his winning smile. "Definitely. Dinner at six?" He made his way to the front door. "Tell your sister 'hi' for me and that I'll meet her officially at dinner—when she's dressed." He laughed. "It looks like you need a change of clothes, as well."

You think? Wise guy! Claire placed her hands on her hips. "Last night was kind of rough."

"Hey, I'm teasing. You're cute no matter what you're wearing."

Claire couldn't imagine that, but the compliment was nice all the same. "I'm glad Geraldine pulled through."

"Me too." Blake pulled the door open, then glanced over his shoulder. "Do you like Chinese food?"

"Love it."

"Good. See you tonight." Blake shut the door behind him and took off for his place.

He cooks Chinese food? Her mouth watered. She couldn't wait.

It wouldn't be long until Blake's kitchen was finished and her meals with him would end. Would he still want to spend time with her? She leaned against the door. Maybe *she* should burn *her* kitchen down.

Claire took one last peek at Blake out the window. A woman slid out of a red Mustang and approached him. Claire moved in for a closer look. The two knew each other by the way they interacted. The woman was familiar. The hair, the figure—*Kristy*. She had called Blake her friend the other night when she and Amber rudely interrupted their date at Capitola Beach. She watched Kristy swing her arm across Blake's shoulder as they entered Blake's house. Claire's shoulders sagged. Friends, huh?

"Okay, now I'm presentable," Haley's voice pierced the air. "Where's Blake?"

With another woman. Claire walked into the kitchen and opened the pantry door. "Cheerios or Rice Krispies?"

"I'm going to run by the hospital to see Mom before I head to the office." Michael gulped the last bit of his orange juice and turned to the morning newspaper. An article jumped out at him.

> The Sheriff's Office and vigilante residents made a small dent in the graffiti problem in Capitola this week when deputies cited three teenage boys suspected in two separate vandalism incidents.

"Good." Michael folded the paper and set it on the table. "Now hopefully my listing in Capitola will sell."

Sandy looked up at him over her plate of scrambled eggs, drew in a breath, and walked away with plate in hand. She had been giving him the silent treatment all morning. Michael thought about her chilling comments the night before. Until he was willing to talk to her about the real issue, she would go about her business and he could go about his.

"Do you have any wedding preparations today?" Michael stood, pushed in his chair, and followed Sandy to the sink. If she wasn't talking, fine. He could get a reaction from her in other ways. Michael approached her retreated back and kissed her on the neck.

"What are you doing?" Sandy rolled her shoulder away from his touch and turned her head in the opposite direction.

"You know I love you, Sandy."

"Do I?"

Michael could hear the tears in her voice. "Yes, of course." He wrapped his arms around her waist and rested his chin on her shoulder. "The other day, at the picnic . . . I was caught off guard. I haven't been around Martin much, and then that darn letter shows up right when we were having such a good time—in front of everyone. What was I supposed to say?"

Sandy pulled away from his embrace and walked to the other side of the island. "You don't get it, do you?" She blinked hard. "I'm jealous of a woman who's dead." Sandy picked up a knife and stabbed the butcher-block counter. "Don't you see something wrong with that? And you're doing nothing to ease my fears."

Michael wanted to run to her, to tell her the whole truth. But he held back. With Julia's wedding fast approaching, he needed to live under the same roof with the mother of the bride, *his bride*. The words wouldn't come. He gripped the granite countertop. A few seconds passed. He let out a sigh. And let his wife walk away.

After breakfast, the red Mustang was still parked against the curb next door. Haley had offered to do the dishes so Claire could take a shower. Nothing like hot water to rinse away her problems—but thoughts of Blake with Kristy still consumed her mind as she fixed her hair.

"I was thinking we could stop by the hospital this morning," Claire called from the bathroom.

Haley appeared in the doorway. "Good idea. Then, I thought we could swing by Babies R Us."

"Don't you think it's a little early? You're barely showing." Claire grabbed the toothpaste and unscrewed the lid.

"We don't have to buy anything, I thought we could look. I'm starting a wish list." Haley pulled her shirt up a little. "There's a bump there. See?"

Claire glanced at her sister's flat belly. "Hey, look! My sister's got a pooch. I thought I'd never see the day—"

"What's that supposed to mean?" Haley pulled her shirt down. "You didn't think Mark and I would have a family?" She crossed her arms.

"That wasn't what I meant and you know it." Claire stuck her toothbrush in her mouth and brushed, then placed it in the starfish holder. "You're the one who brought Mark into the conversation."

Haley tossed her arms in the air. "Great. My own sister doesn't want me to have a baby."

Claire rinsed her mouth with water, and then swiped her face with a towel. "Of course I'm excited about my nephew or niece. But since you brought Mark into this, let's talk."

"You know what, Claire? I came here to check on you. Not talk about my husband."

"Some husband. If he had any sense, he never would've let you leave." Claire pushed her way through the doorway.

"Mark doesn't know where I went. I left before he woke up." Haley grabbed a hairbrush and ran it through her long hair. "I haven't spoken with him since. And I don't know when I will."

Good. Claire tucked her hair behind her ear. "It would serve him right." She came up beside Haley. "He doesn't deserve you or your baby."

"It still hurts." Haley set the brush down and grabbed a tissue. "I don't want to be a single mother—like Mom." She blew her nose. "How will I be able to support a child?"

Claire's heart softened. She knew her mother had had a difficult time raising two girls on her own. Claire touched Haley's arm. "I know, sis."

"I want to be alone for a while." Haley tossed the tissue in the trashcan. "You go to the hospital. Take my Chevy." Haley looked at her with a glint in her eye. "And I'll watch out for Miss Mustang."

"You sure?"

"Positive."

"Thanks." Claire leaned over and gave her sister a hug. "I'll be back before you know it."

31

Michael climbed the steps and walked down the long corridor of Dominican Hospital to room 2125. He turned left and nearly ran into Claire. She held a mauve-colored pitcher in her hand.

"I was getting your mom ice water. You know how she likes her water . . .with ice." Claire stammered.

Michael could tell he made the young woman nervous. It didn't surprise him one bit after the fiasco at New Brighton Beach. "Here, I'll get it. Why don't you go back to the room, and I'll be there in a minute."

The surprise on Claire's face brought a smile to his own. Claire needed to see his softer side. He did have one, even though he didn't show it much. He had tried to give his wife a bit of affection too this morning, but it didn't get him far. Guilt clawed at his insides. He could be nice to Claire, Emily's daughter. "Really, it's no problem."

"Thanks." Claire handed him the empty pitcher. She turned and slipped into Geraldine's room.

With container in hand, Michael walked to the nurses' station. "Where can I find the water—and ice?"

A nurse looked up. It was Nancy. Michael knew her at once. "Michael. I was wondering if I'd see you today. Follow me." Nancy stood and walked down the hall to a storage room.

Michael followed behind, and then entered a rectangular room filled with storage supplies. He filled the pitcher.

"Claire loves your mother." Nancy grabbed a few cups off the shelf. "She acted quickly yesterday. You must be so grateful that your mom has such a wonderful caregiver."

Claire had been doing a great job. The doctor told him it was a miracle his mother was able to have the angioplasty. "You're right, Nancy. Claire is the best person to come along for my mother in quite a while. And I'm going to make sure she knows it." He'd make sure his mother gave Claire a hefty raise.

Nancy handed Michael the cups. "For you and Claire."

"Thanks." Michael made his way to his mother's room.

Mom was asleep, and Claire sat in a chair, one leg curled under the other, flipping through a magazine.

"How long has she been out?" Michael set the pitcher and cups down on the table.

"Not long. I came twenty minutes ago. She was wide awake when I went to get the water." Claire glanced at his mother. Her mouth hung open as she took deep breaths.

"Want to grab a coffee?" The words were out of Michael's mouth before he had a chance to think. Why did he do that? Did he feel he owed Claire after saving his mother? He ran a hand through his hair.

"Sure, why not." She stood and followed him out the door.

"I wanted to thank you for taking such good care of my mother."

"We take care of each other."

The statement warmed Michael's heart. He had noticed his mother fussing over Claire a time or two.

"I owe her a great deal. If it wasn't for your mom, I wouldn't have a job or a roof over my head." Claire kept a good distance from him as they walked side by side down the long corridor.

Michael motioned for her to go first through the entrance of the cafeteria. "How's it working out with Blake cooking in the kitchen?"

"Fine. Really good."

Did Michael see a hint of pink in Claire's cheeks? Blake had the same effect on his eighty-two-year-old mother.

"If I remember correctly, you like mochas?" Michael pulled out his wallet.

"Yes, but—"

"I insist." Michael ordered the drinks. "Why don't you find us a seat and I'll be right there." He watched Claire walk toward the chairs. She was a sweet woman—reminded him of his own daughter Julia in a way, but with lighter features. Now might be a chance to get to know Claire. Find out about her background. Something he should've checked before he hired her.

Michael collected his change and carried the steaming drinks to the table Claire had selected by the window. "Here you go."

"Thank you." Claire brought the cup to her lips and sipped the hot liquid. She kept her eyes averted, then peered out the window.

"Claire, we started off on the wrong foot." Michael rested both forearms on the table, his coffee tucked between his hands. "My mother knew you from L.A., and I know you're Emily's daughter, but that's all I know about you. I'd like to know more. What brought you to Capitola?"

A few seconds ticked by. Claire seemed to be formulating her thoughts by the way she hesitated. Her eyes met his. "Ever since my mom died, I'd been working as a waitress, living with my sister, and wanting to be on my own. Then, when I was fired, my brother-in-law kicked me out. I needed somewhere to go." Claire leaned back in her chair. "I couldn't forget the letter. So, I came here to find out who wrote it."

Michael heaved a sigh. What did this girl want from him? "And? Now what?"

"The man I dreamed about doesn't exist." Claire turned her head toward the window.

"Don't you think you're being a little unfair?" Michael knew his voice sounded condescending. "After all, I was barely out of high school. A kid. Someone who thought he was in love."

"It's not the teenage boy I'm disappointed with, but the man you've become—" Claire shot her hand up to her mouth.

Michael didn't like who he was either. He had to give Claire credit for speaking her mind. Where had the caring family man gone? Michael let out a long breath.

"I can't believe I said that. Please don't fire me. I need this job. Geraldine means the world to me."

"Whoa." Michael held up a hand. "Slow down. I'm not going to fire you—."

"Michael . . . Claire?" Sandy walked toward their table, her outfit perfectly coordinated and her right hand planted on her hip. "Am I interrupting something?"

"No." Claire bolted out of her seat. "I was just leaving."

Michael watched Claire's retreating back as she sprinted out of the cafeteria. "Mom's asleep, so we grabbed a coffee." He motioned for Sandy to sit down.

She didn't budge. "I don't have time. I came to check on your mother. Then I have an appointment with Julia."

At least Sandy was talking to him. "We could've come here together." Michael downed the rest of his coffee, stood, then tossed his cup in the trash. "Maybe Mom will be awake later." He kissed his wife on the cheek.

"Don't make light of the situation, Michael." Sandy straightened her collar. "Until you want to tell me what's *really* going on, you can sleep in the guest room."

"Baby, please." His pet name for Sandy when he wanted to score points rolled off his tongue. "Don't you think you're being a little extreme?" He kept his voice low. He didn't want anyone overhearing his conversation. "My mother is in the hospital, finances are tight, and our daughter is getting married. Life is stressful." Michael grabbed Sandy by the elbow and led her out of the cafeteria.

"I still think you're hiding something from me." Sandy opened her purse and pulled out a tube of lipstick. She applied a thick layer over her perfectly formed lips.

Michael felt as if he were sinking into a mud hole. How could he consider telling his wife of twenty-seven years that he had broken his wedding vows? Was one night with Emily out of thousands with Sandy worth ruining his life—and his future? Keeping the secret from his wife might break up his marriage if the look in Sandy's eyes was any indication.

He needed to do something fast. Michael slipped his arm around her waist. "Sandy, sweetheart, I assure you. You're the only woman I want to be with forever. But we need to work together." He led her to the lobby doors. "Now I've got to go to work. I'll see you tonight."

Michael pulled his keys from his pocket, leaving his wife's empty glare behind him.

"Bye, Geraldine. You take care. I'll see you tomorrow." Claire leaned over and gave Geraldine a hug. The last fifteen minutes had been awkward with Sandy's watchful gaze on Claire's every move. Was Sandy mad at her? The picnic had turned out to be uncomfortable. Claire could feel the tension between Sandy and Michael then, and once again today in the hospital cafeteria. Now, Sandy couldn't keep her eyes off *her*.

"Claire, can I talk with you in the hallway?" Sandy motioned with her hand.

Claire's pulse quickened. Why would Sandy want to talk with her? "Okay. I'll be right there."

Sandy turned on her heel and left the room.

Claire turned toward Geraldine. "Is there anything you need from home?"

"Blake."

"Excuse me?" Claire thought Geraldine must still be under the influence of pain medication.

"Can you bring that handsome man by tonight? I'm going to miss dinner." Geraldine winked.

"He's going to make Chinese food." Claire patted Geraldine's hand. "I'll ask him to sneak you an egg roll or two."

"That would be nice." Geraldine reached up and touched her white hair. "Can you bring my hairbrush and lipstick?"

"Of course." Claire smiled. She loved Geraldine's spunk. "I've got to go see what Sandy wants."

Geraldine frowned. "It was a pretty big blow for her to find out Michael loved your mother."

"But they were only teenagers." Claire hooked her purse on her shoulder.

"He loved Emily for a long time. Too long."

Claire's stomach tightened. What did Geraldine mean? How long? She glanced at the door, knowing Sandy was waiting.

"Go on now. I'll see you tonight." Geraldine waved. "Tell Blake I'm looking forward to my egg roll."

Claire headed toward the doorway. She thought back on the awkward situation at New Brighton Beach. She didn't mean for Sandy to see the letter or for there to be an awkward moment between her and Michael. And she certainly didn't intend for Sandy to find her and Michael in the cafeteria together drinking coffee. Did Sandy think there was something going on between them? Claire recoiled. She would never intentionally spend time alone with a married man. The cafeteria was filled with people coming and going. Surely Sandy didn't feel threatened by her. Claire stepped into the hallway and looked left, then right. Sandy was nowhere to be found. How odd.

Claire walked down the stairs and out to the parking lot. A silver Lexus peeled around the corner. Claire jumped back. She adjusted her sunglasses and strained her eyes to see the driver. It couldn't be? Could it?

Sandy gunned her car out of the parking lot and into traffic on Soquel Drive.

32

The red Mustang was gone. And so was Haley. Claire had used her sister's car, so she knew Haley couldn't have gone far. Did she go for a walk? Claire knocked on Blake's door. She needed a friend, someone she could talk to. There was no answer. Her heart sank. She didn't have a claim on him, so why did the thought of Blake being with Kristy bother her so much? She knocked again. No answer. Strange. His truck was parked out front.

Claire followed the walkway around Blake's house to his carport in back. Her VW Bug's trunk was open.

"Claire, just the person I wanted to see." Blake wiped his hands on a rag. "I think I finally did it."

He *was* home. Her heart skipped a beat. "Did what?" Claire approached. She smiled at the oil-stained jeans and old T-shirt Blake wore. He looked like a regular mechanic.

"Rebuilt your engine." He shut the trunk's lid. "Come on, let's fire it up."

Claire swung around the back of the car to the passenger's side door. She slid in while Blake sat behind the wheel. "Ready?" He flashed her a smile and turned the key.

The hum of the motor brought tears to Claire's eyes. She ran her hand over the dashboard and took in a deep breath. She had her car back because of Blake. She reached over and squeezed his hand. "Thank you *so* much."

"Wait till I give you the bill," Blake chuckled. "You might not be thanking me then."

Claire leaned back in her seat. "You'd accept payments, right?"

"Oh, yeah." Blake looked over his shoulder and backed out of the driveway. "Starting with my first neck rub tonight after Chinese food." He shifted the car into first gear. "Let's see how this baby drives."

"Whoa, buddy. I meant monthly payments." Claire couldn't suppress the smile that tugged at her lips.

"We'll work something out. Don't worry."

A comfortable silence filled the car as they cruised the neighborhood. Claire rolled down her window and let the cool air blow through her hair. She glanced over at Blake and smiled. It felt right—the two of them driving around Capitola.

Blake spoke first. "What's your sister up to?"

"I don't know. She was gone when I got home from the hospital." Claire held up her hand to keep her hair from flying in her face.

Blake pulled up to the end of the street overlooking the ocean and cut the motor. "A taxi came by to pick her up."

A sense of panic overwhelmed her. Haley couldn't go back to Mark now, she couldn't. "Did she have her suitcase?" Claire's pulse quickened.

"No. I think she was only carrying a purse." Blake shifted in his seat, the sound of newspaper crunching beneath him. Claire appreciated the fact that Blake didn't want to soil the upholstery with his dirty jeans.

Relief washed through her. Her sister wasn't going back to Mark. Then where? Babies R Us. Haley had mentioned she wanted to visit the baby store. "Shopping. My sister must have gone shopping."

"And you didn't want to go with her?"

"I was visiting Geraldine at the hospital."

"How is she?" Blake's voice held a note of concern.

"She looked good—there was color to her cheeks, but she was real sleepy."

"It's probably the meds."

"Geraldine wants you to come by the hospital tonight." Claire played with the strap on her purse. "She misses you."

"Me or my cooking?" Blake chuckled.

"I think a little of both."

"Hey, you need to see my new kitchen cabinets. They're beautiful." Blake rested his arm on the open window frame. "And I picked out a counter."

Claire tightened her grip on her purse. She was sure Kristy had something to do with that decision. The brunette must mean more to him than he was letting on. She had to know. "Did you pick them out yourself?"

"Actually, I had help." Blake started the engine. "Let's go back to my place and I'll show you."

The last thing Claire wanted to see was the new kitchen counter Kristy had picked out. Her stomach knotted. Was she jealous? Up to now Blake had been little more than a friend, a good neighbor. Sure, he'd cooked for her, fixed her car, and taken her out on a date, but that didn't mean—. Claire was lying to herself. Blake Coombs had done so much more. He made her feel special. Cherished. Like a person someone could love. And she had blown him off—pushed him when he attempted to kiss her, and then told him she wasn't ready to date. And now Kristy was here to help with his kitchen, which Blake had asked her to do, but she had refused.

"Hey, you're quiet. Lost in your thoughts?"

Claire pulled herself back to the present. "You could say that." Blake's kitchen was almost finished, and her car was fixed. She had a feeling she'd see less of Blake, and more of a red Mustang parked out front.

Blake pulled the VW in front of the rental. He cut the engine and handed Claire the keys. "All yours."

"Thanks." Claire pulled on the door handle and slid out of her car. "Can I see your kitchen another time?"

"Are you sure? It'll only take a minute." Blake walked around her VW.

"I'm going to grab a nap before Haley comes home. I didn't sleep too well last night." Claire covered a yawn.

"Okay, if you say so." Blake held up his dirty hands. "I'm going to grab a shower. See you at six?"

"I'm looking forward to it." Claire started up the walk, then stopped. She turned around and looked at Blake. In a rush of emotions, she ran up to him and hugged him tight. "Thanks for fixing my car. It means the world to me."

"You're welcome." He gave her a genuine smile.

Dirty or not, she felt right in Blake's arms. Did he think the same thing?

Michael looked at the clock on his desk—again. He leaned over his laptop and stared at the empty screen. *I must be crazy.* Why consider admitting to his friend and colleague that he had an affair? After all these years, did it matter now? Michael knew it mattered. A gnawing ache swirled in his gut. It mattered to him, and, more important, to his wife. There was something about Eric that caused Michael to trust. Was it Eric's family values? Work ethic? Faith? A combination of the three? Michael tossed a paper clip into his empty coffee cup. He thought of himself as Eric's mentor—but sometimes, when it came down to the tough issues of life, it was the other way around.

"Hey, man, you ready to go? I'm starving." Eric clapped him on the back.

Michael jumped.

"It's one o'clock. We agreed to go out to lunch, right?" Eric stood with briefcase in hand. "You don't mind running by a house on the way back, do you? It should only take a few minutes."

Michael chuckled, shut his laptop, and slipped it into his briefcase. "Why don't we take two cars? Your few minutes could take an hour."

"All right, wise guy." Eric straightened the stack of folders on Michael's desk. "But no one has accused me of not being thorough."

"You're right on that count." Michael grabbed his cell phone and clipped it to his belt. "Where are we going?"

"Red Apple Café?" Eric led the way out of the real estate office. "Sound good?"

"Meet you there." Michael headed toward his car.

"Michael?" Crown Real Estate's secretary called from behind.

Michael turned.

Valerie waved a small white envelope. "I wanted to give you this. It seemed urgent. A blonde woman dropped it off not two minutes ago. Said it was priority mail."

Claire. It must be an apology from this morning. "Thanks, Valerie." Michael stuffed the envelope into his back pocket.

"Have a nice lunch." Valerie called over her shoulder.

Michael slid into his BMW, opened the sunroof, and slipped on his sunglasses. At age fifty-two, he liked to think he was still young, successful, and could turn women's heads. That kind of thinking is what got him into trouble all those years ago. Michael pulled his car into the restaurant's parking lot, got out, and slammed the door behind him, cutting off the recollection.

He walked into the café and noticed Eric was already seated.

"What took you so long?"

"Valerie stopped me." Michael dropped his briefcase by his feet.

A heavyset waitress came to take their order.

"And for you, sir?" The redhead turned to Michael after taking Eric's order for a hamburger.

"Cobb salad, please."

The waitress took their menus and promised rounds of water coming right up.

Twenty minutes later, Eric took a bite of his burger. Ketchup oozed out and dripped onto his plate. "So, how are the wedding plans coming?"

"My checkbook tells me I'd better sell another house—and fast—if I'm going to keep up with Sandy and Julia's plans." Michael gulped his iced tea and then dug into his salad.

"So, what does a wedding cost these days?" Eric wiped his face with a napkin and popped a French fry into his mouth.

"I'll let you know when the final bills come in. For now, my baby girl's getting married and nothing's going to keep me from giving her the best wedding possible."

"There's a new listing in the Uplands." Eric smiled and raised his eyebrows.

"Don't tell me, you're the listing agent." Michael folded his arms across his chest.

Eric laughed. "What can I say, when I'm hot, I'm hot."

"You dog!" Michael tossed a wadded napkin at Eric. "Is that the house you wanted to check out after lunch?"

"The one and only."

"Do you pay someone to get those listings? Today's market's so slow, I don't know how any of us survive."

"Only the best." Eric took a swig of his Coke and looked deep in Michael's eyes. "Hey, man, you sounded kind of serious the other day. You said you needed to talk."

The turn of conversation made his palms sweat. He didn't know if he could do it. Michael pushed his salad aside, reached for his glass, and brought the iced tea to his lips. He took a long, hard drink.

"Anytime you're ready." Eric leaned back in his seat and rested his hands on his belly.

Michael bit his lip. "I was in love once—or thought I was—to a girl the summer after high school. And then we met again—twenty some years ago."

Eric sat up and propped both elbows on the table. "Go on."

Michael inhaled and let his breath out slowly. "I had an affair." There, he said it. He exposed the secret that caused the ache within him. Michael looked out the window. "We had a one-night stand twenty-some odd years ago."

"And you're still thinking about her?"

"A year ago she died of cancer."

Their waitress stopped in front of their table. "Can I get you anything else? A box for your salad?"

"Yes, please." Michael felt his cheeks flush. Had the waitress overheard his conversation? He looked down at his half-eaten salad.

"You're paying, right?"

Michael nodded. "Yes, it's my turn."

Eric rubbed his hands together. "Okay, then, I'll have a brownie with vanilla ice cream."

The thought of eating dessert turned Michael's stomach.

"Anything for you, sir?"

"No." Michael let out an annoyed breath.

"I'll be right back with your brownie." The waitress turned on her heels and lumbered to the kitchen.

Eric pushed. "Does Sandy know?"

"No, Sandy doesn't know. Neither does Julia."

Eric's brows furrowed.

"I wasn't going to tell you either, but the guilt is killing me."

The waitress brought the dessert, set it in front of Eric, and handed Michael a to-go box. She placed the bill on the table. "Anything else?"

"We're good." Michael held up a hand.

The waitress walked away.

Michael scraped his fork along his plate, filling the box with salad.

"What are you going to do?" Eric crammed his mouth with a forkful of the brownie.

"Nothing. Nothing until the wedding is over, when I can sit down with Sandy and tell her the truth."

"Sounds like a plan." He finished off his dessert with a swig of his Coke.

Eric's cell phone went off, interrupting their conversation. "I've got to take this one. Potential buyer." He stood and walked outside.

Michael dug in his back pocket for his wallet and felt the envelope Valerie had handed him. He pulled it out. Surprisingly, the letter was unsealed. He glided the piece of paper out of the envelope. "Dear Michael . . ." He gasped. The note was in

Emily's handwriting. He checked the date. It appeared to be written right before her death.

> Dear Michael,
>
> Even though I want to stay in this world and be with my girls, cancer has taken over my body. But I have won the fight. God is calling me home.

Michael swallowed the lump that formed in his throat.

> I take the blame for what happened between us. You were a married man, with a child on the way, and I was a separated single mother needing to feel loved.

No, Emily, it was my fault as much as yours. Michael exhaled and kept reading.

> I never wanted to tell you—to burden you, or make you feel obligated to be part of my life—but now I must, because I don't have much longer and I want you to know.

Michael glanced out the window at Eric. He was still talking on his cell phone.

> Nine months after the night we were together, I delivered a beautiful baby girl.

"Hey, man, ready to go?" Eric stood over him. "You don't look so good. Are you sick?"

Michael charged to the restroom. And lost his lunch.

33

Claire nestled under her covers. A nap would do her good. She felt exhausted—between Geraldine's heart attack, her sister coming to town, coffee with Michael, and Blake's possible new love interest, Kristy, Claire could sleep for a week. She rolled over on her left side and pulled the covers under her chin. She closed her eyes, took in a few deep breaths, and tried to empty her mind.

"Mew." The muffled sound came from outside her window.

Claire turned over and settled in a comfortable position on her back.

"Mew." The sound was louder now.

She'd never be able to sleep with that noise. Claire kicked off the blanket and wandered over to the slightly opened window. She opened it all the way and listened.

"Meow."

A cat.

Claire pushed herself away from the window, then sprinted to the front door and around the side of the house. Sitting in the bushes was the most beautiful calico cat she'd ever seen. Claire took a few steps closer. She could see it was mostly white with black and tan markings. And it didn't have a collar.

"Meow."

"Are you hungry, little one?" Claire pushed her hair behind her ear, then gathered the cat into her arms.

It purred and nuzzled Claire's neck.

"Come inside with me." She stood, cradling her find. "I'll pour you some milk."

Once in the kitchen, she filled a bowl and placed it on the tile floor.

The cat lapped the milk up quickly, then walked over to Claire and rubbed against her legs.

"Where are your owners?" She leaned down and scooped the cat up. "I'm sure they miss you." *I know I would.* Claire recalled her pets growing up, and she stroked the cat's fur as she walked into her bedroom and sat on her bed. The cat hopped off her lap, then walked around in circles before settling down in a ball near Claire's feet.

"I'm tired, too." Claire plumped the pillows and sank into them. She stared at the ceiling and felt the cat's soft fur against her leg. Thoughts of her mother's journal invaded her mind. She reached in her nightstand, grabbed the book, and opened it. It felt good to see her mother's handwriting—neat and straight, unlike hers. It reminded Claire of all the times her mother wrote notes and stuck them in her school lunchbox when she was a child.

Claire read the first line.

I'm in love with Martin DeWitt.

Ever since finding out Michael wrote the letter, a nagging feeling told her something wasn't right. Why did her mother write in her journal that she was in love with Martin when Michael was the one who wrote the letter?

Claire looked closer. Wait a minute. The ink in Martin's name appeared to be a shade darker than the ink used for the rest of the sentence. Claire flipped a couple of pages. She found Martin's name once again in darker ink. Who changed it? And why? Claire tossed the journal on her bed and stroked the cat's back. It didn't make sense.

"Claire?" Haley's voice called from the family room.

"I'm in the bedroom." Claire picked up the cat and sat her on her lap. She'd question Haley later, when the time was right. "You'll never guess what I found."

"Oh, no. You let an animal in the house." Haley covered her nose and mouth with her hand. "Don't you know pregnant women shouldn't be around cats?"

"That's only a myth." Claire scratched the top of the cat's head. "Pregnant women shouldn't change the litter box, that's all."

"Where did you find her?"

"Outside my bedroom window."

Haley sat on the edge of Claire's bed. "Are you going to call Animal Services?"

"Yes. Then, if no one is missing a calico cat, I was hoping you'd come with me to the pet store for food and a litter box." Claire held the cat like a baby. "Isn't she the sweetest thing?"

"What do you think Geraldine will say? After all, she lives here too."

"Don't you remember? Geraldine loves cats. She had at least a half a dozen at one time. I'm sure she'd welcome Cali with open arms."

Haley rolled her eyes. "Cali? You named her?"

"It fits, don't you think?" Claire held Cali up underneath her front legs.

"Oh, brother." Haley stood, walked to her suitcase, and rummaged through it.

"Where were you, by the way? Blake said you left in a taxi."

"Blake and Miss Mustang were locked in an embrace, I didn't think he saw me."

Blake and Kristy were hugging? Kristy probably made the first move. "He's an affectionate guy." Claire felt the need to defend him. "I'm sure he didn't mean anything by it." She wished she believed her own words. "Did you go shopping? I don't see any bags."

"I ran an errand." Haley pulled out a baby name book and sat next to Claire on the bed. "I'm thinking of Beau for a boy and Brooke for a girl. What do you think?"

"I like them both." Claire hesitated. "Speaking of names . . ." She didn't want to start another fight with her sister, and yet she wanted to know the truth. "Did you notice the different-colored ink in mom's journal?" Claire opened the book and pointed. "I know Michael wrote the letter, yet there's a reference to Martin in a darker shade of ink."

Haley's cheeks turned pink. She walked toward the window.

"You were the one who sent me mom's journal." The realization dawned on Claire. She joined Haley next to the windowsill. She met her sister's eyes. "Why? Why did you change Michael's name to Martin?"

"Because I wanted you to quit searching." Haley leaned against the wall. "I thought if I wrote Martin's name, you'd leave everything alone."

"How did you know about Martin?" Claire leaned against the wall. "Mom never told me about him."

"Mom mentioned him to me when I was getting my driver's license. She knew that Mark liked to party and she was afraid I'd end up like Martin."

"You didn't think I'd talk to him?"

Haley brought her hand up to her temple. "Mom told me about Martin's car accident. I hoped he wouldn't remember with his brain injury and all."

Claire let out a frustrated sigh. "But why?"

"I miss you. I need you, especially now." Haley touched her pregnant belly. "Won't you come back to Los Angeles with me?"

Why would her sister ask her now, after she had finally made a life for herself? Geraldine needed her. And hopefully Blake did too. "Back to L.A.? You're not seriously thinking of getting back with Mark, are you?"

"No, but my life is in L.A." Haley let out a long, slow breath. "With or without Mark."

"And for now, my life is here in Capitola." Claire touched Haley's arm.

"That's what I was afraid of." Haley gave Claire a hug. "I was wrong. I'm sorry. Do you forgive me?"

"Just one question." Claire folded her arms. "How did you change the names when they were written in ink?"

"I dipped a Q-tip lightly in bleach." Haley grabbed the journal. "I kept the M and erased the rest of the name." She bit her lip and handed the book to Claire.

Did Haley's apology excuse her actions? No. But her sister was frightened. She'd be scared too if she were pregnant, alone, and married to Mark. Haley had made a mistake, but then again, she couldn't remember the last time her sister had admitted she was wrong. Claire felt a surge of compassion. "I forgive you."

"Thank you." Haley smiled. She nodded toward the cat, licking her front paw. "Let's go find out if someone is missing her pet."

"All right." Claire scooped up Cali, grabbed her purse, and followed Haley out the door. "Let's take my car." Suddenly, she had a boost of energy.

Cali's emerald green collar jingled in the backseat. Claire was relieved no one had called Animal Services about a missing cat with Cali's markings. She left her phone number anyway, just in case. But at this point, the cat was hers. And Geraldine's.

The crate, food, and bag of litter filled the backseat of her VW as she and Haley drove home.

"Blake should be by in a little while. Chinese food tonight." Claire loved the feel of the steering wheel beneath her hands. It had been too long.

"Meow."

"I hope Blake isn't allergic to cats." Claire turned off the highway at Bay Avenue.

Haley glanced over her shoulder. "We'll find out at dinner."

"Afterward, I promised Geraldine that Blake and I would come for a visit."

"For a woman who doesn't have a boyfriend, you sure talk about Blake a lot." Haley adjusted her seat belt. "All I can say is, take it slow. Don't follow in my footsteps."

"I'm not eighteen. And I would never elope. No, I would want a wedding on the beach, with my friends and family there." Claire grinned.

"Sounds like a dream." Haley looked out the window. "Life doesn't always turn out the way you want. Look at me." Her voice quivered. "Pregnant and separated from my husband."

Claire hurt for her sister. She couldn't imagine being married to a creep like Mark. And she definitely couldn't imagine raising a baby alone. She knew how difficult it had been for her mother. A few more turns and they pulled up behind Haley's Chevy in front of the rental.

"What is *he* doing here?" Claire caught sight of Mark standing on the front porch before Haley did.

"Mark," Haley whispered.

"You don't have to talk to him." Claire pulled the keys out of the ignition and slipped them into her purse. "Wait right here with Cali."

"I can handle my own husband," Haley argued.

"Of course you can, but now is not the time." Claire opened her door. "You're pregnant. And vulnerable." She stood. "Wait here." *Lord, help me.* Claire took long strides up the walkway.

Mark's eyes bore a hole through Claire "I'm here for my wife."

"I don't think so." Claire marched up the steps.

"I don't know what she's been telling you, but I've been clean and sober ever since I heard I'm going to be a father."

"You're right. That's not what I heard." Claire stood a few feet from Mark, her hands on her hips.

"Haley's wrong." Mark's upper lip curled. "I've been working overtime to save money for the nursery. I haven't touched a drop of liquor."

Claire didn't believe him—didn't want to believe him. She had lived with Mark long enough to know he wasn't strong enough to stay away from the bottle. "It's time to leave Haley alone. She needs to live her own life. Without you." Claire was surprised how calm she felt. Like her prayer was working. "And what about Brett Wilder? Did you go out with him?"

Claire heard footsteps behind her. She turned. Haley carried Cali in her arms.

"I'd like to hear this." Haley handed the cat to Claire.

Mark reached out and ran his fingertips down Haley's arm. "Baby, I didn't touch a drop. Not one sip."

Haley flinched.

"I drove Brett back to his hotel. He's long gone."

Haley looked at Claire, then back to Mark.

"You took off before I had a chance to explain." Mark pulled Haley close. "Come back with me. I don't want to live without you, baby."

Claire nearly gagged. Surely Haley wasn't buying Mark's story again. "Haley, come inside. We've got to talk." Claire put her key in the lock and opened the door. "Mark, wait outside."

Haley's brows furrowed, and her mouth formed a straight line. "Just a few minutes." Haley looked again from Claire to Mark. "I'll be right back."

Once inside, Claire placed the cat on the recliner chair and turned toward her sister. "You don't believe him, do you?"

"It's complicated." Haley sat on the couch, obviously torn. "He's my husband. And the father of this baby."

"You don't need him. Mom did it alone and so can you. And I'll help you any way I can." Claire sat down next to Haley and grabbed her sister's hand.

Haley's eyes filled with tears. "If you could have a relationship with your father, would you?"

"Our father was a low-life. He left us. Why would I want a relationship with *him*?" Claire shook her head. She didn't see Haley's point.

"No, Claire. You didn't know him. You still don't." Haley stood and walked to Claire's bedroom.

Claire followed. "What are you talking about?"

Haley gathered her things. "Your father is here—in Capitola."

What was Haley saying? They shared the same father, didn't they? Claire felt dizzy. Confused. She watched her sister tuck her clothes and toiletries into her suitcase.

"I want my baby to grow up knowing her father, because one day she'll want to find him. And like you, she won't be able to leave the past alone."

"Michael?" Claire's voice was barely above a whisper. Could it be?

"Bye, Claire." Haley hugged Claire tight, then grabbed her suitcase. "Mark is going to take me home."

"Wait a minute. You're leaving me now?" Claire held on to Haley's arm. "How do you know Michael is my father? Did he tell you?"

"Babe, let's go," Mark called from the entryway.

Claire's pulse raced.

"Mom wrote a note to Michael before she died." Haley inched closer to the door. "I was supposed to give it to him at the memorial, but I held on to it—until today."

"The taxi." Claire's eyes narrowed.

"I went to Michael's work and gave it to his secretary. I'm sure he's read the note by now. You're Michael's daughter; Claire."

Tears sprang to her eyes. For a year she had wondered about her mother's relationship with the writer of the old love letter. And it was her father. Haley had known all along. And kept it from her.

"Go. Leave." Claire pointed to the door.

"When you're ready to come back to L.A., call me." Haley walked to the doorway and stopped. "I need you. And so does my baby." She blew her sister a kiss, then left.

Claire heard the front door click shut. She wanted to run after her sister and tell her goodbye, but her feet were frozen to the floor. Claire felt hurt, deceived by her own flesh and blood. *Her half sister.* The thought unnerved her. She sat down on her bed and leaned her head into her hands.

Cali jumped up and rubbed against Claire's arm.

Claire held the cat close to her chest.

Michael. Her father? Her heart felt as though it had dropped into her stomach.

That meant Geraldine, the woman who lay in a hospital bed, was her grandmother. Claire exhaled deeply, set Cali down next to her, and lay back on the bed, allowing the tears to fall.

34

Michael swerved his BMW into a parking space at Dominican Hospital, numb from Emily's note. Why hadn't Emily told him sooner? And what about his mother? Had she known all these years and yet never said a word? His stomach clenched. He had to know.

Glancing at himself in the rearview mirror, he couldn't help but notice the pouches of skin that sagged under his eyes. The last six weeks had taken their toll. He ran a hand through his hair and slid out of the car.

Michael walked into the hospital and up the stairs. The long corridor to the cardiac unit stretched on, making each step difficult. *Sandy and Julia.* Michael broke out in a sweat. How would he tell them about Claire? His heart pounded.

Dear sweet Emily. She must have known it would split apart his family and break their hearts. Michael stopped and leaned against the wall. All these years, did he consider anyone else's feelings? Had *he* thought of anyone but *himself*? He let out a deep breath. The pastor of Capitola Christian Fellowship once told his congregation to live for an audience of one—God. But Michael lived for a different audience of one—himself. He leaned against the wall, tears slipping down his cheeks. *Lord,*

I'm so sorry for the mess I've made of my life. Help me make things right. Michael reached into his pocket for a handkerchief and wiped his face.

"Michael?" Nancy's voice grabbed his attention. "Are you all right?" She laid a hand on his arm.

"I'm okay. Thanks." He tucked the cloth in his pocket. "I was on my way to see my mother."

"Nothing wrong, I hope."

"No." Michael shook his head.

"That mother of yours loves company." Nancy smiled. "She'll be happy to have a visitor. Well, I'm off. Tom is expecting me home. It's our anniversary."

"Congratulations." His tone belied the sentiment. Would he and Sandy make it to their special day?

"Twenty-nine years." Nancy's eyes sparkled. "They haven't all been easy. In fact, they've been downright hard. But God has been faithful, and He's helped us through the tough times."

Michael nodded. "Thanks for the reminder. I needed to hear that."

"You bet. See you later." Nancy waved and walked away.

Michael continued to his mother's room. He peeked his head in the door. The curtain was closed. "Mom? It's Michael."

"Come in, son."

His mother sounded alert. Good. He slipped past the curtain. She was sitting in a chair wearing the blue housecoat he had given her for Christmas. "Look at you. You're doing great!"

"The nurses don't want me staying in bed. I've got to keep this old body moving."

"Did Claire bring your robe?" Michael's voice quivered at the mention of Claire's name. He sat down on the edge of the hospital bed.

"Yes, this morning. Isn't she the most considerate young woman? And she's going to bring my hairbrush, and lipstick." His mother's face brightened. "I have a handsome man coming to visit me tonight."

Michael's brows shot up.

"It's Blake, dear." His mother swatted the air with her hand. "An old woman can dream, can't she? And besides, he's perfect for our Claire. Any amount of time those two can spend together is good, don't you think?"

Our Claire. Did she know how true that was? "Now, Mother, don't go matchmaking. If they're meant to be together, they will. Let them find their own way."

"In the meantime, I plan on looking my best—or the best I can under these conditions." She straightened the collar of her housecoat.

The time had come. Michael couldn't wait any longer. His pulse quickened. "Mom, I have something important to ask."

"Of course, dear."

"Do you remember the night I spent with Emily? I realize it was a long time ago."

His mother's eyes dimmed. "I may forget many things, but I'll never forget that night. I was half sick worrying about where you were. You were supposed to be back in a couple of hours. Instead it was morning."

Michael hung his head. "That's the night." He pulled the note he received from his secretary out of his pocket, then handed it to his mother.

"What's this?"

"Emily's last words to me."

"My glasses." His mother pointed to the small table.

Michael retrieved them. He waited the few minutes his mother took to read the note.

Her mouth moved and her hand shook as she read. Tears slipped down her wrinkled cheeks. She dropped the note in her lap.

"Did you know, Mom?" Michael noticed the strain in his voice.

"How could I have known?" His mother shook her head. "I was a grieving widow and barely holding on." She fingered the note. "I didn't pay attention to anyone else." She let out a breath. "All those years, my own granddaughter lived down the hall from me and I never knew."

Was his mother telling him the truth? How could she not have known? The blue eyes, the wavy hair—Claire reminded him of himself. Then why didn't he know? Why didn't he suspect Claire was his daughter at Emily's funeral?

Why would he suspect he fathered a child when it took him and his wife a few years to conceive? And he and Emily were together only one night. Guilt and doubt clouded his mind.

"When are you going to tell Sandy? And Julia?" His mother brought his attention back to the present.

Michael stood and shifted from one foot to the other. "Sandy suspects something is going on. She's barely speaking to me. With Julia's wedding in a couple of months, it might be better to wait."

"What?" His mother's voice rose. "You can't go on like this, Michael. You need to own up to your mistakes and confess your past to your wife. You owe Sandy that much." She gripped the letter and waved it at Michael. "And there is a beautiful young woman who deserves to know her father—and her grandmother."

Michael sat back down and rested his elbows on his knees, head in his hands. He looked up. "How do I face Claire?"

"The same way—with grit and determination to make things right." His mother's heart monitor beeped a strange rhythm.

"Mom, are you okay?" Michael jumped up and pressed the call button.

"Don't bother, son. I'm fine. This machine does strange things sometimes."

Michael placed a hand on his mother's arm. "Are you sure it's not your heart?"

A nurse walked in. She fiddled with the heart monitor, then checked his mother. "You need rest. I hope this gentleman didn't rile you up." The nurse gave Michael a stern look. She reached under his mother's arms and helped her stand. "Here, let me help you to bed."

The last thing Michael wanted to do was stress his mother's already damaged heart. Time to leave.

She reached up and patted Michael's arm. "Remember what I said, dear."

Michael watched the nurse cover his mother with a blanket. She looked small and frail. "Bye, Mom. Take care."

"My granddaughter is coming for a visit tonight with her handsome beau," his mother said to the nurse.

His stomach somersaulted and his breath caught in his throat. His mother was already calling Claire her granddaughter. If he didn't tell the women in his life the truth, his mother might beat him to it.

"Well, let's get you all rested up so you can enjoy your visit." The nurse's voice sounded gentle, yet firm.

Michael walked out of the room resolved that he was going to tell the truth, even if it killed him.

Claire stood in front of the mirror and brushed her hair. Blake would arrive in twenty minutes. She was refreshed after her nap, yet felt hollow inside. She loved Haley and missed her already, but it would be a while before Claire would speak to her. She needed to sort out her feelings—about Haley, and her father. The thought of Michael being her dad overwhelmed her. What did Haley say? He found out *today*? She didn't understand why her mother never told Michael she was pregnant. Claire might have had a whole different upbringing if her mother had.

Claire looked around the family room. She grabbed a magazine off the couch and placed it neatly on the coffee table, then picked up the afghan, folded it, and hung it over the edge of Geraldine's chair. *Her grandmother's chair.* The thought brought a smile to her face. *Lord, help her to be okay.*

Hanging out with Blake had been great for her prayer life. Before he showed her that praying to God was as natural as talking to your best friend, Claire had hardly uttered two words to the Lord.

Claire stepped outside. The air was chilly. She walked down the walkway to the mailbox, gathered the contents, and flipped through the envelopes. Bills, but mostly junk. A large manila envelope with her name on it caught her eye. She glanced at the return address and saw Vivian's name at the top. Why would Vivian send her a package? Claire shut the mailbox and hurried inside. She placed the rest of the mail on the table, and tore open the manila envelope. A brochure? She pulled out the thick booklet. A yellow sticky note was attached.

> Claire,
> Pursue your dreams. You can do it!
> Love,
> Vivian

Claire remembered Vivian telling her the day she got fired from the restaurant in L.A. that she was college material. Claire opened the Cabrillo College brochure and read the different programs and degrees. Could she do it? Did she have what it took to be a college student? The nursing program intrigued her. After all those years taking care of her mother, and now Geraldine, Claire realized she loved helping people.

The familiar knock on the door sent Claire scurrying. She collected the mail and tossed it in the basket on the counter. Her insides quivered as she thought about spending time alone with Blake. She turned the knob and welcomed him in.

"I hope you like sweet and sour chicken and Szechwan beef." Blake held a bagful of groceries. He had a sly grin on his face as if he already knew the answer.

"Who told you?" Claire closed the door behind him and followed him into the kitchen.

Blake emptied the bag's contents on the counter. "I have my ways."

"No, seriously. How did you know?" Claire picked up the can of diced pineapple.

"I asked Haley." Blake threw her a sideways glance. "Before she left with her husband."

So, he knew Mark came to get her sister. Claire set the can down and leaned against the kitchen counter. "What else did she tell you?"

"To take good care of you." Blake tapped her nose with his index finger. "And I told her not to worry. That you'd be well taken care of."

But what about Miss Mustang? Claire knew Kristy wouldn't go for that. "I can take care of myself." Claire opened the bag of Chinese noodles and popped several in her mouth.

"You'd live on soup and cereal." Blake laughed. "You know you like my cooking."

"Are you kidding? I think I've gained ten pounds since you started." She patted her belly.

"If you'd rather I left . . ." he teased.

Claire enjoyed the easy banter between them. She needed a light conversation after today's events. Her mind shifted. Haley would be halfway home by now, and Michael . . . who knew what he was doing and thinking.

"Hey Claire, you're a million miles away. Anything I can do?" Blake rested his hand on top of hers on the counter.

"Tell me Miss Mustang doesn't mean a thing to you." The words were out of her mouth before she had a chance to stop them. *Think before you speak.* Her mother told her that her tongue would get her into trouble one day.

Blake rolled his head back and let out a hearty laugh. "Methinks the lady is jealous." His accent was a mix of knight in shining armor and bad British drama.

Claire knew her cheeks must be a deep shade of red. How she wished she could duck under the kitchen table. "You're not interested in Kristy? I saw her Mustang parked in front of your house this morning."

Blake rested his arm across Claire's shoulder. "Kristy is an interior decorator. She helped me pick out a countertop. But I love it that you noticed."

See Haley, I knew it was nothing. Or at least I hoped. Claire felt her insides warm at Blake's nearness.

The phone rang.

"Do you want to get that? I'll start dinner." Blake winked.

Claire liked that Blake could be so practical. He was also confident in his decisions and knew what was important in life. She was falling for him and falling hard. Red flag!

She glanced at him over her shoulder, then reached for the phone.

"Claire?"

"Yes?" She looked at Blake and shrugged her shoulders.

"It's Pearl, dear."

"Pearl!" Claire shrieked. "It's so good to hear your voice."

"Yours too. I had a dickens of a time finding your number. Thank goodness for Samantha, sweet girl."

Samantha. Claire needed to call her. Would her friend take her advice and come to Capitola?

"Harry and I are on our way to visit John and Melody in San Francisco."

"I bet you miss the little guy."

"We sure do. Say, we were hoping to spend tomorrow night at New Brighton Beach and we'd like you to join us for dinner." Claire could hear the eagerness in Pearl's voice.

In the past, Pearl had been a source of wisdom. Claire needed to hear what the elderly woman thought of the chaos in her life now. "I'd love to."

Claire heard a loud crash and whipped her head around.

Blake had dropped a pan on the tile floor. He held up his hands in mock surrender. "Sorry about that."

Claire's eyes widened. She lifted her index finger to her lips.

"What's going on over there?" Pearl teased. "Was that a man's voice I heard?"

"It's my neighbor. He cooks for me."

Blake picked up the pan, a sheepish grin on his face.

"You have your own personal chef?" Pearl sounded confused.

"His kitchen burned down so he's cooking at my house till it's repaired."

"Sounds like an interesting arrangement. Why don't you invite him to dinner with us? Tell him Harry's barbequing. I'm sure he'd like a night off."

Pearl had a point. Blake had been cooking her gourmet meals ever since she moved into the rental. He needed a break. Also, it might be good to have someone there to talk with Harry. Then she'd be able to talk with Pearl alone. Claire was sure Harry would like to meet the man who fixed her car. "I'll do that."

"All right, dear. We'll call you tomorrow and let you know of our location at the campground. See you tomorrow night. Around 6:00 p.m.?"

"Sounds good." Claire put the telephone back in the cradle. She stood by the counter and watched Blake in the kitchen. He moved like a professional. Claire chuckled. Maybe she did have a personal chef after all. And Blake was the perfect diversion to keep her mind away from her sister and father.

35

Claire held a bouquet of mixed wildflowers, the ones Blake had purchased, and stopped down the hall from Geraldine's hospital room. *Breathe. Breathe.* Did the elderly woman know she was her granddaughter? Would seeing Geraldine now be any different than it was this morning? The hallway spun.

Blake carried an egg roll in a small paper bag. "Why don't you go first and make sure she's ready for a male visitor."

"She's ready. Geraldine's been waiting all day." Claire handed him the bouquet. "These should come from you. I'll wait right here." She was working her way up to telling Blake at dinner about Michael and Geraldine being family, but the timing never seemed right. He'd be all excited that she lived with her grandmother and had a father close by. Not Claire. She had to make sure they wanted her around before she got her hopes up.

"You don't want to come in with me?"

Claire was positive Geraldine would appreciate having a little male attention by herself. Especially since Blake looked so handsome in his jeans and navy T-shirt. "I'll give you a few minutes alone."

"Anything to help." Blake winked, and then walked the few steps to Geraldine's room.

He knocked. "It's Blake."

"Come in, dear," the elderly woman's voice rose.

Blake shot Claire a grin, then walked into the room.

"Oh, my, what beautiful flowers! And you brought me an egg roll. How sweet."

Claire listened from outside the door. She wrapped her arms around her waist and leaned against the wall. Would Geraldine ask about her? Her throat constricted.

Her thoughts drifted to her mother. Why hadn't she told Claire that Michael was her father? Why write a note to Michael? Did she expect him to tell her? Claire's mind was filled with so many unanswered questions. And her mother wasn't around to answer them.

Haley. She held on to the secret for a year, and then seemed eager to dole out information once Claire was established in Capitola. Haley wanted her to run back to L.A. Her sister had selfish motives. But wouldn't Claire do the same if the roles were reversed? She sighed.

The sound of Blake's hearty voice mixed with Geraldine's occasional guffaw made her suddenly feel left out. It was *her* grandmother. Claire rolled her eyes. Could she walk into the room and act as if nothing had happened? But something had happened. She had found out the truth. Now was the time to be brave and face Geraldine, whether or not she knew. Claire walked through the doorway and past the curtain.

"Blake is so funny." Geraldine brought her hand to her cheek. "You should have heard the story he was telling."

Blake clutched his side.

Claire pulled up a chair and sat down. "Sorry I missed it."

"Where were you, dear? I was hoping to run a brush through my hair and put on a dab of lipstick before Blake came in."

Geraldine pursed her lips and touched her hair. "Did you see?" Her eyes widened and she smiled. "He brought me flowers. Aren't they gorgeous?"

"As beautiful as you." Blake placed his hand on top of Geraldine's. "If you ladies will excuse me. I'm on call tonight." He grabbed his vibrating cell phone, flipped it open, and walked out of the room.

No, Blake. Don't leave. Claire wasn't ready to spend time alone with her grandmother. She unzipped her purse and pulled out Geraldine's hairbrush and lipstick. "Sorry. I should have brought these to you before Blake arrived."

"Oh, phooey." She giggled. "I know that man only has eyes for you, as it should be, but I'm an old woman who appreciates a good-looking man when I see one. He did give me a compliment."

She doesn't know. Geraldine's demeanor put Claire at ease. She stood with hairbrush in hand and placed the lipstick on the small table. "May I?"

"Yes, please do." Geraldine sat real still and closed her eyes.

Claire brushed the white hair with slow strokes. "I have a present for you."

"You didn't need to do that." Geraldine looked up at Claire.

"Actually, it's for both of us." Claire set the hairbrush on the small table. She handed Geraldine the lipstick.

"Now you've got me curious." She applied a generous amount to her lips.

"You'll have to wait until you get home before you see it." Claire bit her lower lip.

"Out with it, Claire. I've never been good at guessing games."

"A cat! I found a cat. She was sitting outside my bedroom window." Claire smiled. "She is the sweetest calico. You'll love her."

Geraldine's eyes lit up. "You know I will. I've been wanting a cat ever since I had to give all of mine away when I moved into the retirement community."

"I named her Cali."

Blake walked in the door, his brows furrowed. "Sorry, ladies. I've been called into work."

"Nothing serious, I hope." Geraldine's voice held a hint of concern.

"We've had several officers out. So, the rest of us have to cover." Blake walked to the foot of the bed and gently patted Geraldine's foot. He looked at Claire. "Want a lift home or do you want to stay a while longer?"

"I'd love my granddaughter to stay." Geraldine turned to Claire. "But it's better to go home with Blake. I wouldn't want you to take a taxi."

My granddaughter? Claire inhaled and held her breath. She does know. Claire exhaled. Either way, she wasn't ready to deal with this new revelation. Not until she talked with Michael. "Blake, I'll catch a ride home with you." Claire leaned over and gave Geraldine a kiss on her cheek. "I'll come back and visit tomorrow."

"Okay, dear. Take care of that cat for me. What a nice surprise." She smiled. "Good to see you, Blake. Come anytime."

Claire followed Blake out the door. Neither of them said a word until they approached Blake's truck.

He reached for the door handle, then turned to look at her. "Geraldine's your grandmother? Since when?" Blake's voice sounded more confused than sarcastic.

"You caught that, huh?" Claire shrugged.

Blake leaned against the side of the truck. "What's going on?"

Claire thought back to this morning when Blake appeared at her door to tell her she was on her own for breakfast. She didn't get a chance to tell him that Michael was the writer of the letter. *And now, her father.* "I don't know if you have time. It's a long story."

Blake put the key in the door. "Tell me on the way."

By the time they pulled up to her front door, Claire had told Blake the condensed version about the picnic, the letter, and Haley's shocking news.

"I wonder if Michael visited Geraldine this afternoon." Claire pulled the letter out of her purse and clutched it to her chest. "She has never called me her granddaughter before."

"Does it matter? She knows you're her granddaughter now." He smiled.

Blake could be so practical. Of course, it mattered! Why didn't Geraldine act like her grandmother as she grew up? She tucked the letter in her jacket pocket.

"I have to go to work, but I'll be off in time for dinner with your friends." Blake stepped toward her and gave her a hug. "I'm happy for you. It's nice to have a close relationship with your grandmother."

She breathed in Blake's musky cologne. At this moment, all she needed was him. She took in another deep breath before pulling back. "The jury's still out on that one. I haven't talked with Michael. His family may not want me here." Claire was definitely not practical.

"What do *you* want?"

"Honestly, I don't know." Claire put her key in the lock and opened the front door. "Be careful tonight. I'll be praying for you."

Blake smiled. "Thank you. And I'll be praying for you."

Michael listened to the message on his cell phone once again.

Why would his wife leave him and go to Julia's? She didn't take any of her things and the suitcases were still in the guest bedroom closet. When was she coming back? The thought of losing his wife of twenty-seven years cut deep. He loved Sandy with his whole being and would never do anything intentional to hurt her. And yet he had. Why wasn't he honest with her all those years ago? He leaned back against the couch and remembered the day as if it were yesterday.

"Honey, I'm home," Michael had said, making sure his voice was steady. His quick business trip to L.A. had turned out to be something he regretted. He searched the house. With his wife seven months pregnant, he had felt comfortable leaving. There was enough of a window before she'd deliver. But Sandy was nowhere to be found. *His pager.* He had selfishly turned it off when he was with Emily and had forgotten to turn it back on. Sandy had paged him. Five times.

Panic set in. He dialed the hospital number, the one he had memorized in case Sandy went into labor. She was only 32 weeks along. *Lord, help me. What have I done?* Michael's hands shook.

Julia weighed 3 pounds 10 ounces at birth. So tiny. And he had missed it.

The ringing of the telephone brought Michael back to the present. He jumped up from the couch and hurried to answer the phone.

"Hi, Michael? Emily."

"Emily?" Was this a joke?

"I'm a friend of Julia's. I'm still at work, but want to go to the shower. What time did it start?"

The bridal shower. Sandy had planned a surprise shower for Julia tonight. Michael had forgotten. He searched the counter looking for a stray invitation. A pink ribbon peeked out from under the morning's newspaper. He pulled it out and scanned the fancy scroll. "7:30."

"Thanks."

Michael glanced at his watch. It was eight o'clock. The party had already started. He needed to talk to his wife now, while he had the nerve. But did he want to interrupt? How long does a bridal shower last? Michael grabbed his keys from his pocket and headed toward his car. If he got kicked out of the all-girl party, he'd come home. Michael hopped in his BMW and started the engine. He shifted the car into drive, pressed the accelerator—and then slammed on the brakes. He was doing it again—thinking only of himself. His head fell back against the headrest. A few minutes passed before he made a decision. A choice that could change his life forever.

36

"Meow." Cali rubbed against Claire's calf as she sat in Geraldine's recliner. Claire flipped through the Cabrillo College brochure. Did she dare sign up for a class or two? She bit her lower lip as she reached down and picked up the cat. "What do you think, sweet kitty?"

Claire's life in Capitola had taken on a nice rhythm before Geraldine landed in the hospital. Now, her emotions were all over the place. She loved her grandmother and hoped she'd be able to stay as her caregiver.

Then there was Blake. She wanted him in her life—not only for now, but for good. Her spine tingled as she dreamed about a future together. But how could she settle in Capitola with Michael, Sandy, and Julia so close? Things were different now that she knew Michael was her father.

Haley had practically begged her to come back to L.A. Her sister wanted family around to be part of her baby's life. Claire suspected it had more to do with free babysitting while her sister shopped for the latest fashion. But Haley did love her and they had a history together. Mark's presence in Haley's life made Claire want to stay in Capitola indefinitely, but if Haley were able to send Mark packing, she'd consider moving back. Claire stroked Cali's back. "What am I going to do?"

The doorbell rang. She wasn't expecting anyone tonight. Claire set the cat down and walked to the door. She peeked out the window. It was a woman. The doorbell sounded again.

Claire turned the knob.

"Surprise!" Samantha held up her suitcase.

Claire wrapped her arms around Samantha's neck in a big hug. "I'm so happy to see you. I needed a friend tonight." Claire motioned her in.

Samantha stepped inside the entryway and set down her suitcase. "I've decided to take your advice and move to Capitola." Samantha's brunette hair was exactly how Claire remembered it—pulled back in a ponytail. "I'm over my job and I'm done with men."

"You've come to the right house." Claire shut the door.

Samantha hung her sweater on the coat rack and followed Claire into the family room. She sat down on the couch and shooed the cat away.

Claire chuckled to herself. She remembered when they were camping how frightened Samantha was of animals.

"It looks like you've got yourself a great place." Samantha craned her neck and looked around.

Claire sat down on the recliner. "I love this house." Her voice was wistful. She twisted her hair between her fingers. "And I've got a great job taking care of the elderly woman who lives here."

"What's going on?" Samantha cocked her head. "I can tell something's bothering you."

"You're right. I have a big decision to make." Claire tucked her foot under her thigh. "My sister wants me to move back to L.A. to help her when the baby comes. And I'm considering it."

Samantha's brows furrowed. "Why? You're on your own. Do you want to go back?"

"I may have to."

"Give me one good reason."

"Remember the letter I told you about? The one signed 'M.'?" Claire stood and walked to the window.

"I do remember. Did you ever find out who wrote it?"

"I did. His name is Michael. And—he's my *father!*" Claire took a deep breath. "But that's not all. He owns this house. And the woman I'm taking care of—Geraldine—is his mother, which makes her my grandmother."

"You're kidding!" Samantha jumped up from the couch and joined her.

"It's true—all of it. My mother had written a note to Michael before she died. My sister Haley was supposed to give it to him at my mother's memorial. But she held off—until today. Meanwhile, Haley went back to L.A. with her husband." Claire pressed her fingers to her forehead. "Now it's up to me—to confront Michael or leave. I'm scared. I don't know what to do."

"I'll be here for you." Samantha laid her hand on Claire's shoulder and squeezed. "Seeing that I have nowhere else to go. Wait, that didn't come out right." She crinkled her nose.

"I know the feeling. You're welcome to stay here. I'd love the company. I get lonely without Geraldine."

"Where is she?"

"In the hospital. She had a heart attack and needed surgery." Claire picked up Cali and nuzzled her cheek against the cat's soft fur. "She should be home in a few days." She set the cat down.

"I'm glad she's going to be okay."

"Me too." Claire led Samantha to the kitchen. "You hungry?"

"Starving."

"How does leftover sweet and sour chicken sound?" Claire opened the refrigerator. "Blake made it for dinner tonight. Oh, and there are a couple of egg rolls."

"Explain to me again how you roped your neighbor into cooking for you every night." Samantha put her hands on her slender hips.

"I had nothing to do with it. His kitchen burned down and he needed a place to cook. I'm one of the lucky recipients." Claire pulled out the Tupperware with the leftovers. "But it's going to end soon. Blake's new cabinets went in. And his counter should arrive soon."

"I can't wait to meet him." Samantha opened the cabinet and pulled out a couple of plates.

"None for me. I finished the Szechwan beef at dinner." Claire grabbed a spoon and emptied the contents on a plate. She stuck the dish in the microwave. "You're going to have to wait until tomorrow to meet Blake. He was called in to work." The microwave beeped. Claire filled Samantha's plate and joined her at the table. "I'm falling for him." Her palms grew moist.

Samantha stuck a forkful of sweet and sour chicken into her mouth. "He definitely can cook."

"That's not the only thing he's good at." Claire giggled. "Say, after you're finished eating we'll get you settled. I want to hear all about what's going on in *your* life."

Later that night, Claire watched one of her favorite movies with Samantha. She'd seen it at least a dozen times. Her mind wandered as she stared at the television screen. If she did go back to L.A., Samantha could take care of Geraldine. Claire glanced at her friend. She was friendly, caring, and needing a job. Yes. Geraldine would definitely like Samantha.

Would Blake? Claire's stomach churned. He needed a woman who knew what she wanted and was ready to settle down. Her imagination ran wild. Claire wanted to be that person. And she knew Blake was interested in her. But was it worth hurting Michael's family in the process? Should she disappear and go back to L.A.—and to her sister, where she knew she was needed?

The college application sat on the end table by Geraldine's recliner. How she wished she could fill out the paperwork and mail it.

She'd have to make a decision—to stay or leave. And soon.

Michael's knees burned.

"Lord, I messed up and now it's caught up with me. You gave me a beautiful wife and daughter, a wonderful home, so many blessings. And I blew it." He paused. "Please forgive me for breaking my vows. Help me." Michael's voice shook. "I don't know what to do or say to make things right again. I've hurt so many people—Emily, Sandy, Julia, and now Claire. If you get me out of this mess, I promise to live my life for you from now on. In your name." He glanced at the clock. The past hour had flown by. Sandy would be home soon.

Michael clutched the comforter and stood. He rubbed his aching knees, then grabbed for the phone. Confession time. He'd call his friend Martin at the nursing facility.

"Martin's room."

A woman's voice trilled over the line. It didn't sound like Debbie. She was probably at the bridal shower with Sandy.

Michael loosened his collar. "This is Michael Thompson. Is Martin available?"

"Just a moment, please."

Michael heard shuffling noises in the background. A couple of minutes passed.

"He-llo."

Michael caught his breath at the sound of Martin's slow drawl. Would he ever get used to the fact that his high school buddy had such a difficult life? Michael's life wasn't exactly easy at the moment, either. "Martin, it's me. Michael."

"I thought you might call." Martin exhaled loudly.

"Why's that?" Michael paced the room.

"It's Thursday. Sandy stopped by to see Debbie. She looked like she had a lot on her mind."

Michael walked over to his dresser and picked up a framed picture of his family. Sandy's arms were wrapped around his waist, and Julia held his hand. His heart skipped a beat. Would it ever be that way again?

"Michael?"

"Sorry, buddy." Michael set the picture down and sighed. "I need to finally tell Sandy the truth." Michael sat down on the edge of his bed. "And there's more." He hesitated. How would Martin respond to his news? "Claire's my daughter."

Michael waited for a response. He heard Martin breathing. Was he going to say anything?

"Trust God, Michael," Martin encouraged. "He'll get you through."

"I'm scared." Michael slid off the bed and sat on the floor with his elbows propped on his knees. He lowered his head into his hands.

"God forgives you."

"Do *you* forgive me?" Michael winced. If he hadn't asked Martin to meet him that night, his friend never would have been in the accident that left him paralyzed.

"Yes, I forgive you."

"But—"

"But nothing."

Michael felt sick to his stomach. Aside from his mother, Martin had been the only one he had confided in until the other day at lunch with Eric.

"I've wanted you to tell Sandy for a long time."

"I know." Michael let out a breath. "Since the accident . . ."

"I never blamed you for what happened to me."

"Thank you."

"For what?" Martin's voice softened.

"For sticking with me. I haven't been a good friend to you. But you've always been there for me."

Martin's tone lifted. "You can make it up to me."

"How?"

"Get me out of this place for a few hours. Let's have lunch sometime."

Michael laughed through his tears "How about next Thursday?"

"You know where to find me."

"See you at noon. And thanks, Martin, for being the kind of friend I want to be from now on." Michael stood.

"I'll hold you to it. And remember, friend, trust God."

Michael looked heavenward, then returned the phone to the cradle.

He walked to the couch, sat down with a stack of photo albums, and slowly flipped through the pages. Michael stared at the lovely image of Sandy on their wedding day. Her white dress hugged her figure. He chuckled at his tuxedo and the goofy grin on his face. *So young. And naïve.* That had been the best day of his life. He loved Sandy with every ounce of his being. Then why? Why did he spend the night with Emily?

Michael turned a few more pages. He ran his hand over a photo of Martin and him before his friend's accident. Michael's eyes clouded. He rubbed the back of his neck with a sweaty palm.

The next album was filled with pictures of Julia. Her tiny body after birth was hooked to all kinds of tubes and wires. How fast life had flown by. His little girl was now a beautiful woman—about to be married. She'd make a wonderful wife to David. He was grateful to Sandy for being such a loving mother. His heart raced. After what he was about to tell Julia, would she even want him to walk her down the aisle?

A car door slammed. Sandy? *Dear God, help me.*

37

Michael's heart pounded. A light sweat crested his upper lip. He closed the photo album and placed it on top of the others. From his place on the couch, he could see the marble entryway. Any minute now Sandy would walk into the house. Was he ready? Was a man ever prepared to tell his wife that he had a one-night stand that had produced a daughter? He'd never be ready, but he had to tell Sandy the truth. He loved her and he owed it to her. The door swung open. "Julia?" He stood.

"Hey, Dad." She came up beside him and kissed his cheek.

"Where's Mom?"

Julia set her handbag on the coffee table and slipped out of her coat. "I'm worried about her. She didn't seem at all like herself tonight."

He took her coat and hung it in the closet.

"Dad, she threw me a surprise bridal shower, and she looked like she didn't want to be there." Julia threw up her hands. "Doesn't she want me to marry David?"

Guilt gnawed at Michael's insides. "Of course she wants you to marry David." He reached for his daughter. "Come here."

She went to him.

He hugged her tight. "Did *you* have fun tonight?"

Julia pulled back. A smile spread across her face. "I was definitely surprised. Most of my high school girlfriends were there—Emily even showed up, late, of course. We played a game where I was wrapped in toilet paper. It was supposed to look like a wedding gown."

Just hearing the name Emily threw Michael for a loop. He walked to the kitchen for a drink of water. His mouth was parched. He tried to listen to Julia describe the party, but he was concerned about his wife. Where was she?

". . . and Mom's friend Debbie gave me a certificate to a spa. I told her I'd go before the wedding. Anything to help me relax before my big day." Julia had followed him to the kitchen. "Dad, are you listening?"

"Something to drink?" Michael offered.

"Do you know where Mom is? I was hoping we could talk. Something's definitely bugging her." Julia reached into the refrigerator and pulled out the milk and chocolate syrup.

"That won't keep you up?" Michael handed her a glass and a spoon.

"I'm so wired from the party right now, I don't think I could sleep. Besides, David wants me to call and tell him all about the shower. I already blew it with sugar today. What's another dose of chocolate?"

"Did Mom drive her car to your house?" Michael took another glass out of the cabinet.

"Wait a minute. No, she didn't. I think she might have come with Debbie. Mom didn't want me to recognize her car." Julia squeezed the chocolate sauce into both glasses.

Michael poured the milk. "You didn't see her leave?"

"Emily wanted me to take a drive around the block in her new Porsche. Mom told me to go ahead. Said she'd finish cleaning. I didn't think I'd be gone long. When I got back, Mom had left."

It didn't sound like Sandy. She wouldn't leave Julia without saying goodbye. Michael picked up a spoon and stirred the milk. The liquid darkened like his life—once white and pure, now heavy and dark. Didn't the Bible say he'd be white as snow when he was forgiven? Michael clung to that thought as he downed his chocolate milk. How would he be able to tell Sandy about Claire? It might put her over the edge. He waited until Julia finished.

"Why don't you go home, honey?" Michael laid a hand on her shoulder. "I'll go look for your mom. I think I might know where she is."

"You're sure she's not upset with me?" Julia grabbed her coat and purse.

"I'm positive." He followed her to the front door. "Hey, do you have time for a date with your old man before the wedding? Just you and me."

According to *his* mother, it would be better if Michael told Julia about Claire before the wedding. He still had his doubts. He wanted Julia to look at him as she always had—as her hero.

"Are you sure you can spare the change?" Julia teased. "You've been rather stressed out lately."

"Just trying to keep up with David's family. It's hard to compete." Michael held the door open.

"You don't have to compete. They're not that kind of people." She gave him a quick hug. "I'd love to go out with you before the wedding." A sly grin crept on her face. "Wait until I tell David I was asked out on a date. I'll let him sweat before I tell him it's my father." She chuckled.

"You take after your grandmother—full of energy. I hope David's ready for you." Michael flipped on the porch light.

"I'll take that as a compliment. I hope I'm exactly like Grandma when I'm in my eighties. I'm relieved she'll be at the wedding. What a close call. I'm grateful for Claire. See you later. Love you."

Michael watched his daughter get into her car. He wished his relationship with Julia could always be this way—lighthearted and comfortable. Why did she have to know Claire was his daughter—her half-sister? He knew the answer. Because he was done with lying and living for himself. Julia started her engine and pulled away. *Please don't drive out of my life.*

The headlights of Michael's BMW shone bright on the back end of Sandy's Lexus. He knew he'd find her parked on State Park Drive overlooking the beach and the city lights of Santa Cruz. It was her favorite place when she needed time to think. Michael's too. He'd asked Sandy to marry him on the beach below. When he pulled up next to her car, Sandy was looking straight ahead, seemingly unaware of his presence. *Dear God, what have I done to her?* He prayed, then put the car in reverse and parked his car behind hers.

Michael slid out of the driver's seat and shut the door. He kept his eye on Sandy as he approached. She stirred. He stood nearby and waited for her to notice him. The streetlight illuminated her face. Sandy turned and looked at him. Michael could see the sadness in her eyes.

He blinked hard. Now was his chance. Michael tugged on the door handle. It was locked. He could see the indecision on Sandy's face. Would she let him in? Then, the button popped up, and he pulled the door open. Michael crouched down and laid a hand on her thigh. "Talk to me, please."

"I don't know what to say." Sandy's voice was void of emotion. "I don't feel I know you anymore."

"Will you come out? Sit on the bench?" Michael stood and reached for Sandy's hand. Surprisingly, she took it and followed him.

Michael linked her hand around his arm. They approached the bench. He didn't want to let her go.

"Michael, I want the truth." Sandy stepped back from his grip. "Is there another woman? Are you seeing someone else?" She looked down and kicked the dirt with her foot.

Michael raked his hand through his hair. "No. I'm not seeing anyone else."

"All those late nights at the office, your preoccupation with Claire—who by the way is young enough to be your daughter—"

His breath caught and hung below the mass in his throat. Did Sandy think he was in love with Claire? The thought jarred him. He grabbed Sandy by the shoulders and gently led her to the bench. "Please, honey, sit down." He sat next to his wife and wrapped his arm around her shoulder. Sandy might not want him after tonight, and he needed the feel of her body next to his. "Can we enjoy the view for a minute?"

"What for?" Sandy's shoulders slumped.

"I need to tell you something." Michael's voice shook. "But I'm scared."

"Haven't I waited long enough?"

Speaking the words he had to say might send his wife away forever. Could he risk that? There was no easy way to tell Sandy what had happened. His heart pounded.

"Do you remember when I went down to L.A. for a Realtor's convention?" His hands shook.

"Which one?" Sandy inched away from him.

"When Julia was born—"

"That was years ago."

Michael hoped her response was in his favor. "It was—many years ago." He turned to look at the view. The city lights glistened in the distance. The romantic setting called for kissing his wife, not breaking her heart. "I went to visit my mother, and I met up with an old friend." Michael couldn't look Sandy in the eye.

"Who?"

A heaviness crushed his chest. Michael faced Sandy. "Emily."

"The woman you wrote the letter to when you were teenagers?"

Michael bit his lip and nodded. "Sandy, I spent the night with her. One night. I've regretted it ever since. We both knew it was wrong."

"And you're finally getting around to telling me?" Sandy let out a breath.

Michael pressed his fingers against his temples. "I never wanted to tell you. It was a mistake, a terrible mistake."

Sandy stood and walked to the edge of the cliff. "And I had our baby alone. No wonder I couldn't get a hold of you. You were holding someone else!"

Michael came up behind her.

"You've been playing me for a fool for over twenty years."

Michael grabbed Sandy around her shoulders and pulled her back. He held on to her. "No, I've been the fool. Don't you see? I've carried around the guilt of breaking my promise to you."

"How many others have there been?" Sandy spat, jerking herself free.

Michael's mouth hung open. "None. I promise. I've been faithful to you ever since."

"I don't know if I believe you." Sandy shook her head. "Your promises obviously mean nothing to you."

Michael gasped for air. He clutched his hands behind his head. This moment was as awful as he imagined it would be. And he hadn't yet told Sandy that Claire was his daughter.

"I've prayed to God to forgive me for my selfishness." Michael kneeled in front of her in the dirt. "I don't expect you to forgive me right now. But I want you to know that I'm truly sorry."

Sandy stood over him, silent and still.

Michael looked up. "I love you, Sandy. With everything I am."

Sandy's body shook. "Do you mean that?"

Michael rose. He cupped her face in his hands. "I'd do anything for you." Tears streamed down Sandy's cheeks. He kissed them away.

Sandy looked into his eyes. "Michael, why are you telling me *now*? It happened so long ago . . . I wish you had never told me." She sucked in a breath.

Should he tell her about Claire now or wait until another time? She was already distraught. Needles pricked his eyes.

"Can we go home now? I'm cold." Sandy made a move toward her Lexus.

Michael grabbed her arm. "There is one more thing." He questioned his words, as he took off his jacket and draped it around his wife's shoulders.

Sandy clutched his coat tight with white knuckles. Her body stiffened.

Michael took a breath and talked on. He couldn't go through this pain all over again. "I recently found out—that Emily had a baby nine months after we were together. Sandy, I don't know how to tell you—except to say it. Claire is my daughter."

Sandy's knees buckled.

Michael caught her before she hit the ground.

38

Red Apple Café's omelet rivaled Blake's. Claire dug in her purse for tip money. "Oh, no, you don't." Samantha produced a few dollars and laid them on the table. "My treat."

"But you already paid the bill."

"It's the least I can do for letting me crash at your house."

"You're welcome anytime." Claire stood and led her friend out the door. "See you this afternoon. And good luck with your interview." It was so like Samantha to have an interview all lined up the first day in a new town. Claire waved and reached into her purse for her car keys.

"Claire," Vivian called from the restaurant's doorway. "I'm so glad I caught you." She motioned Claire to come toward her.

"What's up?" Claire's breath caught in her throat. Vivian's face was ashen next to her burgundy Red Apple Café T-shirt.

"It's Blake. I overheard a couple police officers. He was stabbed. Blake's at Dominican Hospital."

Claire's heart pounded. *Blake was stabbed.* The news didn't compute. She must get to the hospital—and fast. "Vivian, I've got to go." She was on her way to visit Geraldine, but she'd have to check on Blake first.

"Keep me posted, honey. And drive safe." Vivian's words fell on Claire's retreating back.

She ran down the cement stairs that led to the parking lot. Claire glanced at her watch. 8:30. When did Blake enter the hospital? He was called in to work last night while they were visiting Geraldine. Claire put her key in the lock and opened her car door. She flung her leftovers and her purse on the passenger seat, her adrenaline shifting into overdrive. Claire couldn't lose him, too. There were already too many losses in her life. She peeled out of the parking lot and into traffic.

The fifteen-minute drive to the hospital jostled Claire's nerves. The traffic was stop and go. She found herself praying for Blake's injuries, Geraldine's health, and her upcoming talk with Michael. Could she leave them all behind?

Claire merged off the highway and onto Soquel Drive. The hospital was on her immediate left. She pulled into the parking lot and cut the engine and a few minutes later approached the information desk on shaky legs. "Officer Blake Coombs, please."

The elderly woman wrote Blake's name on a piece of paper. Then she typed on the computer keyboard.

Claire drummed her fingertips against the counter. Why was the woman taking so long? She couldn't wait to see Blake. The smell of his cologne from last night's hug lingered in her mind.

"I'm sorry, but I don't have him listed." The woman looked up from behind the small glasses that pinched her nose, giving her the appearance of an ostrich. "Are you sure *he* was the patient?"

Claire let out a breath. "Are you sure you spelled his name right? C-O-O-M-B-S?"

The woman checked again. "Oh, wait a minute. I see he came in early this morning to the emergency room but was released. Anything else I can help you with?"

Blake was released. That was a good sign, wasn't it? "He's all right then?" Claire gripped the counter with both hands.

"That's all I can tell you." The woman shook her head.

"Thank you." Claire stepped away and called Blake's cell phone. No answer. She'd try him again after her visit with Geraldine.

Claire climbed the stairs to the second floor. She walked the hallway and then peeked inside Geraldine's room. The bed was empty. What was going on? Everyone who mattered to her seemed to disappear. She spoke to the nurse sitting in the hallway thumbing through a stack of paperwork. "Excuse me. I'm looking for Geraldine Thompson."

"They moved her to Dominican Rehabilitation on Frederick Street. She needed physical therapy before she could go home."

"Where is the rehab center located?" asked Claire.

"You can head straight down Soquel Drive toward Santa Cruz or take the highway and get off on Morrissey Boulevard."

"Thank you." Claire bit her lip. Her frustration mounted. Should she call Geraldine first to make sure it was a good time to visit? She searched for her phone.

A folded piece of paper was inside her right pocket. Claire turned away from the nurse, walked down the hallway toward her car, and pulled out the paper. It was an envelope. *The letter.* In a way, she wished she'd never pursued the writer of the letter. It had only brought heartache.

Michael was not someone she could respect as a father. From what she saw of him, he was selfish. Claire wouldn't be surprised if he'd known all along she was his daughter. She was sure he abandoned her mother the minute he found out she was pregnant. Wasn't Julia older than she was? The thought disturbed her. Why would a married man give it all away?

Claire sat in her VW, her thoughts drifting to her mother. Why would her mother have an affair with a married man? She hit the steering wheel with her fist. Didn't her mother think she deserved better? Haley followed in her mother's footsteps, except she chose a man who drank his troubles away.

It was time to confront Michael and make a decision whether she should stay in Capitola or return to L.A., but her heart told her to first check on her neighbor.

Blake's white Ford F-150 sat in his driveway. Claire pulled up next to the curb in front of her house. She slid out of her car, ran up the sidewalk, and knocked on Blake's front door.

"Coming."

At the sound of Blake's voice on the other side, Claire sucked in her breath. What was she going to say? *Thought I'd check on you. By the way, I may be moving back to L.A.* The idea seemed crazy whenever she was near him. Claire could list a dozen characteristics she admired about Blake—his relationship with God, for starters. She'd never met a man who put God before everything else.

The door swung open. "Claire, what brings you by?" Blake's right forearm was covered in gauze.

"I heard you were stabbed. I rushed to Dominican Hospital, but you weren't there." Claire hurried to him and threw her arms around his waist, her head resting on his chest. "I was so scared."

"I should get hurt more often." Blake slipped his left arm around her and squeezed her tight. "I like all this attention."

Claire stepped back. "What happened?"

Blake motioned her inside. Claire hadn't been in Blake's house more than a handful of times. She liked what she saw. It needed a feminine touch, but it was comfortable. She sat down on the black leather couch. Blake joined her.

"Capitola police have been dealing with gang members tagging signs, restaurants, trash bins, anything they can get their hands on." Blake looked down, then back at Claire. "Last night was rough. I thought I had it all under control until the guy pulled out a knife. He sliced my arm pretty good, but I was fortunate. He was aiming for my face."

"No." Claire was suddenly nervous. "Did you call for backup?"

"Amber came, but by that time it was too late." Blake's torso deflated. "In self defense, I shot the guy. I'm on a paid leave of absence until they investigate."

"You could have been seriously hurt." Claire brought her hand up to Blake's cheek.

"They caught the two other gang members who took off running. All three of them were carrying weapons." Blake held her wrist and kissed the inside of her hand. "Do you know what flashed through my mind?"

Claire's pulse quickened. She shook her head.

"I didn't want to die without telling you how I felt about you."

Was Blake going to kiss her? She wouldn't push him away this time. No, she'd welcome the intimate moment. But would she give him false hope when she could be moving back to L.A.?

"Claire, I know you're scared of a relationship. I can see it in your eyes. But I want you to know—"

Oh, no. He's not going there. "Your kitchen is amazing!" Claire bolted off the couch. She rubbed her hand over the granite countertop. "When was this installed?"

Blake stood next to her, his nearness making her regret her actions.

"Claire, you sure you want to talk about my kitchen now?" Blake's husky voice moaned in her ear.

"It's perfect. And these cabinets are beautiful. I love maple." Claire fingered a handle and opened the door.

Blake blinked hard. "Okay, Claire. I get the message. You're not ready."

Oh, yes, I am! Claire knew the real reason she held back. Fear.

"Kristy knew of wholesalers trying to get rid of their extra granite. I got a deal."

"You have great taste." She knew she was being overly dramatic. Why couldn't she allow Blake to open up to her?

Because of Michael. If her father didn't want her around, she'd hit the road. Whether back to L.A. or another California town, she'd leave. Every other man who mattered to her had rejected her. Why would Michael, or Blake for that matter, be any different?

One look into Blake's eyes told her the truth. He would never hurt her. She longed to love him with her whole heart. "Blake, I've got to run." She needed to talk with Michael. Her future depended on it. "I'll talk with you tonight, okay?" Claire stood on her toes and kissed Blake's cheek. It was rough from stubble, but she didn't mind. To be near Blake sent a rush of emotions through her.

"Why don't we drive to New Brighton Beach in my truck?"

"Are you sure you feel up to it?"

Blake walked Claire to the door. "Definitely. Any time with you is worth it. But you'll need to drive, okay? I'm on pain meds."

"Harry and Pearl can't wait to meet you." She took a few steps, then looked back. "Oh, and by the way, my friend

Samantha will be joining us. She's in town. We'll knock on your door at a quarter till six."

"You can get me anytime." He leaned against the doorframe, a silly grin on his face. "I love you, Claire."

He loved her? Her hands grew clammy. She didn't know what to do with those words. Did she love him too? She opened her mouth to speak. "See you tonight."

Was Blake's love enough to keep her in Capitola?

The scribbled note hung haphazardly on the front door.

> Samantha,
>
> I'll be back soon. There's something important I need to do. It couldn't wait.
>
> Claire

With white knuckles, Claire gripped her steering wheel and drove to Michael's house. Would he be home? Surely he didn't work every day of the week. Maybe that's what it took to drive the kind of cars he and Sandy drove. And who'd want to clean such a big house? People with money hired help. She'd take her small house by the beach, with tons of character, any day.

Claire stopped on the street in front of Michael's house. What if Sandy was home? Claire definitely didn't want to hurt Michael's wife as she had at the picnic. Sandy was a nice woman. She could tell Sandy she wanted to speak to Michael privately about Geraldine. In a way, it was true.

If Claire were honest with herself, she was surprised Michael hadn't made any effort to contact her since Haley had given him the note from her mother. Of course, he had a family to consider. Were they begging him to go on with their lives as if nothing had happened? Claire looked up. The sloped driveway and trees blocked her view. She let out a nervous breath. *Michael is my father!*

Dear God, give me strength. The only other time she'd been at Michael's house was when she was hired to take care of Geraldine. Blake had prayed for her before they went in. And now she was praying to God all on her own.

Claire hit the gas pedal and drove up the driveway. She didn't see Michael's BMW. Was it in the garage? Claire's stomach tied in knots, and her pulse raced. She second-guessed herself. Her car idled while she sat staring at the flagstone steps that led to the front door.

With a surge of courage, Claire turned off the engine and stepped out of the comforts of her VW. She gently shut the door and walked up the steps. Her hands shook. She balled them into fists, then relaxed. She'd watched her mother die of cancer, lived with her sister and her sister's alcoholic husband, and moved to a new town. Claire could face Michael and find out if he wanted a relationship with her. She brought her hand up to knock. But before she did, the door swung open.

39

Her eyes bore through Claire like daggers. "What are *you* doing here?" Julia stepped out of the house. "Do you have any idea what you've done to my family? I'm getting married in a couple of months. And you've ruined everything."

Julia knows the truth. Claire took a step back. She wasn't prepared for such an attack.

Julia threw up her hands. "Why did you move here?"

Claire slipped her hand into the pocket of her jacket. If Julia read the letter, maybe she'd understand. "I was fired from my job as a server and kicked out of my sister's house. I had to make a life for myself somewhere, so I came here. It made sense at the time." Claire pulled out the envelope and pointed to the upper left corner. "The return address is your father's rental."

"You mean *our* father," Julia spat.

The thought tightened her gut. "Listen, I didn't come here to fight." Claire attempted to keep her voice even.

"Why show up at all?" Julia folded her arms across her chest. "Do you expect to waltz right in and become part of the family?"

"No, I—"

"I've been consoling my mother all night."

Claire gripped the letter. "I'm sorry. I never meant for anyone to get hurt—"

"We are hurt." Julia flopped down on the flagstone steps.

Claire sat down beside her. No words would come.

"While my mom was delivering *me*, my father was in L.A. with *your* mother." Julia lowered her head, her arms resting on her knees.

Claire pressed her fingertips to her forehead. "At least you still have a mother. *My* mother's dead."

Julia turned her head. Her voice softened, "Can I read it?"

Claire handed Julia the letter. For a split second, Claire changed her mind. "Maybe you shouldn't. It's from—"

"My dad, I know." Julia's eyes darted from Claire to the letter. Her lips moved as she read silently.

Dad. The endearment slipped easily from Julia's lips. Would Claire ever call him that? She stared at Julia's face. Their noses were alike—small and slightly upturned, but they were totally different in every other way. Julia's dark features contrasted with her lighter ones. Her half sister was definitely Sandy's daughter.

Julia handed Claire the piece of paper. "It's a sweet love letter written by a teenager. Why couldn't you leave it at that?"

"My mom never wanted to tell him I was his daughter because she knew he had a family, but Michael would've found out sooner or later. She wrote him a note when she was dying of cancer."

"So, you weren't the one who told Dad?" Julia's brows furrowed.

"No. In a way, my mother did." Claire slipped the letter back into her pocket. "My sister Haley was supposed to give the note to Michael at the memorial, but she held on to it. I guess she felt I had a right to know. I wouldn't purposely do anything to spoil your wedding."

Julia pushed herself to standing and wiped her hands together. "I need time. You're a good companion to my grandmother. She needs you. But don't expect a wedding invitation. Look, I've got to go. David is waiting for me."

"Is Michael home?" Claire twisted a strand of hair.

"No, he's not. Neither is my mom." Julia stepped into the house and held on to the doorframe, her knuckles turning white. "On second thought, maybe you should go back to L.A. where you belong." The door closed with a bang.

With stooped shoulders, Claire walked to her car. "Where do I belong?" she muttered under her breath. Her car crept out of the driveway as her heart sank.

The note on the door said she'd be right back. Michael raked his hand through his hair as he sat on the porch steps waiting for Claire to return. Where was she? He'd been sitting there for a good half hour contemplating what he'd say.

Michael never thought he'd have more than one child. For years he and Sandy tried for another baby, with no success. They came close to filing papers to adopt, but life always seemed to get in the way. It was an excuse. Michael didn't know if he could love a child that wasn't his own flesh and blood contrary to what many adoptive couples said. But it was all about him. Always had been.

And now, he had another daughter. What about Sandy? Where did that put her in all this? Michael's stomach clenched. It didn't seem fair.

The night before, Sandy had made it clear that she needed time to wrap her mind around all that he had told her. Michael tried to put himself in her shoes. He'd be patient. His mother was right. The hard part was telling Sandy. He needed grit and determination—and humility. Michael's pride had gotten in the way many times in their marriage, but last night he needed to admit his mistakes. And by God's grace, he did. Sandy was the love of his life, and he vowed to prove it to her—whatever she wanted or needed.

"Hi. Can I help you?" A brunette approached.

"No, thank you. I'm waiting for my daughter." The words rolled off his tongue easier than he imagined.

The woman nodded in acknowledgement. "I'm Samantha. Claire's friend." She extended her hand.

Michael stood. "Nice to meet you. Michael Thompson."

"Do you want to wait inside?" Samantha reached into the potted plant and produced a key.

Michael's eyes widened.

Samantha glanced at the key in her hand. "I'm only visiting. Claire wanted me to be able to get into the house if I beat her home."

"Ah," Michael nodded. "You go in. I'll wait here."

"All right. But let me know if you need anything." Samantha disappeared behind the door.

Michael sat down on the porch steps and glanced at his watch. Sandy would be home in half an hour. She wanted to check on his mother at the rehab center. That gave him time to speak with Claire before meeting her back at the house.

Claire pulled up to the curb in her VW. He watched his daughter get out of the car, her coloring so much like his own. What would he say? His heart felt as if it were in his throat. Would she accept him?

Claire's shoulders drooped. Tears streamed down her face. When she looked up and saw him, she froze.

With hands on his knees, Michael stood. He shoved his fingers in his pockets and took a few steps. "Hi, Claire."

She continued to stare.

He inched closer. Michael could hear Claire's rapid breathing. Was she going to run away?

"I know what you're going to say." Claire's voice squeaked. "I'll go pack my bags."

"Wait a minute. Hold on." Michael held out his hand. "Join me. On the porch. Please."

With tentative steps, Claire moved toward Michael. He placed his hand on her shoulder and guided her to a place next to him. Claire clasped her hands in her lap, her back completely straight.

"I know this is hard for both of us. But I need to talk to you." Michael swallowed hard, then took a deep breath. Claire hadn't said more than a few words since she arrived. He decided to skip the small talk.

"At seventeen, Emily was one of the prettiest girls I'd ever met. She was full of energy, loved to drive her VW and go to the beach. She was something. All the boys had a crush on her, Martin and I included." Michael noticed Claire's posture relax a little. "Emily was a regular around here for two summers, and I looked forward to seeing her. You could say she was my first love. I kept in touch with her throughout the year. One time I sent her a picture." Michael chuckled. "My mother was so angry that I took one of her picture frames." He rested his elbows on his knees and glanced at Claire.

"Then what happened?" Claire leaned forward.

"We grew apart. I went to college, your mom to beauty school in San Diego. We decided to date other people."

"Why did you find her again?" Claire shrugged her shoulders, her brows a straight line.

"I found out she lived in my mother's apartment building." Michael raked his hand through his hair. "I was in L.A. for a Realtor's convention. One thing led to another . . ." He hung his head.

"You had a wife. And child. So did my mom. Didn't that matter to either of you?" Claire's voice shook.

"Emily and I both knew it was wrong. But we couldn't change what had happened between us. We agreed never to contact each other again." Michael kept going. "I've made many mistakes in my life. But hurting my wife was inexcusable." He picked a leaf off the ground and twirled it between his fingers. "Claire, I can't say that I wish I'd never spent time with your mother. Otherwise, you wouldn't be here. But I can tell you that if I had it to do over again, I wouldn't. And now I have to prove to Sandy that our marriage is worth saving. I want her to learn to trust me again. Julia too."

"Where do *I* fit in the picture?" Claire's gaze fell away.

"Sandy and Julia may take a while to warm up to you." Michael reached over and touched Claire's shoulder. "But I want us to get to know each other. As father and daughter."

"Haley wants me to move back to L.A. I haven't decided what to do."

Michael felt as if he'd been punched in the gut. Now that he'd found his daughter, she might leave. "I want you to stay. Please tell me you'll think about it." He stood and held out his hand. "I promise, we'll take our relationship slowly. I'll let you call the shots."

Claire placed her hand in his, and he pulled her up. He reached around her shoulder and gave her a sideways hug. "I'm your father. And I want to take care of you."

He felt her body relax against him. It was a start.

40

The smell of Michael's aftershave mixed with the clean, fresh scent of laundry soap. A warm rush of emotions came to the surface of Claire's mind. Her father wanted to get to know her. Now, in his embrace, she saw hope for the future.

"I need to go, but please consider what I've said." Michael gave her shoulder another squeeze. "I want you here, Claire. And my mother needs you."

Claire still hadn't been able to visit Geraldine. Would she be as open as Michael to a relationship? According to what she said the other night, Geraldine knew Claire was her granddaughter. "I plan on visiting her this afternoon."

"Good. She loves you. Blake too." Michael took a step back. "Speaking of your neighbor, how are you two getting along?"

A smile hovered at the edges of Claire's mouth. She glanced to her left. "Okay. Fine. Really good."

Michael laughed. "Which one is it?"

Claire let out a sigh, her voice low. "One part of me wants to jump in with both feet and see where our relationship takes us. And the other part wants to run."

"I understand. I felt the same way when I met Sandy. She challenged me to be a better man like no other woman I've known. And yet, I was scared. I knew that once I committed my life to her, there was no looking back."

"But you stumbled." Claire brought her hand up to shade her eyes from the sun.

"I did." Michael shifted. "The problem was I took my eyes off God and kept them on myself. You can learn from my mistakes. If you love Blake, trust him. And keep your eyes fixed on God. He's the one who'll keep your paths straight."

Claire's insides warmed. She was receiving advice and encouragement from her father. "Thank you for listening."

"That's what fathers are for." Michael smiled. "See you soon. Keep in touch." He turned and walked toward his car.

Funny, she didn't notice his BMW parked across the street when she first arrived. It was probably a good thing. She might have kept going—all the way back to L.A.

Claire burst through the doorway. "You won't believe—"

"I can't wait to tell you—" Samantha turned, her ponytail flying through the air.

Claire flopped on the couch next to her friend and burst into laughter.

"You go first," Samantha tapped her on the arm. "I want to hear all about your visit with your dad. It surprised me to see him sitting on the porch when I came home."

Claire kicked off her flip-flops and hoisted her feet on top of the coffee table. Cali sprung onto Claire's lap, circled around a couple of times, and settled into a ball. "He told me about his relationship with my mom. It was a little hard to hear, but he answered my questions. The best part is that he wants to get to know me as his daughter. It's almost too much to handle, especially after my visit with Julia this morning." Claire rested her head back against the couch. "She doesn't like me."

"She probably doesn't like the situation. It has nothing to do with you." Samantha was the voice of reason. She was methodical, organized, *and* discerning.

"Well, it may take time for her to accept me as part of the family." Claire stroked Cali's back.

"So, you're staying?" Samantha leaned in.

Claire's mouth hung open. "How'd you know I might be moving back to L.A.?"

"You were mumbling to yourself during the movie." Samantha straightened her collar.

"I love that movie, but I admit I've seen it at least a dozen times. I didn't want to tell you. After all, you had just arrived." Claire pressed her lips together, then chuckled. "I was mumbling, huh?"

"I sure learned a lot about you . . . how much you care for Blake, how worried you are about Haley and Geraldine, how much you care for Blake . . ." Samantha teased as she listed them off on her fingers.

"Oh, you." Claire grabbed a throw pillow and playfully hit Samantha on the arm. Cali leapt off Claire's lap and scurried down the hall. "I want to hear all about your interview. You look great, by the way." Samantha's gray suit and green blouse were a perfect complement to her complexion. "Professional through and through." Claire tugged on her plain white T-shirt that hung a few inches over her skirt.

"*HCP Resources, Inc.* wants me to come back for a second interview." Samantha stood and glanced at her watch. "And I've got another interview in twenty minutes. Who knew food and nutrition services were so big here in Santa Cruz."

"Oh yeah, we like to eat." *Especially with Blake.* Her mind drifted to the man who had stolen her heart. Claire glanced wistfully at her kitchen. Blake had looked so tired and defeated this morning. His job meant the world to him. And apparently so did she. The three little words he said to her had a huge impact on her decision. He loved her.

Samantha cleared her throat. "Earth to Claire, come in, Claire." She waved a hand in front of Claire's face. "Girl, you need to come back down. Something tells me you've got it bad for your chef."

Claire smirked. "Good one. My chef. I get it." She walked Samantha to the door. "I hope you get a job. It'd be nice to have such a good friend close by."

"Thanks. But before I agree to work here, you're staying, right?" Samantha's brows shot up. "Because *I* want to have at least one friend in this town."

"I'm staying, no worries." Relief flooded her at the admission. The decision felt good, right.

"Great. Now I can go." Samantha twisted her ponytail into a bun, her purse dangling on her arm.

"If I'm not home when you get back, you know where to find the key. I need to make a visit to Geraldine." Claire shut the door behind her.

Her familiar ring tone chimed. Claire scrambled to find her phone inside her purse. She glanced at the screen. Haley. It was time to tell her of her decision. Claire was staying in Capitola. She flipped her phone open. "Haley, what's up?"

"So, when are you moving back?" Haley's anxious tone unnerved Claire. Ever since they were little girls, her sister had acted like a mother ordering her around and assuming Claire would do whatever she wanted.

"No hello? How are you?" Claire rolled her eyes.

"I'm sorry. How're you doing?" Haley's voice softened.

Now Claire felt like the heel. She wouldn't want to be pregnant and living with an alcoholic. "No, Haley, *I'm* sorry. I'm fine. More than good. Michael and I talked. He wants to have a relationship with me."

"I'm happy for you."

Claire heard sniffles in the background. "How are you doing?" Claire didn't know if she was prepared to hear her sister talk about Mark and how much he'd changed, when it was clear the other day that he hadn't. Haley took a ragged breath.

"I kicked him out."

"You did?" Claire sat down on a dining room chair. "When?"

"The second we got home. I told him that until he went to Alcoholics Anonymous he wasn't welcome here. He moved in with his uncle." Haley sobbed. "I miss you so much, Claire. I can't do this on my own. I need you to help me be strong. *Please* come home."

The words wouldn't come. Claire had barely reconciled with her father and recently found the man of her dreams. And now she was being asked to let them go. "Haley, please. Pull yourself together." Who was the mother now? "You are stronger than you think." Her eyes drifted to Geraldine's recliner. She needed to talk with her grandmother. Geraldine would know what to do. "Can I call you back tonight? I'm on my way out the door."

Haley hiccupped. "Don't forget. Okay?"

Claire stood and grabbed her purse. "How could I forget my sister? I love you and your baby."

"Thanks, Claire. Talk to you later."

Claire clicked her phone shut. She had heard words of wisdom from her father today, and now she needed to talk with her grandmother. Claire sagged against the door. She remembered telling herself she'd consider moving back to L.A. if

Haley kicked Mark out. She'd done it. Now what? The last thing Claire wanted to do was move.

God, what are you trying to tell me?

The smell of the antiseptic turned her stomach. Claire hurried down the hallway of the rehabilitation center to Geraldine's room. She was excited about visiting her grandmother. The nerves she had felt the other night were gone.

The doctor had ordered daily physical therapy to improve Geraldine's muscle strength. Claire was now eager to help Geraldine get strong enough to come home—and soon.

"Come on, Betty, you need to eat something." Geraldine's voice drifted into the hallway.

Claire chuckled. Her grandmother was busy helping someone else. So typical. That woman had enough spunk for the both of them.

Claire walked in holding one of Geraldine's favorite teddy bears. "I thought I'd bring Mr. Teddy to cheer you up."

Geraldine's eyes lit up. "Claire! Come here, dear, and give this old woman a hug."

Claire gladly went to her. With Geraldine's arms around her, she took in her grandmother's baby powder scent. She was related to this woman. It felt good. Comforting. A sudden urge to get to know her grandmother—from her childhood until now, welled up inside of Claire. She knew bits and pieces, but she wanted to know the whole story of this woman's life.

"Thank you for bringing Teddy. He'll cheer me on so I can get out of here."

Claire sat down on the edge of Geraldine's bed and looked around the small room. Two twin beds, two nightstands, and a small bathroom filled the space—adequate for recovery, but her grandmother needed her home and the fragrance of the salty ocean air. "How long will you be here?"

"Depends on how much trouble I give the physical therapists." Geraldine chuckled while fixing Teddy's bow. "They want me to be able to walk without my walker. 'Stand up straight, Mrs. Thompson. Stop shuffling your feet, Mrs. Thompson.'" Geraldine glanced at the old, frail woman next to her. "Oh, how rude of me. Claire, this is my roommate, Betty." She gestured to the other side of the room and lowered her voice. "Poor thing. She's blind and is recovering from pneumonia. Can you believe she's ninety-seven?"

Betty's breathing deepened.

Claire peeled her eyes away from the old woman. "I think she's asleep, Grandma."

Geraldine grabbed Claire's hand. "You called me Grandma." Her eyes softened. "Michael told you, then." She smiled. "Good boy. I knew he could do it."

"Actually, Haley told me . . . the same day she gave Michael the note from my mother." Claire gently squeezed Geraldine's hand. "I was completely shocked. Then the realization that *you're* my grandmother dawned on me. I was so happy . . . and scared."

"Scared of what, dear?" Geraldine hugged the teddy bear to her chest.

"That you wouldn't want me. And that my presence here would ruin your family," Claire whispered, her words wavering.

"Oh, pooh. This family has been needing someone like you with your carefree spirit and spontaneity for a long time." She cupped her hand around her mouth, "If you haven't noticed, we're a tightly wound group."

"Not you!" Claire shook her head. "If there's anyone in this family who is full of energy, Grandma, it's you."

"You and I are made from the same mold." Geraldine smiled.

The time was right. Claire needed to speak to her grandmother about her sister. "Haley wants me to move back to L.A." Claire looked down. "With Mark going through AA and living with his uncle, she says she can't make it on her own." Claire brought her eyes to meet Geraldine's. "She needs my help to keep her strong."

"Do you believe that?" Her grandmother cocked her head.

"Haley has always needed someone. When my mother was sick, Haley needed Mark. When my mother died and Mark started drinking, she needed me."

"Sounds to me like Haley does need someone in her life." Geraldine pressed her lips together, her brows forming a straight line.

"I know. That's the hard part. I don't want to move away from you, Michael, and Blake." Her voice quivered, and she looked down.

Geraldine touched Claire's arm. "Oh, no, dear. Haley doesn't need *you* right now. She needs a Savior."

Claire tilted her head and met Geraldine's gaze. "You mean God?"

The edges of Geraldine's mouth turned up. "Yes, dear. She needs Jesus."

Claire blinked back tears that threatened to spill down her cheeks. "So do I."

"Claire, hand me my Bible." Geraldine pointed.

Claire stood and grabbed the worn-looking book from the nightstand.

Geraldine flipped through the pages and read 1 John 4:9-10. "This is how God showed his love among us: He sent his one and only Son into the world that we might live through him.

This is love: not that we loved God, but that he loved us and sent his Son as an atoning sacrifice for our sins."

God loves me so much he sent his Son to die for me. The realization washed through her. Claire slipped off Geraldine's bed and knelt on the floor. She desperately needed Him in her life.

Right there in Geraldine's room, with Betty lightly snoring to her right, Claire prayed the prayer to accept Jesus into her heart. And when she opened her eyes, she knew her life was changed forever.

41

Michael lit the candles on the dining room table. "Come join me. The lasagna is ready." He pulled out a chair for Sandy. She scooted herself in but didn't say a word. Michael let her be. She needed time. He knew that.

That afternoon, he and Sandy had worked side by side in the kitchen layering the noodles and cheese and sauce. It was like old times when they were newlyweds. Michael smiled to himself simply thinking about it. They couldn't afford to eat out so they made their favorite dishes at home—together. He warmed at the thought of how much he loved doing simple things with his wife.

Michael grabbed a mitt, opened the oven door, and took out the French bread, then gathered the dressing and salad off the counter. He hoped their conversation over dinner would consist of more than the weather. It would be up to him to keep the dialogue moving.

Sandy looked beautiful. A strand of her raven hair was tucked behind one of her delicate ears. He glanced at her neck. Was that the diamond he bought for her on their last wedding anniversary? The simple gesture of wearing the necklace gave him hope. She reached up and touched the diamond before putting her hand back down in her lap. Was Sandy nervous? Michael didn't want to have that effect on her. He wanted this night to be perfect.

Michael set the food down, then joined his wife at the table. He searched her eyes. When she finally looked at him, he held out his hand.

Sandy hesitated, but then slipped her hand in his.

"I love you." Her hand was soft, dainty, and feminine. He stroked it with his thumb. "And I want to earn your trust."

Sandy's eyes glistened. Was she going to say anything? The silence made his stomach turn. It was as he thought. He'd need to keep the conversation going.

"At Julia's wedding, I want to be able to stand in front of our friends and family as a stronger, more confident couple. It would be good for us—and for Julia." Michael gave his wife's hand a gentle squeeze before letting go.

Sandy grabbed her napkin and dabbed at her eyes. "I want that too."

Michael felt as if he could dance the tango. "You do?" He touched her arm and smiled.

Sandy let out a long breath. "Yes. I've thought all day about those hard years when we were first married. Your affair with Emily was as much my fault as it was yours. I pushed you away while I was carrying Julia. I remember feeling so scared. Scared to be a mom. What if I couldn't do it? So much responsibility. I shut you out." Her voice shook. "I never meant to hurt you. I was in my own world. I had no idea I was driving you into the arms of someone else."

Michael stood. He held out both of his hands this time.

Sandy came to her feet. And walked into her husband's embrace.

"You're not to blame for what I did." Michael kissed the top of her head. "You had a difficult pregnancy." He touched his lips to her cheek. "And I made a terrible mistake." Michael looked into Sandy's brown eyes. "And I will never hurt you like that again. I promise." He cupped her face between his palms and kissed her gently, then deeply. He wanted her—all of her—right then. He loved his wife's spirit, the very core of her, and he loved her body. "Sandy, I-I—"

Sandy blew out the candles. Then she grabbed Michael's hand and led him upstairs.

Claire rapped on Blake's door. Her insides quivered even though the temperature outside was a comfortable sixty degrees. All afternoon she had ached to see Blake again, especially now that she had accepted Jesus and had decided to stay in Capitola. Samantha stood by her side. Her dimples creased, and she bounced up and down.

"Stand still, you're making me nervous." Claire nudged Samantha.

"I'll know if he's the right one for you. Who knows, I could be meeting the man you marry—"

The words were barely out of Samantha's mouth when Blake opened the door.

"There you are." Blake looked as if he had taken a shower. His hair was still damp, and his chest was bare. "Come in. I'll just be a minute."

Claire and Samantha stepped inside.

Blake disappeared to the back of the house.

"So far so good. That man's got one nice set of abs." Samantha bumped Claire's elbow.

"For your information, that was the first time I've seen him without a shirt." Claire giggled. "But he does, doesn't he?"

Samantha chuckled. "It will be fun to watch the two of you tonight. I'll get a good picture of your relationship."

"Please, Sam, don't pressure me. It'll be hard enough to let him know how I feel without a pair of eyes watching our every move."

"You'll be in your own little world. You won't even notice me."

"Of course we'll notice you." Claire rolled her eyes in a playful gesture.

"How long does it take Blake to get ready?"

"Remember, he's injured. I wonder if he needs help." Claire walked toward the hall. "Blake?"

"I'll wait right here." Samantha took a seat on the leather couch.

A soft moan came from the back room.

"Blake?" Claire called again. She peeked her head into his bedroom.

He wrestled with a shirt. Every time he lifted his right arm, a moan escaped his lips. He tossed his shirt in the corner of the room and lay back on his bed. He was a sight. Claire reined in her thoughts.

"Need a little help?"

Blake sat up. "You could say that." His tone was cool.

Claire strode across the floor and picked up his shirt. *So, even you, the most even-tempered man I know, get a little frustrated, huh?* "Button-down might be easier." Claire walked to his closet and hung up the polo shirt. She fingered his clothes and pictured herself as his wife, picking out his wardrobe. Her cheeks flushed.

"I like the navy blue one." Blake pointed.

Claire unhooked the shirt from its hanger and held it up to him.

Blake slipped his left hand easily through its armhole. His face contorted as he brought his right hand back. Claire guided his arm into the sleeve and pulled the shirt over his shoulders.

She stood in front of him and started buttoning. Standing so near him made her heart race. She needed a distraction. Now was a good time to tell him her good news. "I accepted Jesus into my heart today." She cocked her head coyly.

Blake grabbed Claire with his left arm and swung her around. "Claire, that's amazing!" His grip was strong, and comforting. He set her down. "Tell me about it."

"I was visiting Geraldine. She reminded me that as much as people need each other, we need God more. I realized I wanted Jesus to be the boss of my life."

"I'm so happy for you, Claire. You don't know how much this means to me. My prayer has been answered."

"You prayed for me?" She continued buttoning his shirt.

"Every day."

"You are a good man, Blake Coombs."

"Hey, your salvation is more important than life itself."

Claire looked deep into Blake's blue eyes.

"I want to spend eternity with you."

Claire's heart raced. He cared for her. Was now the time to tell him how she felt? "There's something else I realized—"

"There's more?" Blake raised his brows.

"Excuse me?" Samantha stuck her head into Blake's room. "If we don't get a move on, Pearl and Harry will wonder if they've been stood up." She winked at Claire.

Claire fastened the last button. "Blake, I'd like you to meet my good friend Samantha."

Blake turned around. "It's nice to meet you." He held out his left hand.

Samantha took it and leaned in. She whispered something in Blake's ear.

What did Samantha say?

"Shall we go?" Blake handed Claire his keys and grabbed his jacket. They followed Samantha out of the house. "You brought along your bodyguard, huh?" he whispered in Claire's ear.

"What?" Claire scrunched her nose.

"Samantha told me she'd injure my other arm if I hurt you." Blake flashed her a wide grin.

"No!" Claire watched her athletic friend walk toward Blake's truck.

He laughed. "Actually, she said it was nice to finally meet your chef."

"That's more the Samantha I know." Claire allowed her fingers to intertwine with his. "And I do have the best chef in town."

"Not for long. The only thing left on the kitchen repair is for me to pick a paint color."

Claire unlocked the truck's doors. Her stomach twisted. Would she be able to spend as much time with Blake once his kitchen was finished? Not if she didn't make her intentions clear.

Samantha climbed into the back, while Blake sat in front. Claire turned the key and revved the engine. Could she live with herself if she let her fears run her life? She glanced in the rearview mirror for oncoming traffic. It was time to look through the front windshield of her life. She was done being stuck in the past.

Thirty minutes later, Claire sat in front of a campfire. Harry stood next to Blake barbecuing the steaks while Pearl knitted.

Samantha set the table. Claire felt Blake's eyes on her. Would he always look at her that way? She hoped so.

"That Blake is one nice young man." Pearl straightened in her chair, her braid resting over her right shoulder. "I'd say you caught yourself a good fish."

Claire smiled at Pearl's choice of words. Even her comments had to do with being in the great outdoors. "I agree. But I haven't caught him yet."

"I see the way you two look at each other. I'd say you're both in the net." Pearl chuckled and continued to knit the baby blanket. "Who knows, one day I might be knitting one of these for you."

"Maybe one day." Claire tucked her hair behind her ear. "Pearl, it's so good to be with you. I needed a night like this." She slumped down in her chair and laid her head back. "It feels good to be with friends."

Harry's voice boomed, "Now, I don't agree with you, Blake. I know how to barbecue. Don't I know how to grill the perfect steak?" He turned and looked at Pearl.

"Yes, dear. If you liked charred beef. Sorry, honey." Pearl shrugged her shoulders. "If Blake thinks it's ready, you should listen to him. Claire says he's quite the cook."

"He's quite the cook, huh? Well, if these steaks are still mooing, we'll know whose idea it was to take them off the grill." Harry speared a piece and set it on a platter.

"You're cooking tonight, Harry." Blake chuckled. "I didn't mean to cause a problem." He held on to his sore arm.

"No problem." Harry stacked the steaks and covered the grill. He grinned. "I do tend to overcook. You ready, Pearl?"

"Land sakes." Pearl tucked her knitting in her tapestry bag. "I'm not used to the meat being done so quickly. Come, Claire and Samantha. Help me gather the rest of the food."

Claire followed Pearl to the RV. Was it only a few months since she had rammed into Pearl and Harry? So much had changed. She was truly independent now, with a roof over her head and a great job helping Geraldine. Not only had Claire found the writer of the letter, but she had found herself too. She was thankful her father was open to a relationship with her. And because of her grandmother, she had accepted Jesus into her life. Her mother would be proud. *Thank you, Lord.*

Pearl handed Claire the potato salad and a liter of root beer. She carried the items to the picnic table. Blake was already seated. He winked at her when she approached. "Do you mind handing me my jacket?"

Claire spied the coat sitting on a rock. She needed to talk to Blake about how she felt about him. But first she'd enjoy the dinner Pearl and Harry had prepared. She grabbed the jacket and helped Blake shrug into it, inhaling his familiar scent.

Samantha set the bowl of baked beans on the table. Pearl joined her with the green salad and a platter of watermelon wedges.

"You outdid yourself, my dear." Harry slid in next to his wife, then said a blessing for the food.

"Pearl and Harry, did you hear the news?" Samantha raised her voice. "Claire found her father and grandmother?"

"Here in Capitola?" Pearl's mouth hung open. "How wonderful."

"Claire is her grandmother's caregiver. Can you believe it?" Samantha piled a mound of salad on her plate.

"It's all amazing." Claire poured herself a glass of root beer.

"Didn't I tell you the Lord provides?" Pearl placed a thick wedge of meat on her plate.

"Yes, you did." Claire nodded. "And I want to thank you for that." So many people had impacted her life the past few months—Pearl and Harry, Samantha, Tom and Nancy, Vivian, Geraldine, Blake, and Michael.

"And he provided Blake to teach us how to prepare steaks—medium-rare. They're perfect." Pearl gave Harry a peck on the cheek.

Harry wiped his face on a napkin. "All right. All right. I've learned a lesson, but don't let it get to your head, son."

Blake laughed. "No worry there. This woman keeps me humble." He gestured across the table at Claire. "I've been trying to get close to her ever since I laid eyes on her."

Claire took a swig of soda to swallow the lump in her throat. "I had a good talk with Michael today." Why did she always see the need to change the subject? Trust. Isn't that what her father had instructed her to do?

Blake sat across from Claire and leaned in. "I saw you with him out front earlier today."

"Are you spying on me?" Claire tried to keep a straight face.

"Who, me?" Blake grinned.

"It's a nice night for a walk. Why don't the two of you let us clean up?" The corners of Pearl's mouth turned up. "Come on, Harry. You too, Samantha."

Did Samantha say something to Pearl? Was it a setup?

"I'm not done with my steak." Harry glared at Pearl.

"You can finish inside the RV. Come on, now." Pearl tugged on his arm.

Samantha took her plate and stood from the table. She winked at Claire before she followed Harry and Pearl to the motor home.

Two minutes later, Claire sat alone with Blake. Did she dare tell him her true feelings? He looked vulnerable sitting across from her at the table. She stood and held out her hand. "That walk sounds good."

Blake pulled a small flashlight from his jacket and turned it on. "Want to hit the trail to the beach?"

"Are you sure you're up to it?" Claire pointed to his arm.

"If we take it slow." Blake rested his left arm around her shoulder and allowed her to navigate the path with the flashlight.

Take it slow. That was exactly how Claire liked it. If she was going to trust Blake with her heart, she needed to take it one step at a time.

They stood on the trail overlooking the city lights. Claire knew Blake was in pain. She noticed him wince when he thought she wasn't looking. "Let's stop here." She leaned against the railing. "Blake, I—"

"Claire—"

"You go first." Claire looked up at the moon. It was full, casting a glow on the ocean.

"I hope I didn't make you uncomfortable earlier. I want you to know how much I care for you. And if I have to wait, I will." Blake gently touched her cheek.

"Yellow." Claire reached up and held his hand. "Your kitchen should be painted yellow."

"What?" Blake laughed. "You want to talk about my kitchen?"

"Remember when we were at Bella Roma? You asked me to help you pick out kitchen cabinets."

"Oh, yeah. Who'd forget that night? You weren't too happy with me."

Claire hesitated. "It wasn't you. I wasn't happy with myself. Blake, I'm scared. But I want to trust." She took a step forward, clasped her hands behind Blake's neck and stood on her tiptoes. "I love you and I promise I won't push you away if you want to kiss me." She closed her eyes, and tilted her chin. And waited.

"The question, honey, is if *you* want to kiss *me*?" Blake rubbed their noses together.

She peeked. "No doubt in my mind."

When their lips came together, Claire's heart nearly burst. The kiss was soft. Gentle. Like a warm caress. She couldn't believe what was happening. She was in love.

Epilogue

"I now pronounce you man and wife. You may kiss the bride," said the Pastor from Capitola Christian Fellowship.

Claire clutched Blake's hand as she watched Julia and David kiss. Her heart warmed at the genuine affection the bride and groom shared. She glanced at Blake and couldn't help but dream of her future.

Blake gave her a crooked grin. Was he thinking the same thing?

"And now, may I present to you: Mr. and Mrs. Richards," announced the Pastor.

Julia took her bouquet from her friend Emily, linked arms with David, and proceeded up the aisle. The crowd erupted in applause.

"She made such a beautiful bride." Haley, who sat on Claire's right, whispered in her ear. "I don't want to stand next to her. I'd look like a beached whale."

"You're barely showing." Claire patted her sister's pregnant belly. "And you're beautiful."

Haley kicked off her heels. "Thanks. You do wonders for my self-esteem."

Claire remembered their phone call a couple months back. Haley had begged Claire to return to L.A. But after a visit with her grandmother, Claire realized Haley needed to make it on her own. The healthy glow on Haley's cheeks was a clear sign Claire had made the right decision. Mark continued to live with his uncle, making great strides toward sobriety. Hopefully, Haley and Mark would work out their differences by the time their baby arrived.

Michael walked up the aisle with her grandmother on one arm and Sandy on the other. Claire noticed the way Michael and Sandy had looked at each other during the ceremony. If Claire wasn't mistaken, she saw renewed love.

Geraldine smiled at Claire as she walked past. Her grandmother was one determined woman. Not only did she get out of rehabilitation after only a week, but she also demanded Julia invite Claire to the wedding.

She grinned back. Claire loved her grandma with every ounce of her being.

"Ready?" Blake held out his arm, his wound completely healed.

"I've been ready for a long time. I just never knew it before today." Claire pressed a kiss on Blake's cheek, held his arm, and walked up the aisle.

Someday—when the time was right, she'd walk in the opposite direction—and Blake would be waiting at the other end.

Discussion Questions

1. The story begins in L.A. with the memorial of Claire's mother, Emily. Have you lost someone you love? What was it like at the memorial? Do you relate to Claire's desire to be alone?
2. When Claire is fired from her job as a waitress and kicked out of her sister's home, do you think her decision to go to Capitola is based on becoming independent or her desire to hold on to her mother's memory? What role did the old love letter play?
3. Vivian encourages Claire to pursue her dreams. What do you dream about? What is stopping you from going after what you want?
4. Relationships are difficult and take work. Communication is key. Describe Claire's relationship with her sister Haley. What about Michael and his wife, Sandy? How do these relationships change as the story evolves?
5. Money is a topic that is brought up in *Delivered with Love*. How does the lack of money affect Michael? What could he have done differently? What does the Bible say about worry in Matthew 6:25-34?
6. Harry and Pearl, as well as Tom and Nancy, are basically strangers and yet they help Claire in different ways when she's in need. Have you ever been the recipient of a stranger's kindness? Tell about a time you showed kindness to a stranger.
7. Besides being a romantic interest, Blake shows Claire the importance of prayer and having a relationship with God. How does his consistency and example help Claire grow spiritually? Is there someone in your life who's done the same for you?
8. Michael wants to forget his past. How does one lie lead to another? Why is it so difficult to forgive ourselves

for our past mistakes? In what way does guilt play a role? Courage?

9. What is your impression of Geraldine? Why do you think her character is so important to the story? How does she encourage Claire? Challenge Michael?
10. Claire had a big decision to make—whether to stay in Capitola or go back to L.A. Do you think she made the right one? Why or why not? What would you have done in her situation?
11. The information Michael receives finally causes him to take the high road. What do you think is the most important factor or person in this transformation? Did you learn anything from Michael's journey?
12. Proverbs 3:5-6 says, "Trust in the LORD with all your heart and lean not on your own understanding; in all your ways acknowledge him, and he will make your paths straight." How do these verses pertain to the main characters in *Delivered with Love?* What is one way you can apply these verses to your life?

Want to learn more about author
Sherry Kyle and check out other great fiction
from Abingdon Press?

Sign up for our fiction newsletter at
www.AbingdonPress.com
to read interviews with your favorite authors, find tips for starting a reading group, and stay posted on what new titles are on the horizon. It's a place to connect with other fiction readers or post a comment about this book.

Be sure to visit Sherry online!

www.sherrykyle.com

Abingdon Press fiction